James Kennedy

Memoir of Margaret Stephen Kennedy

I0564623

James Kennedy

Memoir of Margaret Stephen Kennedy

ISBN/EAN: 9783743305366

Manufactured in Europe, USA, Canada, Australia, Japa

Cover: Foto ©Raphael Reischuk / pixelio.de

Manufactured and distributed by brebook publishing software
(www.brebook.com)

James Kennedy

Memoir of Margaret Stephen Kennedy

MEMOIR

OF

MARGARET STEPHEN KENNEDY.

BY HER HUSBAND,

JAMES KENNEDY, M.A.

LATE MISSIONARY IN NORTHERN INDIA.

LONDON:

JAMES NISBET & CO., 21 BERNERS STREET.

MDCCCXCII.

PREFACE.

MORE than a year has passed since the subject of this biography, now presented to the public, was taken to her home above. Remembering the strong testimonies to her worth and usefulness conveyed in letters addressed to me on occasion of her death, it occurred to me, in my loneliness, with my abundant leisure, I should attempt to give, with some fulness, an account of her long and chequered career, with its varied experiences of work, toil, and suffering, at times of sore trial, great perplexity, and great peril. On making known my wish to intimate friends, in whose judgment I could trust, I received letters strongly approving of my design, and expressing the opinion that such a record was fitted to be eminently useful.

In 1884 a work of which I was the author was published under the title of " Life and Work in Benares and Kumaon, 1839-1877." A large edition was issued, which had a gratifying sale. The publisher informs me he cannot supply me with a single copy. The work now sent to the press may be considered the complement of that volume. In both works I have followed the chronological order. Frequent references are made to the same events. I have very occasionally quoted from myself, but the details are widely different.

In this volume prominence is given to my dear wife's domestic character. All who knew her were aware her domestic feelings were unusually strong and tender. These, instead of being a hindrance in her efforts to do good outside the family circle, inspired her with a tenderness, a sympathy, and a pity, which greatly contributed

to fit her for ministering to others, and gave her a power
for good which she could not have otherwise possessed.
No biography could truthfully present her in which prominence was not given to this aspect of her character,
and, if I mistake not, no part of this work will be more
acceptable to readers.

The experience I have acquired in Deputation work for
the London Missionary Society and in conversation with
Christian friends, has led me to the conclusion that information about the circumstances in which we prosecute
our work, incidents of travel, the climate, aspect of the
country, native and European society, have been very
welcome, and have stimulated the missionary spirit by
enabling friends at home to realise our position and action.
In former times the circumstances of Indian life were in
several respects widely different from what they are now.
In these days, when the appetite for fiction is so keen
that no paper or periodical can succeed without ministering to it, with very full, often most minute, details of
domestic life in the personages portrayed, I think a place
is still due to somewhat full information about an actual
career of worth and usefulness.

All friends of Missions rejoice in the new access obtained to native homes in India. Mrs. Kennedy, while
thankful for the many opportunities for usefulness she
had with women and girls, was bent on getting into the
houses of high-caste Hindoos, but was foiled in her every
effort. We knew at Benares many of that class, some of
the highest in the community. They visited us, Mrs.
Kennedy conversed with them, and asked permission from
them to visit their families, but in the most courteous
manner, with various excuses, her visits were declined.
So far as I am aware, while many doors formerly shut
are now open, the families of the highest class in Benares

are still inaccessible to the ordinary zenana teacher; but while she is excluded an entrance is now and then obtained for the lady-doctor. The great gloomy mansions are yet the prisons of their female inmates.

Towards the close of this volume my readers will find a touching tribute to Mrs. Kennedy's memory from Ram Chandra Bose, M.A. As I send this work to the press information has reached me of his death in his sixtieth year. I mourn his departure. There was no native of India to whom I was more warmly attached, and whom I had more reason to regard as one of my most affectionate friends. In the *Harvest Field* for July, a missionary periodical published at Madras, I find a sketch of his life. I transcribe a few sentences from it.

" Beneath some defects of temperament there was an unswerving fidelity to the Master he served, and an un-tiring zeal in presenting the Gospel of Jesus Christ to his educated fellow-men." After resigning his place as head-master in our Central School at Benares, he entered Government employment. " While serving the Government he received a higher call to work for the Master. He gave up his worldly prospects with the large salary he enjoyed, and for a comparatively small amount he gave himself to the work of God amongst his educated country-men. . . . His last work was to give a course of lectures to the students of Duff's College in Calcutta. He could not complete the course on account of an attack of fever. He returned to his relatives in Lucknow. He was con-scious to the end, and bore unmistakable evidence of his faith in Christ. . . . He had a mind of great power, and intellectually he was one of the foremost sons of India. His literary productions evince keen thought and great mastery of philosophical problems. . . . His death has been lamented by all classes of the community, and many appreciative notices of his life and worth have appeared in Christian, Hindu, and Brahmo papers. His self-denial, his zeal, and his devotion to Christ were greatly needed to stimulate his fellow-Christians, and to them his departure is the greatest loss."

Many were the letters we received from him and sent to him. Mrs. Kennedy wrote to him frequently. I greatly regret I did not at a sufficiently early period ask him to send these letters to me. They were highly prized by him, and I believe proved very useful to him. In the case of others, as well as of this Indian friend, I regret I have not succeeded in getting letters which would enrich the Memoir. Many of Mrs. Kennedy's most intimate friends are dead, and the surviving members of their families cannot lay their hands on their correspondence.

With hesitation, and yet with conviction that I am acting wisely, I have given place to Mrs. Kennedy's most secret and sacred feelings, and her loving and ardent aspirations for the spiritual good of her children. Nothing was further from her thoughts than that a Memoir of her should be written, but I think the Memoir now sent to the press is fitted to promote the great object of her life—the glorifying of her Saviour and the spiritual good of her fellow-creatures. The biographies of consecrated lives demand prominence for the utterance of holy thought and feeling, and have been eminently useful in urging readers to strive for spiritual excellence. With this aim and prayer this work is submitted to the Christian public, and especially to the promoters and agents of Christian Missions to the women of the heathen world, in which our honoured and loved society, the London Missionary Society, is taking an active part.

J. K.

16 CHRISTCHURCH ROAD, HAMPSTEAD,
September 1892.

CONTENTS.

CONTENTS.

CHAPTER XIV.
1869–1877.

CHAPTER XV.
1877–1891.

CHAPTER XVI.

CHAPTER XVII.

MARGARET STEPHEN KENNEDY.

CHAPTER I.

EARLY LIFE AND EARLY CHRISTIAN EXPERIENCE.

1814–1838.

My beloved wife and I talked so frequently with each other about our early life, our parents, brothers and sisters, friends, circumstances, feelings, education, and everything which affected us, that we felt as if we had been companions from the commencement of our earthly career. In our later years our early life became increasingly the subject of conversation. In very precious documents, written for our children at my earnest request, but not read even by me till after her departure, she has left for them a touching account of her early religious experience. On her death-bed she directed my special attention to these papers, and told me where I would find them. They have been since her death read and re-read by myself and our children with feelings I will not attempt to describe. Of these I will make use in the sketch of her life I am now to attempt.

She was born in Aberdeen on January 18, 1814. Her father, Mr. John Walker, was engaged in business, and at the time of her birth, and for years afterwards, was in

prosperous circumstances.   Her mother, in love to her
children, was all that a mother, a Christian mother, could
be.   She was sent at an early period to the best school
in the town for girls of her age, but according to her
own account, she was too fond of play, too romping in
disposition, to make progress.   She kept steadily and
contentedly at the bottom of her class, till one day, by a
happy hit, to her great surprise, she found herself at the
top.   Her ambition was roused, and the lowest place was
no longer hers.   Her sisters often reproved her for her
wild ways, but the sobering period soon arrived.

That the change which came over Margaret Walker may
be understood, some account must be given of her religious training, common in the communion to which her
parents were attached.

This is no place for entering into detail regarding the
history of Presbyterianism in Scotland since the Revolution of 1688.   All we can say about it is, that while the
Presbyterian Church was re-established at that period,
and the vast majority of the people were unanimous in
regarding it as Christ's order for the government of His
Church, marked divergences of opinion manifested themselves from the beginning.   A small number were utterly
dissatisfied with the settlement then made, as they maintained that the Solemn League and Covenant, binding
all succeeding generations to the adoption of Presbytery
for the whole of the United Kingdom under a Covenanted
king, had been utterly disregarded in the arrangement.
These dissentients called themselves the Reformed Church
of Scotland, and remained a separate community down
to our day, when, with the exception of three or four
congregations, they have been merged into the Free
Church.

In 1732 some eminent ministers seceded from the Established Church on account of what they deemed its maladministration, its contempt of the rights of the people, its forcing of ministers on congregations protesting against them, and its tolerance of false doctrine.

This seceding body called themselves the Associate Presbytery. In 1745 an unhappy division arose as to the lawfulness of taking the burgess oath exacted in royal burghs. The oath required all admitted to municipal office " to profess and allow with all their heart the true religion presently professed within the realm." One party maintained the "true religion" meant the religion established in Scotland, notwithstanding all faults in its administration; while another party held it meant the Church as it then was, with all its corruptions. The contention was so sharp that it led to open rupture in 1747. The party consenting to the oath were called Burghers, those opposed to it Anti-Burghers. This division lasted more than seventy years. In 1820 this oath was abolished. "Even in their divided state these two communions were true lights in many parts of Scotland. Their ministers were educated men, zealous for the maintenance of the ancient standards of the Reformation, preached the unpopular doctrines of regeneration by the Spirit of God and justification by faith in Christ's righteousness, and maintained a high personal character."

After 1747 there was secession after secession, unions effected, and then dissenters from the unions, the great question at the root of prolonged eager, angry discussion being the relation of the Church to the State. Margaret's father belonged to the party that clung tenaciously to what they deemed the original constitution of the Church, binding down the entire nation to the continued acceptance of the Solemn League and Covenant. They called themselves the Original Secession of Anti-Burghers. They were commonly called Auld Lichts, a name made lately familiar to English ears by a well-known novelist. Their leader was Dr. Thomas M'Crie, the author of the "Life of John Knox," and of many other valuable historical works. He was on intimate terms of friendship with many outside his own communion, and was widely and most justly esteemed, but, along with the whole of his denomination, he could engage in no act of public worship with any from whom they differed in ecclesiastical matters. Their ministers were, as a class, able and faithful preachers of the Gospel, and stood high in their respective places of abode; but while at liberty to hold friendly intercourse with all, they deemed themselves bound to keep themselves so separate from others, that even when no service was held in their own church, or distance prevented attendance, members going to any other place of worship, even that of the party approaching them most nearly in their views, became subject to Church discipline. A lady in Aberdeen, the wife of one of the most prominent citizens, had three sons and two sons-in-law who became eminent ministers in the Church of Scotland, and her conscience would not allow her to hear one of them preach.

In this very conservative community there were, as my wife often told me, as might be expected, some persons fanatically attached to the Westminster Confession of both doctrine and Church government, ever ready to fight for it, who gave little evidence of true godliness in either temper or life. Many were, however, most devout, earnest, well-instructed Christians, who lived a life accordant with

their profession. They were warmly attached to the Westminster Confession and the Shorter and Larger Catechisms,
as setting forth Divine truth in the most Scriptural form
in which it was ever presented, and it was a first principle
with them to indoctrinate their children and households
into these views. Margaret's father belonged to this class.

In these families Christianity was ever kept in the fore-
ground. God's blessing was invoked before and after
every meal. However busy the family might be, worship
was conducted by the head of the house morning and
evening, when a passage from the Psalms was sung, a
portion of Scripture read, and prayer offered. Singing was
deemed an essential part of worship. They sang with the
heart, however inartistically with the voice. A favourite
expression was, "Sing you with your art, and we'll sing
with our heart." The Lord's Day was most strictly
observed. They attended public worship forenoon and
afternoon, and the evening was devoted to the instruction
of the family and household.

In Mr. Walker's family this order was carried out with
the best intentions, in a way, however, which showed little
appreciation of the capacity and peculiarities of the youthful
mind. After two long services in church, separated from
each other by an hour, in the evening came the catechising
and teaching of the household. This service extended to
nearly three hours. There was singing, reading a portion
of Scripture, and prayer at the beginning and the close.
They were examined about the sermons. The Shorter
Catechism had been by the more advanced children committed to memory, and was repeated with closed book.
The Larger Catechism was learned by some. Long portions
were read from Watson's "Body of Divinity" and such
works. In this way, in the course of time, the whole of

Dwight's "System of Theology" was got through. Now and then, to the great relief of Margaret, passages were read from Mosheim's "Church History" or the "Life of John Knox"—bright moments in a service which was, Margaret said, "awfully wearisome, but it was considered very wicked to feel so." Up to her twelfth year, and a little longer, this Sabbath-evening service was dreaded by her. On Monday there was the feeling of emancipation, which decreased as the week advanced towards the service she felt so irksome. In after years, she often referred, with thankfulness, to the large measure of instruction she thus received, though it was at the time largely against her will ; but, with a full appreciation of the motive which prompted her father to this long laborious service, she deemed it very injudicious, because it tended to make that repulsive which ought to be most winning. The effect in the management of her own children was to lead them to observe the marked difference between the Sabbath and other days of the week, but to make it throughout, by ingenious devices, a day of pleasure, and not of gloom.

Mr. Walker's conduct in this matter was in close accord with that of his brethren, though I should think the great majority did not carry it out to the same extent. The charge against Scotch Sabbatarianism—a charge which there is less and less reason to make in our day, the tendency now being to the opposite extreme—that it made religion repulsive to the youthful mind, was not without evidence to support it, though not to the degree it often assumed. In many, I trust in most, Christian families, there was a love which largely counteracted the austerity of the form religion put on ; and from these families went out, and continue to go out, many deeply thankful for having been early imbued with Divine truth, and thus prepared by Divine grace for the warfare and work of life.

When a little more than thirteen, Margaret Walker began to be deeply impressed by Divine truth. The change began in a singular way. Her father had a much larger library than most of his class had. It was chiefly composed of solid theological works. A few were of a different order. She told me that on one occasion her minister, Mr. Aitken, called, and observing among the books a good edition of Burns' poems, said, "Ah! that spoils your entire library." Margaret, looking at the books one day, was delighted to observe a novel, Mackenzie's "Man of Feeling." She read it with intense interest. She succeeded in getting two or three other light books, but the supply speedily failed. She was bent on getting something to read, and her eye fell on Boston's "Fourfold State," of which her father often spoke in high terms. She set to its perusal, and as she read her interest increased. Her mind awoke to the highest subject, the claims of God on her love, trust, and service. Religion, before so distasteful, became the subject of intensest interest. She gave up the worldly pleasures of girls of her age, and her supreme desire was to be good. She attended her pastor's monthly Bible-class, and from it and his Sabbath-day ministrations received much benefit. Her religious experience cannot be better given than in her own words in the paper she left for her children, written at my request years before her death. I have slightly abridged her statement :—

"I strove to work out my own righteousness. I got up at 5 A.M. in the cold winter mornings, and sat up at night to read and pray. I studied, with self-application, what is required and

forbidden in the ten commandments, as set forth in the Westminster Larger Catechism." [Let any one look at that Catechism,
and he will see how minutely, and even bewilderingly, these
requirements and forbiddings are set forth. I proceed with
Margaret's statement.] "The Sabbath was now a delight to
me. I attended every week-day sermon and meeting, so far
as I could. I could not understand my terrible headaches on
Sabbath evenings; but I understand them well now. And yet
I was in bondage and had no rest. 'What lack I yet?' That I
did lack something was evident. I felt as if all my reading,
praying, and striving had been in vain. I came to the conclusion
I had, notwithstanding my mental unrest, that love to Christ
which entitled me to avow myself His. I applied to Mr. Aitken
for membership, and was accepted. For weeks previous to the
half-yearly Communion "—[The Lord's Supper, as was common in
Scotland, and is so widely still, was held in Presbyterian churches
only twice in the year]—" I was so intensely in earnest, that my
attention had to be recalled to my daily duties. I went to
the Lord's Table, expecting some almost visible manifestation
of the Divine presence and token of my acceptance. Not
finding this, I was sadly distressed and disappointed, being sure
I had communicated unworthily. This lasted for six weeks,
when my emancipation came. It was the instant revelation of
Christ while hearing a sermon of Mr. Aitken from the text,
'Jesus Christ, whom we preach.' One of his particulars was,
'Christ preached as the only foundation of the sinner's hope for
eternity.' About the middle of the sermon the whole Gospel
scheme flashed into my soul. It seemed as if the sun had burst
out in the darkness of midnight. I was in a new world. I saw
my own righteousness to be as filthy rags, and felt Christ to be
all in all. I had found the pearl of great price, and everything
beside was esteemed by me as less than the dust of the balance.
The world and all in it appeared as nothing. To win Christ
and be found in Him seemed alone worth living for.

"For some six weeks I seemed to live on the very threshhold
of heaven. I had no care or concern about anything earthly.

I was like the Israelites when they crossed the Red Sea—I felt as if almost in the promised land.

"At the end of six weeks commenced a season of unutterable trial and temptation. The thought suddenly flashed into my mind—'It is all a myth.' The thought was agony. For about eighteen months I was in a sea of indescribable doubt and temptation. I feared I had committed the unpardonable sin. I prayed constantly. I read all sorts of books on Evidences, Paley, Leslie, &c., but found them miserable comforters. Like Bunyan in the Valley of the Shadow of Death, I did not know my own voice. The doubts were not my own. I hated them, and would have given the world to get back my old joy and peace. Still I charged myself with them all, and believed they proceeded from my own mind. Oh, that I could be assured beyond doubt that the Bible was true, that the glorious Gospel was God's message! I read much and prayed much. I sometimes at night looked out upon the sky, and almost expected some visible manifestation to put an end to my unbelief.

"Various means were used for my relief. I got much help from an old woman, Jean Mitchell, whose experience had been like my own. I was also much benefited by perusal of twelve sermons by Ralph Erskine, entitled 'The Sinner's Conflict,' from the text, 'As he was coming the Devil threw him down and tore him.' All along I had lived on the text, 'If any man will do my will, he shall know of the doctrine.' Gradually the tempter left me, my former peace returned, and in that light of life I have walked ever since, obscured only by my own want of watchfulness, and closer walk with God. Sixty years have come and gone since I have had these various experiences; but the clear view of the way of salvation, and my joyful acquiescence in it, has never left me. I have never had since a shadow of doubt that it was a direct revelation by God's Spirit."

This account of Margaret Walker's experience, being familiar to me, was at my earnest request written by her

in 1888, and written solely for her children and myself.
I now copy it somewhat abridged, as it gives the keynote
to the life of excellence and usefulness which she led all
through her subsequent career. Her piety was intense, deep,
and thorough, by the Gospel having been heartily accepted,
and assimilated by her intellect, conscience, and heart. It
was maintained by close habitual communion with God.
The Lord Jesus Christ in His glorious person, and in
His redemptive and sanctifying work, was the object of
her most profound reverence, her supreme love, and her
glad obedience. It was to her inconceivable how any
one could separate the doctrine of Christ from the person
of Christ, and how the doctrine could be held and the
character remain unchanged; no love to Christ exercised,
no conformity to His image attained, no obedience to
Him rendered. With her doctrine and practice were
inseparably united; the one the root, the other the fruit;
the one the fountain, the other the stream. Many, both
in India and in our own country, who knew her well, are
ready to testify to the dominating influence of the Gospel
of God's grace, acceptance by God on the ground of
Christ's work without any deserving of our own, in
moulding her character, and fashioning it to a holy,
consistent, loving, generous, self-denying life.

While strongly attached to her communion, and to the
last regarding her pastor, Mr. Aitken, as one of the most
estimable and lovable of men, whose ministrations had
been of signal service to her from the commencement
of her Christian life, Margaret Walker refused subjection to their narrowness. She was probably helped
to look beyond her own denomination by the circum-
stance that her eldest sister was engaged to be married
to a young man who had been accepted for missionary

service by the London Missionary Society. She never left her own place of worship when service was conducted in it, but on Sabbath evenings and week-day occasions she went to sermons and meetings which promised to benefit and interest her. She told Mr. Aitken what she did. He simply shook his head and smiled. The Solemn League and Covenant was deemed binding, and on one occasion all the members were called on to declare their adhesion to it; but Margaret felt that, however demanded by the time when it was formed, it had no binding force for our day, and declined to take part in the engagement. They had no Sabbath-schools, and no Missions. She wrote a paper expressing her dissatisfaction with what she regarded a marked dereliction of duty. Sabbath-schools were not altogether condemned, but heads of families were deemed the divinely-appointed teachers of the young, and Sabbath-schools were regarded as a necessary evil, caused by parents unfit by their ignorance and ungodliness to perform primary parental duty. The want thus caused they made no effort to supply. Their one aggressive effort, and that only a short time previously, was the supporting of an evangelist in the Western Islands of Scotland. The opinion commonly held was that foreign missions could be Scripturally conducted only on Presbyterian principles.

From my wife I heard so much about the minister of her young days, her people, and the church of which they were members, that I felt as if I knew them as well as she herself did. I do not think my readers will be displeased by my giving the information I thus obtained.

A favourite novel of our day, found in all libraries, and read by all novel-readers, brings to the knowledge of a

host of English people a class of religionists in Scotland
of whom they had never heard previously.

"The Little Minister" was pastor of an Auld Licht
congregation in Kirriemuir, a small town in the north-
east of Scotland. The old minister who is mentioned
with so much respect was Mr. Aitken, the father of Mr.
Aitken of Aberdeen,—Margaret Walker's pastor. She
had often heard him preach in his son's pulpit. She said
he was a man of noble appearance, of lofty Christian
character, and was regarded with love and reverence by
all who knew him. The last time she heard him he was
very feeble. According to the manner of the time, at
the end of the sermon he gave an epitome of what he had
said. The epitome was only half given when he paused
and said, "My friends, I cannot remember what I said,
but I hope you do."

The people to whom this worthy man ministered called
themselves the Original Secession Church. They were
called Auld Lichts, because they refused to accept some
views about Church and State which the great majority
of their brethren had adopted, and which they deemed
unscriptural innovations. Narrow though their views
were, they had a high character for sterling principle
and great excellence. An expression often used by them
was, "New licht is nothing but auld darkness."

A Kirriemuir paper gives an account of the old
minister, which was copied into the *British Weekly*.
From it we learn that the community was small and
poor; that the minister's income was never above £40,
and a manse and garden, and that when it was proposed to
raise it, he rather deprecated their action. In addition
to this information, my wife told me that on one occasion
his elders came to him and begged him to leave, as they

were at the time so impoverished (they were weavers) they could give him no stipend. He said he had sinned with them and would suffer with them. For three years he had no income from the Church. Between the produce of the garden, a daughter taking in dressmaking, the servant dispensed with at harvest-time, that she might then get good wages elsewhere, and probably a little money of their own—he had married into a very respectable family —they held on till the time of great scarcity came to an end.

There is one touch in the old minister's advice to the "Little Minister" which English people will not understand—"Do not give out the paraphrases." This was a most characteristic counsel, but it was scarcely necessary.

At the close of the last century or beginning of the present, a number of ministers in the Established Church longed for an addition to the Scotch metrical version of the Psalms, which alone up to that time had been sung in public worship. A committee was appointed to make a collection of hymns, and after a time they proposed the adoption of a selection called Paraphrases, with a passage of Scripture named above each to show that only those hymns were recommended which rested on God's Word; in fact, the greater number are hymns found now in all selections. This selection, I believe, never got the sanction of the General Assembly, but for many a day it has been bound up with the Scotch version of the Psalms in all Bibles printed in Scotland.

To the present day the great body of people in the northern counties are resolutely opposed to the use of hymns. The Auld Licht people so utterly rejected them that no counsel against their use was needed.

Mrs. Kennedy told me that while her fellow-members

held tenaciously to the principles of their Church, they
had much less social intercourse with each other than she
afterwards found in Congregational churches.

One summer she spent in the Cabrach, a district west
of Huntly, in Aberdeenshire, and there she saw a great
deal of families attached to Auld Licht views. The people
deemed truly religious were all more or less imbued with
them. Early in the century there was an Anti-Burgher
in Huntly, the Rev. George Cowie, known far and wide as
a man of apostolic zeal and labour. He was at last deposed because he gave encouragement to lay evangelistic
work. Most of his people clung to him, but in the Cabrach
there were a number who refused to follow him. Margaret
found some of their descendants very orthodox, of most
doctrinal precision, but, with marked exceptions, far from
being exemplary Christians. There was much smuggling
in the district, and they took their full share in it, and
gloried in their exploits. They could contend for justification by faith alone, but had loose views of what faith
should produce. Some, however, were truly excellent.

Margaret had much conversation with an old woman
who walked twice every year to the church in Aberdeen
to the Communion in Mr. Aitken's church, but never
entered any other place of worship. She had a great
sorrow. Her two sons, very worthy men, became Baptists.
Though so narrow, there was much which was beautiful
in the character of this old woman. Her husband died.
Margaret sat with her during the funeral. The funeral
attendants returned to an ample meal which had been
provided. A great snowstorm came on suddenly, and
they were for the night storm-stayed. The time was
spent in reading, praying, some dozing in their chairs.
At last one said, "We are hungry; put the remains of

the dinner into the pot." All was thrown into a pot on the fire, and then, without plates, knives, or forks, each took out a piece of mutton or leg of a fowl, or whatever came to hand. It was a sight which Margaret never forgot.

Stirred up by a pious lady in the neighbourhood, Margaret secured a school-house for a Sabbath-school. A number came, boys and girls, but men also came. They remained outside close to the door and windows, where they could hear what she said. She begged them to go away—she could not teach the children if they stopped— but go away they would not. "You are a stranger. We don't know you. We are not sure you are sound in the faith. We must know what you teach our children."

At a missionary meeting Margaret heard for the first time the hymn—

> " Jesus shall reign where'er the sun
> Does his successive journeys run,"

and she begged for a copy of the book that she might commit it to memory. This was the commencement of her acquaintance with hymns, with which in the course of time she stored her memory, and which were to the end of life in an eminent degree means of grace. She had a singularly retentive memory. By reading a hymn twice or thrice she so remembered it that for years it became her sure possession, to be recalled at her will. She thus travelled to Zion refreshed by the songs of Zion.

Serious reverses in business, to which business people are so often subject, affected her father's position and proved a great trial to her. It did not affect to a great degree the prosecution of her education, what was lacking in opportunities for learning being supplied by increased diligence. She engaged at an early period in teaching, which was beneficial to herself, and I know was highly appreciated by those whom she taught. Those trials were felt keenly at the time, but in after years she often referred to them as needful discipline by which her Heavenly Father was preparing her for her subsequent life.

CHAPTER II.

VOYAGE TO INDIA AND ENTRANCE ON INDIAN LIFE.

1838–1847.

MARGARET'S brother-in-law, Mr. Buyers, and her sister, Mrs. Buyers, had often requested her to join them in India, and the way was opened to compliance with their wishes. Towards the end of 1838 she set out for India, and after a long voyage, during which she suffered greatly from sea-sickness, she reached Calcutta. Previous to her departure, friends in Aberdeen, members of the Church of Scotland, who knew her well and esteemed her highly, wrote to the Scotch Church Missionary Committee in Edinburgh, strongly recommending her for female teaching in connection with their Calcutta mission. This recommendation was very favourably regarded, and on her arrival in India she found the Scotch missionaries disposed to engage her for zenana work. While the matter was being considered, her brother-in-law and sister wrote her in urgent terms, entreating her to join them in Benares, and she thought it well to comply with their invitation.

There were two ways of travelling to the North-West Provinces in those days—one way by palanquin, borne on the shoulders of men, relays being found at about every eight miles, and the other way by steamers on the Ganges, established a short time previously, which went to Allahabad, about a hundred miles beyond Benares. The pal-

anquin journey for nearly five hundred miles was formidable for a stranger who did not know a word of the
language, but was especially formidable for a lady. The
river route was generally preferred. Previous to the establishment of steamers, many made their way to the Upper
Provinces in native boats, when the voyage was often more
prolonged, and not infrequently more perilous, than the
voyage from England. Margaret Walker travelled by a
steamer, and after three weeks was welcomed by her
Benares friends before the end of March 1839.

In 1837 there had been a terrible famine in the North-
West. Many orphans were rescued by the authorities, and
for the most part made over to the different Missions. A
great number were entrusted to the Church Mission at
Benares, and a few were placed under the charge of the
London and the Baptist Missions. The orphans in the
charge of Mr. and Mrs. Buyers after a short time were
taught by Margaret. She set at once to the diligent
study of the native language, and made rapid progress
in its acquisition. She was greatly helped in getting
command of simple Hindoostanee by a child of her
sister's ayah, eight years of age. The ayah (female
servant) was a native Christian. Mrs. Buyers had no
school at this time, but she had taught this girl to read
the Roman, Hindi, and Persian characters. This little
girl, very bright and advanced for her years, was always
at hand, so that Margaret was able to talk and read with
her from day to day. Thus commenced an early and
thorough acquaintance with the colloquial language, and
with the characters in which it was written, which was
of signal service to her throughout her missionary
career.

On 1st May 1840, Margaret Walker changed her name

and position by becoming my wife, an event regarding which I can only trust myself to say it has proved an inestimable blessing to us both, and to all nearly related to us and connected with us, for which we have abundant reason to thank our Heavenly Father, and for which we shall be thankful to all eternity.

At the time of our marriage we had only orphan boys in our charge. After the departure of Mr. and Mrs. Buyers to England towards the close of the year, we removed to what was called the Mission House, and a number of girls were made over to us. The girls were in a little house near ours, and the boys were at a short distance. To the instruction and management of this large family Mrs. Kennedy gave herself with all her heart. The girls were her special charge.

At that early period, with our experience to learn, there was much which was very perplexing and trying in the management of these children. It was difficult to teach them tolerable habits of cleanliness. They had in their famine-hunger partaken of things at once disgusting and deleterious, and when good food was supplied, when not closely watched, they ate in preference what proved most hurtful. Their digestion was so bad that even good food had to be given most sparingly. The result was great sickness and mortality. We were told that a short time previous to our arrival a Church missionary had taken fifty to the country for change of air; cholera broke out, and in the course of a week only one survived. In our Mission the sickness and mortality were most depressing. On one occasion four little orphan girls were at the native service one Sabbath morning; half an hour afterwards, while we were at breakfast, word was brought us that they were very ill. We went to them at once, and found they had been seized with cholera. They had no strength to resist it, and within an hour all three were gone. The fourth died in the course of the day. Those who survived the early period of their stay with us entered, for the most part, on a season of health.

In addition to the orphanage a day-school for girls was commenced towards the end of 1840, and was taught in the little mud chapel in which the services with our native Christians were conducted at that period. In an article written for the Girls' Mission Guild of the Congregational Church at Acton, which was published in the *Quarterly News of Woman's Work*, Mrs. Kennedy says of this school: "I gathered a few little girls, naked and dirty gutter children—no others were accessible. They had to be paid for coming an equivalent for what they would have earned by carrying little baskets of earth, or anything else by which they could make a few pice. A woman had to be paid for bringing them and to ensure our doing them no harm; the idea of getting good in any way beyond the pice was far beyond them. At that time no woman who could read was to be had as assistant, and having a man in a girls' school was in every way objectionable. It was uphill work, but after a time the children, at first so stolid, began to show signs of intelligence. The little school grew till we had fifty or sixty on the roll. So far as I am aware it has never been given up, though now it is one of many, instead of being the only one."

For years Zenana Missions, conducted by women for women, have had a prominent place in the Foreign Missionary enterprise. For a long period the name was not assumed, and no separate organisation was formed to conduct them; but they were actually commenced and carried on by the first missionary who had a wife of the right spirit, and they have been thus conducted ever since by missionaries' wives.

Before our going to India a Society had been formed, unconnected with any of the great Missionary Societies, to send unmarried ladies to India, and several went who did excellent service. On our arrival I remember hearing of a lady, Mrs. Wilson, the widow, I believe, of a missionary, who had collected orphan girls at Agarpara, near Calcutta, and who also, if I remember rightly, had commenced a day-school for girls. Her labours were spoken of with high praise.

At Benares, on our arrival, we found Mrs. Smith and Mrs. Leupolt of the Church Mission zealously engaged in this good work. Mr. and Mrs. Leupolt had a large orphanage under their charge, and Mrs. Leupolt was indefatigable in her exertions. Mrs. Smith's daughters, as they grew up, Mrs. Sandberg, Mrs. Fuchs, Mrs. Lockwood, Miss Ellwanger, and other ladies gave themselves to the same department. With them, with the ladies of our own Mission, and with Mrs. Small of the Baptist Mission, Mrs. Kennedy was in deepest sympathy. They met often, told each other of their doings, their difficulties, and their success, and took counsel of each other as if they were all members of the same Mission. Nothing could have exceeded the cordiality of their intercourse. Mrs. Kennedy had the honour of being one of that band of pioneers in Northern India. Since that time Female Missions have become an integral part of every Missionary Society, in addition to special Societies for that object.

An orphan girl ten years of age, sent to us by the civil surgeon, Dr. Butter, whom we were at first unwilling to accept lest at her age she might corrupt the other girls, became in the course of time Mrs. Kennedy's most efficient assistant, by her quickness in learning, her docility, and her excellent character. She was afterwards married to one of our catechists, and to the end of her life was one of the brightest and best of our native community.

From 1840 on to 1847, when we went for six months to Almora, a sanitarium in the Sub-Himalayan range, was to Mrs. Kennedy a time of great activity, happiness, and usefulness, and yet, from various causes, of severe trial. The intense heat of the weather during more than half the year was, during that period, and indeed ever afterwards, very oppressive to her.

At the commencement of our married life we lived in what is called a bungalow, a house elevated a few feet above the ground, having all the rooms on one floor, with a high sloping roof covered with tiles, the roof being hidden from view inside by a cloth ceiling drawn where the sloping roof begins. This was and is the most common style of dwelling still in the North-West. It is deemed much cooler than the flat-roofed houses, of which there are some in every station. This, our first abode, threatened to be our last in this world. The timber of the roof had been eaten through by white ants, and as its decayed condition was concealed by the cloth ceiling, we were quite unaware of our danger, though somewhat startled by pieces of mud falling on the cloth. About midnight, on a Sunday night, we were startled by a tremendous crash, and almost smothered by the dust. Mr. and Mrs. Buyers and their children, in anticipation of their departure for England, were with us. We all rushed out, and soon discovered the roof had given way, the rooms occupied being covered with dust and pieces of brick, which happily had not hit any of us, while three unoccupied rooms were buried under the broken timber.

In one of these rooms we had sat during the day, and the sofa on which we had been was broken by a large piece of wood. We had a most narrow escape. Afterwards, we were again and again the occupants of bungalows, and we always took special care to have the condition of the roof examined. During the rest of the night we remained in the open air, and when morning came, kind friends took us to their house. Shortly afterwards we removed to the Mission House, which had a flat roof, and had been most substantially built, but had the disadvantage of being much hotter than the house from which we had escaped.

During a considerable part of this period Mrs. Kennedy suffered much from ill-health. Towards the end of 1842 she had a severe attack of dysentery, and for two or three days her life was in great danger, but by God's blessing on the means employed she recovered. She suffered during the first six years, not from acute disease, but from great weakness and prostration, forcing her to keep during a part of every day to her couch. Her Christian principle and cheerful hopeful spirit did much to keep her up, and to enable her to lead an active life. From day to day the orphans were brought to her couch to be taught by her, while our two children, as they grew, played near her in the large central room of the house. Again and again our doctor told her she must give in, and one hot season she was so prostrate that it looked as if yielding was imperative; but heavy rain fell, there was a marked fall in the temperature, her spirit revived, and all thought of yielding was abandoned.

The sights and scenes of that period were a great trial to her. How she felt cannot be better described than in her own words. Referring to the terrible famine, by which so many perished previous to our arrival, she says, "Some of the missionaries' wives did noble work in the fight with disease and death, but at what suffering to themselves! Little do those at home know the effect of such times on the nervous system. Though the worst of this was over when we went to Benares, enough remained to make us feel that we were living as much among the dead as among the living. Cholera was always with us, and now and then it was fearfully prevalent. We had constant applications for medicine, and death came with startling suddenness. On one occasion when we were at dinner, the man who was serving us disappeared. He had been seized by the disease. We went to him at once, and found him apparently dying, his jaws locked, so that no medicine could be put into his mouth. A large reserve bottle of strong hartshorn was applied to his nostrils, which had the desired effect. He swallowed the medicine and recovered. Funerals, with uncoffined dead, on their way to the Ganges—where all Hindus, high and low, the high caste and no caste, if sufficiently near the river, find a grave—were often passing near enough for us, as our house was less than a hundred yards from one of the great roads leading to the city, to hear the wail of the mourners, and the shout, *Ram nam sat hai*, which means, 'The God Ram' (deemed an incarnation of the Deity), 'his name is true, abides, is our stay.' Those who have heard this cry can never forget it. Occasionally we went on the river. In front of the city the burning ghat, and below it crowds of carrion birds doing their dreadful work on bodies half burnt, made us give it up. My nerves got shattered. After eight years on the plains, one hot season in Almora gave me a new lease of life, and after that I never suffered as before."

On the last short trip on the river in the neighbourhood of Benares, Mrs. Kennedy was so distressed by what
she saw, that she begged me never to take her out again
in that way. For several reasons, for comparative safety
among them, land trips were much preferred.

The cold weather is the season in Northern India for
travelling, whether it be by water or land. Our river
trips were in that season, and, while taken for the refreshment of my family and myself, were turned to some
account for evangelistic purposes. We always landed in
the evening, and walked on the bank, conversing with
those whom we met. These walks the children greatly
enjoyed. Every now and then I set out for a village at
some distance, and got back as night was setting in. On
one occasion I had a narrow escape from trampling on a
serpent. I was walking warily on a narrow path merely
covered with grass; three or four men were behind me.
I suddenly halted, seeing something like a rope before
me, and immediately a large serpent moved away in
fright. That evening, before getting to the boat, I saw
quite a number of serpents playing on an old ruin. I
moved quickly, not caring to disturb them.

Long before Mrs. Kennedy had any anticipation of being
engaged in mission work, from the time of her conversion she took a very warm interest in mission enterprises.
One primary qualification for missionary services is a
deep loving interest in the people to whom the Gospel
is brought. This qualification she had in a high degree.
In her words which I have quoted, reference is made
to the dispensing of medicine. I suppose there is no
missionary without a medicine-box, from which he gives
out what he thinks needed for the diseased who apply to
him. We had a good supply of medicine, and all around

among the native population it became well known that
we were ready to help all who came.   In this work Mrs.
Kennedy took great delight.   Not infrequently when our
store was low we said, " Why not go to the Government
Dispensary ? " and often we got the reply, " Your medicine is far better."   It was better, I believe, solely because
dispensed with greater kindness.   In fever cases we had
constant applications for quinine, and as this was an expensive medicine, we were obliged to be both sparing in our
giving, and to be sure it was taken by the fever patient,
as it was so highly valued, it could easily be turned into
money.   We had two kinds, a coarser and a finer, the
coarser and cheaper being, I believe, as good for healing
purposes as the finer and more expensive.   The people
knew the difference, and it was amusing to observe how
often the request was made, " Please to give us *Lūmber
Ek* (Number One), instead of *Lūmber Do* (Number Two)."
Many a time we had to tell them " *Lūmber Do* is as
good as *Lūmber Ek*, and that is what we have to give
you."

CHAPTER III.

WORK AMONG NATIVE WOMEN, CHRISTIAN AND HEATHEN — CO-OPERATION WITH FELLOW-WORKERS.

For years the number of native Christians was very small. They were regarded as our special charge, and in them we took a special interest. How faithfully, wisely, and lovingly Mrs. Kennedy did her part towards them has been attested by the few who survive in a letter of condolence written on hearing of her death. This letter will be given at the close of this biography.

For some time previous to our departure from India in 1850, Mrs. Kennedy had two meetings every week, one with heathen women, composed chiefly of the mothers of the children attending the day-school, and of women in our compound, servants' wives, and the other of the native Christian women and grown-up girls. The attendance at the former meeting was small and irregular; the second was attended by all who could attend.

In this work Mrs. Kennedy had an excellent example in her sister, Mrs. Buyers, one of the most kindly and loving of women, whose memory is still cherished by the few survivors who knew her well. Often after her death in 1857 she was spoken of in terms of the warmest affection and gratitude.

Mrs. Kennedy, like most Europeans, missed greatly for a time the society and associates of her early home, but gradually obtained a large measure of compensation in

the new society into which she had entered and the new
services in which she engaged. In addition to constant
and very pleasant intercourse with the members of our
own mission—for a short time Mr. and Mrs. Lyon, and
for a much longer period her sister, Mrs. Buyers and Mr.
Buyers, and Mr. and Mrs. Shurman—we became soon
well acquainted with the members of the other Missions
in Benares, the Church and Baptist Missions, and the
acquaintance ripened into a fast friendship. From the
beginning we met with them monthly for prayer, and
after a time there was a weekly evening-meeting, which
we greatly enjoyed. That evening was reserved for
spending two or three hours together. After pleasant
intercourse at tea, we studied a portion of Scripture
together and engaged in prayer. We looked forward to
those meetings with pleasure, and they left an impression
on our minds which has never been effaced. The distinction between Churchman and Dissenter, to use con-
ventional terms, was not merely overlooked—it did not
seem to throw even its shadow over us. We felt we were
one, the followers of Jesus, engaged together in obeying
His last command to make known the Gospel of His grace.
Of those with whom we were so closely bound in our early
years in the Baptist and Church Missions, the sole survivors
are our dear friend the Rev. George Small of the Baptist
Mission, long retired from Foreign Mission work, and the
widows of the Rev. B. Leupolt and Rev. J. Fuchs of the
Church Mission, with Miss Ellwanger of the same Mission,
now retiring after many years' service in zenana work,
first in Benares, and latterly in a remote part of the
Punjab. With two of these ladies Mrs. Kennedy formed
a very fast and intimate friendship, interrupted only
by her death. These two friends, Mrs. Fuchs and Miss

Ellwanger, we had the pleasure of entertaining as guests at Acton. A short time after Mrs. Kennedy's death it was very affecting to me to receive a letter from Miss Ellwanger acknowledging a letter she had just received, and expressing in very strong terms love and gratitude for the love and kindness shown her.

Beyond the able and devoted missionaries of our own Society, Buyers, Shurman, and, in Benares for only a short time, Budden, we had much and increasingly intimate intercourse with Smith, Leupolt, and Fuchs of the Church Missionary Society, and Smith and Parsons of the Baptist Society—all gone to their rest and reward. Our dear friend D. G. Watt still survives. His stay in India was very brief, but in this country he has had a long and honoured career.

Foreign Mission service has many disadvantages, but its advantages are great also, and among these is the close intercourse held with Christians who from their Church connections keep aloof from each other at home. Nothing strikes missionaries on coming home more painfully than to find the Christian fold into which they are brought so narrow compared with the fold in which it was their happiness to abide abroad. No one would believe me— it would be so abnormal in our very strange, abnormal human nature—if I were to say the intercourse of missionaries of different Societies with each other is always unruffled. In Benares, as elsewhere, our perverse human nature did at times show itself, but I can say that, with very rare exceptions, our bearing towards each other was most friendly, and when difficulties arose, they were soon adjusted. In our later years this friendship was peculiarly intimate.

The readers of the charming volumes the "Autobiography of John Paton, Missionary to the New Hebrides," have a striking illustration of the softening and conciliating effect of Christian intercourse in the Foreign field.   He was a member of what was called the Reformed Church of Scotland, which, as we have observed, had never formed a part of the reconstituted Church.   It protested against William of Orange being crowned King of England, Scotland, and Ireland, because he would not swear to the Solemn League and Covenant.   This Church was composed of persons who regarded black Prelacy with abhorrence, as the enemy of the true Church of God.   It was a principle with them to obey the law of the land, but not to take any office under such an Erastian, prelatic government.   With all their sternness, they could not resist the softening influence of time, and since John Paton's entrance on missionary work the great majority, as we have mentioned, have joined the Free Church.   This very worthy missionary took kindly to Bishop Pattison, and felt that in him he had a Christian brother.   He did not abandon his Presbyterianism, but it appeared wonderfully small in the presence of the bond by which all believers are one in Christ Jesus.

The *British Weekly* of March 3rd has given insertion to a long earnest letter from Mr. Paton, in which he pleads for unity at home as well as abroad.   In his view of the state of the world, so unhappy, and refusing to go to the source of happiness though urged to do it, in view of the vast majority of the human family under the sway of the Evil One and entirely ignorant of the Saviour, he is amazed Christians can contend for the small things which keep them apart, instead of throwing their utmost energies into the glorious enterprise for the extension of Christ's kingdom.

Mrs. Kennedy had been in her early days a member of the Church nearest to the Reformed Church in its Presbyterian strictness. Till she went on board ship for India, she had never attended a service conducted with Church of England forms. She never to the last took kindly to Prelacy, but the strong aversion to it of early years entirely gave way. We met successive Anglican Bishops on their visits to Benares, and in conversing with them she felt no moving of Anti-Prelatic sentiment. She heard with much pleasure old Bishop Wilson's faithful Evangelical sermons. On two occasions—I believe only on two—she communed in the Church of England mode, and on both occasions she stood, refusing to kneel, which she had been taught to regard as adoration of the Host.

As time advanced, she adopted what may be called latitudinarian views on Church government. She thought the New Testament simply indicated the principles of Church government, and left details to be settled by the adaptation of these principles to the needs and circumstances of different periods. She thought a very limited Episcopacy justifiable in difficult and trying times, the wisest of the Presbyters acting as superior leaders appointed to guide their brethren.

Where there is decided piety of the Evangelical order, lay, and for the most part clerical, members of the English Church become greatly liberalised, and are quite at home with their fellow-believers of other Churches. This catholic spirit they have taken home with them, as we have found wherever we have met them in this country.

While Europeans, as a rule, are courteous to missionaries when they meet, the great majority take no interest in Christian missions, and do not seek the society of those engaged in conducting them. Very different has been the case with individuals, as we know from happy experience. They were one with us in faith and aim. We met them frequently and greatly enjoyed their society. By both Europeans and natives they were known as our friends. Some of them occasionally attended our native services, and were present at our Christian social gatherings. They were ever ready to aid us by their contributions, and by every way in their power.

Mrs. Kennedy often contrasted this mutual Christian attraction with the isolated position of early years, and, so far as the Anglican Church is concerned, with the experience of her home life, after her Indian career had come to an end. With a very few members of the English Church she formed an acquaintance at home, and these she greatly esteemed and loved.

During the early years of our married life we were in a very favourable position for showing hospitality. Indeed, at that period, all over India, European residents of a hospitable disposition had opportunity for its exercise to the full bent of their spirit. With the exception of the great cities, with their considerable European population, there were no hotels for the accommodation of new arrivals. There were what were called "staging bungalows," rest-houses under charge of a native, called "Khansamah," who combined in his person landlord (by office, though not proprietor), cook, and waiter. They had generally two rooms, with bath-rooms attached, each room containing a bedstead (no bedding) and a couple of chairs, both bedstead and chairs being often rickety. The English of these native butlers, as I may call them, did not go beyond the names of a few ordinary articles of food. It may be supposed that persons who had just arrived in India and could not speak a word of the language, were often perplexed when prosecuting their journey to their respective destinations, and were not a little relieved when taken by the hand by their own countrymen, as they often were. I am not entitled to speak about *all* India, but this was the state of things in the North-Western Provinces, where we resided.

Benares was the first great halting-place for travellers to the North-West, and after a weary journey by the Trunk Road of more than four hundred miles, they stood much in need of rest and of a fresh supply of provisions. The only public place for their accommodation at Benares was such a bungalow as I have described, and it stood immediately opposite to the gate of our compound. The result was the occupants of the Mission House were often called to render help to their travelling fellow-countrymen who had not been invited to the houses of others in the station. Not unfrequently persons with whom we had no acquaintance, in their difficulty to make their wants understood, and, when understood, to get them supplied, seeing a European residence opposite, sent to us for aid, which we were ready to give.

We had a special pleasure in receiving our missionary brethren and sisters of different Societies, and of forwarding them "after a godly sort." They had no occasion to betake themselves to the strangers' house opposite ours. We were commonly, but by no means always, prepared to receive them, by their coming being foretold. Though sometimes not very convenient, it gave us exceeding pleasure to do all we could for their comfort and help. I can look back to our having thus made the acquaintance of missionaries of the Propagation Society (one at least), the Church Missionary Society (though, as a rule, they went to their own missionaries, two miles off), Baptist, Methodist, American

Episcopal Methodist, Presbyterian, Scotch, and American, and members of our own Mission. In addition to these, we were visited by other Christian friends and by friends' friends. From the character afterwards shown of those who came to us, we knew we had received "angels unawares." In this work of Christian hospitality Mrs. Kennedy had special delight. It involved her in a good deal of toil and expense, but it was rendered without grudging, and had most ample compensation. In several cases something far beyond acquaintance was formed. We became united with our visitors by the bond of warm Christian friendship, which in feeling, though seldom in person, was maintained throughout our subsequent career. A few yet survive who are ready to testify to the kindness shown them by my dear wife, when, on arriving in the land of strangers, they stood much in need of kindness. The hospitality we thus rendered we often enjoyed during our frequent journeys. We were very kindly treated guests in the houses of brethren, Episcopal and non-Episcopal, English, American, and German. We were engaged in one common glorious enterprise, which bound us to each other in Christian love.

From her earliest days Mrs. Kennedy had a taste for flowers, which gave her great enjoyment throughout her Indian career, and on, indeed, to the end of her life. Her father's house was in a part of Aberdeen where there were no gardens, and she had therefore no garden of her own to which she could go to see her favourites. She often told me that when she got a penny as a child, it was her delight to buy a little bouquet with it. In the Mission House compound there was a piece of ground laid out for a garden of some size. It had a vinery, orange-trees, and bushes of various kinds. We tried to grow vegetables but their constant watering from a well at some distance was too expensive for us to keep up. From the want of water, vinery and orange-trees gave us no fruit worth gathering. Immediately in front of the house and behind it were spots favourable for flowers, and in cultivating these Mrs. Kennedy had exceeding pleasure. The necessary watering was carried on at so moderate an expense that it was no burden. There was scarcely any part of the year in which we were without roses or flowers of some kind; and in cultivating these, in watching them, looking at them, and plucking them, Mrs Kennedy took great delight. They were like a part of her home life, of her early joys, transplanted to India for her enjoyment. She had erected a little wooden house, supported by wooden pillars and covered with a creeping plant, to which we resorted in the evening, when the weather permitted and we were at leisure.

The Mission House, both before our time and after it, has had occupants as hospitably inclined as we were, but the number of later years visiting Benares had been so great, that it has become impossible for private persons to entertain them. There has been, also, no need for showing the hospitality of our early period, as Benares has now excellent hotels for the accommodation of Europeans. The old staging bungalow was sold, and it was bought by our Mission. It has been for many years the abode of the head-master of our High School. A new and far better staging bungalow was erected in a more central place.

CHAPTER IV.

TRAVELLING, ITS JOYS AND TROUBLES.

INDIA is now increasingly visited in the cold months, from November to February, by many of our countrymen, called "Globe-trotters," by perhaps too disrespectful a name. They come back to tell their home brethren of the charming weather of that season—clear, bright sunshine, a little too warm in the sun's rays, but delightful in the shade, and bracingly cold at night. People who judge of the whole by a part—that part very unlike other parts—conclude that the climate is all that could be desired. When the late Dr. Norman M'Leod visited India, we had the pleasure of entertaining him as our guest during his short stay, and I did as I best could the part of cicerone. Driving up from the Ganges to my house in the morning, he said to me, " You missionaries complain of your climate ; I only wish we had such a climate in Glasgow." I said to him, " Dear Doctor, do prolong your visit till next cold weather, and then you will be able to proclaim right and left in what a splendid climate these growling missionaries prosecute their work." If required by duty to do it, I have no doubt the good Doctor would have done it, but he was not put to the test.

Dr. M'Leod, if I remember rightly, died within a year of his return from India, and it was said his death was hastened by his Indian tour. Sir Richard Temple, in his interesting work, " Men and Events of my Time in India," mentions his pleasant intercourse with Dr. M'Leod, and says of him, " He was delighted with his visit to India, and seemed to have much capacity for enjoyment; but manifestly his constitution was not one calculated to withstand the disadvantages of the Bengal climate." This visit was paid in the cold weather, and of the climate at that season Sir R. Temple himself says a few pages afterwards in another connection, " Those who are acquainted with the whole of India know that Calcutta, having the sea-breezes and some winter cold to be set against the heat of other seasons, presents as many climatic advantages as any other place of equal magnitude in the plains of India." It is very likely that Dr. M'Leod was injured by his Indian tour. He was fêted everywhere, kept late hours, especially in the great Presidency cities, preached and addressed meetings constantly, travelled with undue haste from one place to another, and thus underwent very hurtful fatigue. It is very likely the life he led while in India undermined his health and hastened his death, but it cannot be traced to the climate.

It was said that Mr. Wilson, who was sent to India to put the finances into order after the Mutiny, was delighted with the country and the climate till the hot weather came on, but declared before his death in autumn it was the most detestable climate in the world. When emerging from the furnace heat of what we call the hot weather, and the succeeding close, muggy, often stifling weather of the rains, which is felt by many to be more trying than the heat, European residents in the plains of Northern India inhale as if they were inhaling the very breath of life the cool refreshing air of the coming-in cold weather, and look forward with delight to the next three or four months.

During the cold months, missionaries as well as other Europeans are happy to avail themselves of the opportunity presented to them of sallying out to be refreshed by the invigorating air of the open country and the varied scenes and sights of country life. When home duties permitted, which they did not always, it was our delight to get away from the city for a time, and this delight was greatly enhanced by the opportunity afforded for prosecuting missionary work among people who rarely saw the face of a missionary. Often our tours were in districts easily accessible, and did not extend over two or three weeks. At other times we travelled over a great distance, and were away from home for two or three months.

As this narrative is sure to fall into the hands of persons who have never been in India, it may be well to give an account of our mode of travelling. My account refers to the North-Western Provinces. In other parts of India the conditions of travelling are somewhat, in some cases, very widely different.

Our ordinary mode, when circumstances permitted, was to travel *en famille*, as thus not only did all get the benefit of a change—a change much needed by all—but the expense was less than if they were divided by some remaining at home. For home purposes, a conveyance was indispensable, and when we journeyed, a second horse was required to meet the additional work. When we were at Stations where there were missionaries or other Christian friends, we were hospitably entertained by them, but they were at a great distance from each other, and as a rule we were dependent on our own arrangements for accommodation, food, and everything. We had to take everything with us, our abode, our furniture, our cooking vessels, our attendance, and in some cases a considerable part of our necessary provision. Here and there on the great Trunk Road there were staging bungalows for travellers, but these were far from each other, and we were most frequently where no such accommodation was available. We had tents, which, with all we needed, were laden in carts drawn by bullocks. When the family travelled, two tents were required, one to accommodate us in the daytime, and another to be forwarded over-night, to be ready on our arrival next day. In the morning, if the road was good, we reached our destination early. As a rule, we travelled early. We were up before dawn, all in the camp were roused, the tent was quickly struck, and the cart was being loaded as we set out in our more swiftly going conveyance. The North-Western Provinces are well supplied with groves by the roadside. Near the grove there was often a good well, and a village or town near. If all was in good trim, we got to our halting-place early, and there we found the tent being erected. Very often we breakfasted under a shady tree, a man with a basket of provisions having been sent on over-night. When the weather at all permits and the place is at all suitable, natives delight to cook and get their food in the open air, and, with fire and provision obtained, manage affairs very deftly.

Is there any self-denial, any hardship in thus moving about in patriarchal fashion, with many more conveniences than the patriarchs had ? Certainly not. It is very enjoyable *when the conditions are favourable.*

What are these conditions ? They are good roads, trustworthy, careful, capable attendants, horses that will pull the conveyance, instead of jibbing and backing, bullocks that will not break down, fair weather, no storm, little rain, and villages near, from which necessary supplies can be obtained.   When any one of these conditions fails, there is discomfort and touring is somewhat marred; when several fail, enjoyment gives place to a struggle to get on; and when nearly all fail, it looks as if, in spite of all effort, progress was impossible.   In our many Indian journeys during our long Indian career, we have known the failure some time or other of every one of these conditions, and at times there was such a complication of troubles that we were brought to our wits' end.   As I think of them, I now wonder how we ever got over them. By the good hand of our God upon us we generally emerged from them without any serious harm.

Of touring life we had much experience on both short and long journeys.   During our first term, from our arrival in Benares on to our departure for Europe in 1850, we had two long journeys—one to Agra and back, of about 800 miles in the closing month of 1842 and the first two months of 1843, and to the foot of the Himalayan range in 1847, and return to Benares six months afterwards.   These were in various respects very remarkable journeys to us.

Many were the incidents that befell us on these journeys, some very pleasant, not a few very unpleasant and trying. If I were to attempt to relate them, I should be filling this narrative with material only remotely connected with its object.   They are fitter, indeed, for recital when sitting with friends round the fire on a winter night, as they have sometimes been, than for insertion in the biography of my beloved partner.

One very pleasant, very delightful thing was the acquaintances we made with fellow-Christians, missionaries and Christians thoroughly interested in missions.   As at

Benares, so in other places, the one bond was unity in Christ and in Christ's work, with entire forgetfulness of ecclesiastical position. In our tour to Agra our principal halting-places were Cawnpore and Agra. At Cawnpore we were the guests of Mr. William Muir, then a junior magistrate, and afterwards for many years known as Sir William Muir, occupying in succession several of the highest places in Indian official life, now Principal of the Edinburgh University. My early acquaintance with him as a student of the Glasgow University was renewed, and henceforward a friendship was formed by Mrs. Kennedy and myself with him and Lady Muir, which was very gratifying to us and of signal help in our work.

At Agra we were very kindly entertained by Mr. and Mrs. Urquhart. In his later years he was well known and highly respected in Edinburgh, in charge of a branch of the British Linen Company's Bank. He and his excellent wife have been recently taken to their heavenly home.

Wherever there were missionaries we were sure to make our way to them, and spend as much time with them as we could. We were braced and cheered by intercourse with brethren and sisters, some of whom led for many subsequent years a life of great usefulness in the mission field.

Of many of my interviews with the people (well on in the afternoon towards evening was the best time for them) I have a vivid recollection. It was saddening to me to hear the remark now and then made, "All this you tell us is very good, and we would like to know well about it : but what is the use ? We hear now, we shall forget it all to-morrow, and no one will care to remind us of it and instruct us further." On one occasion I had been preaching in a village, and had been endeavouring, as my habit was, to make known the great, the true Autar, Jesus Christ, the Incarnate One, with His one great aim of delivering man from sin. Next morning we set out for our next stage, twelve miles distant. I had been up very early, long before dawn with my family, accomplished the journey, had breakfasted, and I lay down on our portable bed to rest before setting out to reconnoitre the neighbourhood. I shortly heard a noise at the curtain door of the tent— "Sahib, sahib!" I said, "Come in;" and in came a tall well-dressed native, who had the appearance of fatigue as if he had been walking fast. There were no chairs in the tent, but that is not a difficulty. He sat down on the tent carpet. I asked him the object of his visit. He said, "Last night you were at my village. I was not present. A friend of mine who was present told me you had said strange things. You spoke a great deal about an incarnation for the purpose of effecting man's deliverance from sin. We have had many incarnations, but not one of them has had that for its object. I often feel an unbearable burden. I have performed many ceremonies, have gone on pilgrimage to famous shrines, have given presents to Brahmins, but the burden remains. There is something wrong with me. Is there an incarnation such as you have spoken of? If so, tell me of him. I have hastened this morning after you to hear about him." Such was the substance of this man's remarks. I need not say with what deep interest I looked on this seeker for deliverance, and how I strove to set before him Jesus the Saviour. He listened most attentively, and when the time for his departure came, finding he could read fairly well, I gave him some tracts and a book containing Luke's Gospel and the Acts of the Apostles, praying that Jesus might reveal Himself to him, and draw

him into His fold. He seemed afraid to tell me his name
or the name of his village, lest he should be suspected of
apostasy from his religion. Such is the fear often shown
by persons in deep earnest about their state, so crushing
is the tyranny exercised by the social constitution of the
people. I never saw him afterwards, never heard of him,
but he has often come to my recollection, and my hope
has been that the seed sown in that quiet hour in the
tent did germinate and bring forth fruit.

Again and again in India seed sown by the wayside,
the Gospel declared among persons who had never heard
it previously, and have never heard it again from human
lips, has been watered by God's Spirit, and been found
productive after many days, but never heard of by the
sower in this world.

In these journeys Mrs. Kennedy was with me, and
was my very sympathetic and efficient fellow-worker in the
Gospel. She could not go with me to the villages, often
at some distance, but she often spoke to women and
children who gathered around our tent, and tried to
interest them. When I returned to our tent in the
evening, the first question was, "How did it fare with
you?" I had not infrequently to tell her my hearers
were very stolid, heard as if they heard not, without even
a gleam of interest. At other times my report was I
had met with keen opponents, who, in proportion to their
ignorance, condemned my doctrine in fierce, sometimes
insulting terms. At other times I came with better news,
that I had been well received, and the remarks made
indicated a measure of interest and intelligence. Whatever my reports might be, I was sure of thorough
sympathy, the sympathy of a heart beating in unison
with my own in earnest desire for the heathen to betake

themselves to the Redeemer of mankind. This sympathy greatly cheered and braced me for my work.

The European lady when travelling in India in tents with husband and children has much difficult and trying work imposed on her. The commissariat is a great concern. In most cases flour can be got of the cereals which form the food of the people, and ghee (clarified butter, a very different thing from our butter), but often nothing more. The lady has to look well ahead, to see that what has become to us well-nigh indispensable articles of food be taken with us, and that no trust be placed on obtaining what we need where our tent may be pitched. It is not infrequently beyond her power, with all the persuasion or authority she can exercise, to obtain a little milk for our tea or for the children. Beef and mutton are of course not to be thought of. If there be low-caste people within reach, half-starved fowls may be generally procured. Very rarely a kid is obtained, and is deemed a great boon. When milk is obtained, it is often so smoked that only necessity could lead us to think of using it. Servants are indeed often very zealous in their efforts to secure supplies, for which, so far as they can, they pay little and charge much, and which they extort from the people in the name of the Sirkar, the ruler. Such was the case in our day, and no doubt such is the case now wherever an opportunity is afforded. In this matter my dear wife had much to do, and by her foresight and tact did it well, leaving to me the general superintendence, the rousing of the camp in the morning, loading of the carts, the erection of the tent, and the other arrangements requisite for the prosecution of our journey.

I have mentioned the enjoyableness of camping out in

cold weather in the North-Western Provinces when the conditions are favourable, and the discomfort when these conditions cannot be secured, especially when there is a combination in failure. Like all who travel much, we knew from experience what failure implied. This unpleasant experience we had now and then on our long journeys during our first tours in India, to Agra in 1842–43, and to Almora in 1847.

When at Agra we had much pleasant intercourse with Christian friends, and saw the sights of the famous city— the Taj, the Pearl Mosque, and the Tomb of Akbar at Secundra.

CHAPTER V.

*JOURNEY TO ALMORA—STAY IN KUMAON—
RETURN TO BENARES.*

1. *Journey to Almora—Leave for a Visit to the Hills.*

AFTER eight continuous years in the Plains, we were very thankful to our Directors for the ready permission they gave us to spend a large part of 1847 in the Hill province of Kumaon. Previous to our departure from Benares, we were glad to see the completion of a work which had for more than a year required much of our thought and attention, and caused us great anxiety. I have mentioned the little mud-built chapel in which our native services were held and the first girls' school was conducted. The time had come for the erection of a much more commodious and better built place of worship in another part of the compound. The old building was so hot that during the fiery part of the year our native evening service was held in the Mission House. An English week-day service had been held for years in the large room in the Mission House, which was well attended by English residents. The Mission had resolved to erect a new place, where both native and English services could be well conducted. Our inexperience led to many mistakes and to unexpected expenses, but just before our departure for the Hills it was opened, to our great joy. The opening services were very successful, both as to attendance and contributions, and within eighteen months the entire debt was cleared.

The difficulties encountered on our journey to and from the Hills in 1847 were far more formidable than those encountered in 1842–43 on the journey to and from Agra. We were advised to proceed in the most direct line through Rohilcund *via* Futteyghur and Bareilly—a very good route for persons on horseback, or in a small springless conveyance, or carried in a palanquin, but very unfit for us with our conveyance. Over a considerable part of the way there were only tracks with deep ruts, and in some places they were so numerous, we could not make out what track we should follow. These rough tracks were not, however, our main difficulty. The numerous unbridged streams coming down from the mountains, happily fordable at that season, but often with high banks, seemed to present insuperable obstacles to our advance. At one place where the banks were very high, we providentially came up with a company of Sepoys under the charge of a European officer. The medical officer, we were delighted to find, was our excellent friend Dr. Guise. He and the military officer at once kindly said they would see us across, and so they did. The Sepoys were set to our assistance. They let down our conveyance on the one side, and by sheer united strength lifted it up to the top of the opposite bank, from which for some little way our course was plain before us.

On we went for successive days, making about ten miles every day, in a very slow and laborious fashion. We had several times to halt and seek help from some neighbouring hamlet or village, which extricated us from our difficulty. Here a stream with the mud or sand so deep that we could not make the wheels turn, and there a ditch into which we had got by not observing how much water was in it.

I must here be allowed to mention an incident with a comical aspect, though our position, which could not be called tragic, was nearer the tragic than the comic. The sky was clear; the mountains of the Snowy Range, rising, as they looked, into the very heavens, were coming gradually into view. My dear wife, so long accustomed to the Plains, whose only sight of hill scenery for years had been low hills not far from Benares, was delighted with the sight, and was feasting her eyes on it in spite of our struggle to get towards these "delectable mountains." She said to the groom, who with the rest of us was straining his utmost to get us out of the ditch, "Groom, don't you see the mountains?" He replied with a grave tone, not lifting his head from the ground, "Mem Sahib, madam, what can I see? We are stuck in the mud." The contrast between the romantic lady and the unromantic groom was so comical that I had a hearty laugh; and it occurred to me that if I had been a correspondent of *Punch* I had material for a sketch.

At length we were told we had only two remaining stages, each under twelve miles, but we found them very formidable. The first was to the edge of the great forest and underwood, with its swamps, which lie immediately under the Sub-Himalayan range. The road, or rather the track, was execrably bad, so that it took us about ten hours to get over less than twelve miles. At last, thoroughly worn out, we got towards evening to the place, where we were happy to find our little tent had reached before us, and a man with a basket of provisions. A more dreary spot could not be conceived. We were close to the region of jungle and swamp, in which wild beasts abounded. There was a small police-station, where two native police-men were located to help on travellers when getting into the jungle. We found a number of native carts had arrived before us, laden with goods for a market which was to be held at the foot of the Hills. We were told by the policemen that a wild elephant—a rogue elephant, as it is called—was in the immediate neighbourhood, which had made it perilous for days for any person to advance. That night, owing, I suppose, to the fatigue of the day, I became ill, had a sleepless painful night, but I struggled to rise in the morning, and the necessity for exertion helped me in getting ready for the work before me. Our tent was struck early, the native cartmen had started at a still earlier hour, and as they went before us they made the forest resound with their shouts to drive away the elephant and any wild beasts that might be near. We found labour had been spent on the road, without which it would not have been passable, and we succeeded in getting to our destination, after hours indeed spent in travelling, but more easily than we had anticipated.

That day's journey had a very happy termination. We had emerged from the forest; we found a rest-house, and were independent of the tent; but, what delighted us much more, we were near a brawling stream rushing over a gravelly bed. Close to us was a pool in the stream, where we could see in the clear water the fish gambolling about. The sight was most pleasing to us all, and threw the chil-dren into an ecstasy of delight, the contrast being so great to what they had seen in the Plains. One of them went on exclaiming, "Water pure and bright, water pure and bright." A native lad caught a few of the fish, which added to their joy.

D

That night we experienced what we afterwards experienced often at the foot of the Hills, in places opposite to
one of the great gorges in the mountains. The lowered
temperature of the night caused the wind to rise, and to
come down by midnight with almost the force of a gale,
the sky at the same time remaining quite clear. We were
struck with the howling of the wind; but happily we were
in a strongly built house, very plain and humble, but a
contrast to a tent.

We had now four stages in the Hills before reaching
our destination, Almora, the capital of the Hill province
of Kumaon. We were no longer dependent on horses,
wheeled conveyances, and tents. We were shut up to
an entirely different mode of travelling. We could not
move without help, and the only help available was men's
heads and backs. Very unpleasant it was then, and often
afterwards, to use human beings as if they were beasts of
burden, but we were obliged to do it or not attempt to
travel in that region. The people we found so accustomed
to such toil that they felt no degradation in submitting to
it, though many of them were of castes so high in their
own estimation that no money bribe would induce them
to take a particle of food with their European employers.
At that time, so primitive were their habits, we were told
that those who had not ventured out of their hills had
never seen a boat or a wheeled conveyance—not even a
wheel-barrow.

Some days before our arrival at Bamouric, the name of
our halting-place at the foot of the Hills, I had taken the
precaution of writing to an official at Almora, whose name
we had got, requesting him kindly to issue instructions for
the sending of men to help us. We were told men had
come, but they had got other loads to carry and had dis-

appeared. All the forenoon on into the afternoon messengers were sent in all directions to gather bearers, with
the promise of good pay. At length a sufficient number
were raised to carry the necessary things, our bedding,
cooking-vessels, and clothing, and also to carry Mrs.
Kennedy, our three children, and a native servant-woman.
For them to go up the very steep road before us in any
other way was impossible. Our friend and fellow-traveller,
Mr. Watt, and myself were ready to tramp it. It was
too late in the day to set out on such a journey, and
we never ventured again on anything of the kind when
travelling in the Hills.

We succeeded in getting a chair, to which poles were
attached, and in it Mrs. Kennedy travelled with her babe
in her arms. The servant-maid and children were put
on a native bedstead turned upside down on poles, carried
by four men. Out we set when the sun was rapidly
nearing the horizon. We were not more than a mile from
the rest-house when Mrs. Kennedy requested her men to
halt at the mouth of a gorge as she had to attend to her
child. She sat down under a high tree. We observed a
small platform in it, but had no idea of the object for
which it had been put there. After a little Mrs. Kennedy
got into her chair and proceeded. Next day we learned
the meaning of the platform. A man-eating tiger had
taken up its position as evening came on in the dense wood
of the gorge, and from it sprung forth on travellers, of
whom it was said that no fewer than thirty had perished.
So great was the alarm that for days no one would travel
by that road. The authorities at Almora sent a few Sepoys
to watch and kill the tiger, and two or three of them, we
were told, sat up night after night on this platform, in the
hope that from it they might shoot the destructive brute.

A goat was tied night after night to the tree to draw the tiger, but the tiger, after the manner of its kind, had discerned danger and disappeared from the neighbourhood. Little did Mrs. Kennedy think she was in a spot where a short time before many had been killed.

That night's journey was to us very memorable. We could not have been more than two or three miles from the rest-house when overtaken by night, and on we struggled by a very steep, rough, narrow road till we reached the next rest-house. It was well on in the night —rather, I suppose, in the early morning. There was dense wood on both sides of the road, which had the advantage of keeping us to it and preventing us from going astray. All our carriers were Hill people, and when they travel at night, which they are very reluctant to do, they light branches of the pine tree, and with it they see the path before them and scare away wild beasts. Their loud shouts are as useful as their lights in securing their safety. Mrs. Kennedy and the children had arrived first at our destination, and she was not a little anxious about Mr. Watt and myself, as we had remained behind to urge on the carriers. At last we were very thankful to find ourselves under shelter, and soon got the rest with which toil is rewarded.

In our after journeys to and from the Hills we always travelled by another route; but in 1874, on one of my missionary tours, I had occasion to go over the ground travelled that night from Bamourie. I went over it in the daytime, and was told the road had been in the interval much improved. As I held on, I wondered how, in its unimproved condition, we had accomplished it without injury to health or limb. In 1847 there was not a mile in the whole province designed for a wheel conveyance.

Very tired though we were, the very thought of our being now really in the Hills was so stimulating that it awoke us early and made us sally out. We were delighted with our surroundings. We found ourselves close to a small beautiful lake, Bheem Tal, embosomed in lofty hills. The sky was clear above us, and the air so fresh and bracing that it seemed to breathe life into us. After years spent in the Plains, everything around had a strange fascination and was most exhilarating. As I was a child of the Scottish Highlands, my early impressions were revived; but my delight did not surpass, if it came up to, that of my wife, who had in her early days seen a good deal of the high hills of Aberdeenshire, and for whom hills had a charm to the end of her life. Our two boys in their own childish way were in as high spirits as we were.

We had still three stages before us before reaching Almora. We had succeeded in getting a few fresh carriers, and as our journeys were in the daytime, the scenery was full in our view, and on we went with a comfort in marked contrast with the discomfort of the night journey, though with a measure of toil which we bore very cheerfully. Our way lay over a lofty range, and from it we descended to the next rest-house, perched on a low hill, with forest and mountain all around. We found a good deal of snow in clefts at the top of the ridge. Mrs. Kennedy had got before me, and when I came up she saluted me with a snowball, to the horror of our people at a wife showing such disrespect to her husband. The children, who had never seen snow before, first supposed it to be sugar, and were startled by its cold when a little of it was put into their hands. It was well on in the afternoon when we got into the rest-house, and we were well ready for rest and refreshment.

These hill rest-houses—staging bungalows, as they are called on the Plains—were tolerably good buildings for the first few stages; but beyond Almora, as we afterwards found, very poor, ill-built, ill-kept little houses, with a native bedstead (a charpoy), a broken table, and rickety chair for furniture, in charge of a hill-man, whose duty it was to supply travellers with wood and water. Often he was out of the way on our arrival, and time was spent before we could get entrance. In none of them in our day was there any one to supply and cook food, and thus we were dependent on our attendants.

When we reached our third stage we were only six or seven miles from our destination, Almora. We had a good view of it on a hill separated from us by a very deep valley. We descended easily enough, but were very tired by the great ascent up to the town, the capital of the province. There, by the kindness of an official to whom I had written, we found a house of some size, very sparingly but sufficiently furnished for our accommodation.

In this biography the reader may think these travelling incidents, and much more which will be found before the close of this narrative, irrelevant, or only remotely and casually connected with my subject. My reason for their insertion is that our lives, not merely as husband and wife, but as engaged in missionary work, were so intertwined, that it is impossible for me to think of her except in connection with myself, travelling with me, sharing in all my experience, sympathising with me in all my plans and doings, and performing duties which were of the highest value to us both, which it was beyond my power to discharge. The journey to and in the Hills which I have described, and our subsequent stay and wanderings of about six months, conferred signal benefit on Mrs. Kennedy's

health, and, as she often said, gave her a new lease of life
and vigour. She never suffered again, in any great degree,
from the painful nervousness with which she had been
distressed in her previous years in the Plains.

2. *Six Months in the Hills.*

Our first months in the Hills were very enjoyable. We
were all in excellent health, and the change from the
scenes of Benares was exhilarating and life-giving. Then
a trial of great sorrow came. A precious little boy, born
in November of the preceding year, in perfect health up
to that time, was taken ill of a disease prevalent in that
hill-region, and after a few days' suffering was taken from
us in June. We had the abiding comfort of Christian
parents in such bereavements. "Of such is the kingdom
of heaven." This sorrow cast a shade over the whole of our
remaining stay in Kumaon. It impressively reminded us
that unmixed enjoyment is not allowed us here, and that for
it we must wait till our pilgrimage ends and we reach our
home above, where we can safely have perfect pleasure
without the admixture of a single drop of sorrow or of pain.

At that time, 1847, there was no missionary in the
province, and Mr. Watt and myself were very thankful for
opportunities of prosecuting mission work in Almora, and in
journeying through that hill-region. The language of the
courts is Hindi, and this, too, forms the substance of the
spoken language; but the dialect differs so widely from
that to which we were accustomed at Benares that it was
very difficult for us to make ourselves tolerably understood.
For ordinary purposes we had no difficulty, but when
religion was the subject the difficulty was almost insuperable. When, years afterwards, we were residents in the

province, the difficulty was still felt, and was a great bar to making ourselves intelligible, but not at all in the same degree.

I had many talks with our landlord, a wealthy native, very sharp in business matters, as such men generally are, very desirous to increase his stores, and very attentive to what he deemed his religious duties. He listened patiently enough to all I had to say, but did not profess to take any interest in it. Our religion might be very good for us, and it was right for us to cling to it, coming as it did from our fathers; but his religion was good enough for him, and he had no desire to know about any other. His purpose was to live and die in the religion of his fathers. Both in the Hills and in the Plains we were familiar with similar utterances. In our own land there have been, and are, multitudes who rest in their religion, rather in their profession of it, like the Hindus, for no better reason than that it is ancestral.

At Almora there was a small English population, composed of officials, military and civil, and with them several East Indian subordinates. The officer in command of the station granted us the use of the mess-room, in which on Sabbath forenoon Mr. Watt and I conducted service. We esteemed it a great privilege thus to minister to our own people, whose opportunities for public worship were confined to the very occasional visits of a chaplain from the Plains. This work mainly devolved on me, as Mr. Watt had set out on a long tour to two famous shrines—Kedarnath and Badrinath—in the heart of the Snowy Range. My tours, till towards the end of our stay, were mainly short ones, and were accomplished within the week.

On some of these tours I struck out of the main tracks,

with a man to cook my food and a man to carry on a light native bedstead some night-clothes, but without a tent, hoping to fall in with hill people, who are great adepts in the erection of booths. I had several adventures, which told me that, though in early middle life, and after years in the Plains retaining some of my Highland ability for climbing steep ascents, I was far from the attainment of the hardiness required for travelling in the native fashion. Natives could put up for the night in places which to me were intolerable, as I was made to feel. One day after a long and fatiguing walk, when afternoon was well advanced, I reached the ridge of a hill, where the men with me set to the erection of a booth with the branches of trees close by. The afternoon was threatening, and by the time the booth was ready a thunderstorm came on with torrents of rain. I asked, " Is there no shelter for us near ? " I was told that a very little way down the hill there was a farmer's house, and to it with my umbrella up I made my way. The owner met us, and took me to the door of the cow-house, in which I have no doubt he could feel quite at home. Far different was the case with me. I advanced two or three steps and came on the cow. The smell almost took away my breath, and I started back saying, " I can stand the storm rather than the companionship of the cow." I returned to the booth, expecting a night of exceeding discomfort, if not of danger. The booth was as poor a shelter to me from the storm as Jonah's gourd was to him from the sun and the east wind. I trust I did not murmur, like him. A man came saying there was a grass-house belonging to a banya (a native grain-seller) half a mile in another direction, and to it we made our way. It was a very small grass hut, made well-nigh water-tight by its close thatch, with a very low,

narrow entrance. The owner for a consideration gave it
to me for the night. My things were got in. I crept
into it. Happily the entrance was on the lee side, and I
had one of the most refreshing sleeps I ever had in my
life. The storm had now abated, though there was still a
high wind. The men with me disappeared, each with his
blanket, which a hill-man, when he travels, always carries
on his shoulder, and they came back to me in the morning
looking as refreshed as I was. A fire was lit. I got some
refreshment, and on we went some sixteen miles to Hawil-
bagh, a valley on the north side of Almora, where the
British officials first took up their abode after the con-
quest of the province. I knew there was there good
accommodation. The first essay at tea-planting was there
being made at Government expense under Government
management. When I reached it, I found a man with a
note from Mrs. Kennedy telling me one of our boys was
unwell, and wishing me to return as quickly as possible.
Tired though I was, after getting a cup of tea, I set out
for the six miles which was to bring me to Almora, up as
steep an ascent as that on the southern slope, which I
have already mentioned. Happily I met the tea manager's
assistant on horseback, told him my difficulty, and begged
of him to give me his pony, which he kindly did. I was
glad to find on my arrival my boy was better. The
messenger sent me was instructed to be sure to get the
usual conveyance for me, that I might be carried up the
ascent on men's shoulders, but he told me he could not
get bearers. Then and afterwards we often found that
whatever might be the good qualities of these High-
landers, they never put themselves about to carry out
instructions given to them, except when this could be
done with entire convenience to themselves.

During this period Mrs. Kennedy, as her habit ever was, looked around her to see what she could do for the good of others. Her time was necessarily much taken up with her own little boys, but domestic work, which she deemed then and always of primary importance, from which no outside claim should divert her, never so engrossed her as to fill up all her time and thought. We had a good deal of intercourse with the officials, especially with those who were married, and it was her intense desire to drop with them a word now and then, which would indicate where her heart was, and where she was sure their hearts ought to be. She gathered around her the children of the subordinates in the public offices, chiefly East Indians, on Sundays and other days, when she could get them, and tried in her own winning way to interest them.

Before returning to the Plains, we resolved to travel to the east of the province, which we were told had a large population. This journey was accomplished *en famille*, and extended to about three weeks. Many striking incidents occurred on the journey, and are so vividly remembered by me that I have difficulty in selecting two or three for my narrative. In travelling east, we had a good deal of cloud and rain, which hid the Snowy Range from our view. In returning, we had clear weather and such magnificent views of the snow, that once and again we looked on for some time in silence, with delight and awe. We passed two military posts, each garrisoned by a company of Sepoys under the charge of a British officer. At one of these places, a woman cutting grass close to the house in which we were was killed by a tiger in the middle of the day in a dense jungle half a mile off, to which she had gone. We were afterwards some three days in a house on the top of a hill, approached through dense wood, where no person would come to us with milk from the terror caused by the tiger that had killed the woman and some bullocks.

On one occasion a sufficient number of bearers had not been secured to take us on, but unwilling to stay, we set out without bed or bedding. We had an uncomfortable night in consequence, though in a house sheltered from the weather; but when one is tired, sleep comes on, however deprived of usual comforts and night conveniences. Very early in the morning, as day was breaking, we were delighted to see a trustworthy man, a Muhammadan, who had come with us from Benares, and had been left behind in charge of our loads. He had succeeded in getting persons to carry our goods. We said to him, "Were you not afraid to travel at night through a country where a tiger was prowling?" He coolly said, "If I am to be eaten by a tiger, I shall be eaten by it, whether I travel by day or by night. If I am not to be eaten by it, it cannot touch me." This fatalism has taken firm hold of both the Hindu and Muhammadan mind; both Hindus and Muhammadans are indoctrinated with it from their earliest years; it has got into their very blood, and it no doubt has a soothing and stupefying effect, at times an emboldening and strength-giving effect; but there is much in human nature to fight against it, and every one who has seen much of the people has seen displays of character and conduct which have proved it has not borne the strain of life.

3. *Return to Benares.*

The time had arrived for our departure from the Hills, and notwithstanding all the pleasure they had given us and the benefit they had conferred on us, we gladly turned our faces towards our Benares home. We had been instructed to consider the claims of Kumaon as a mission-field, and our report was not such as to induce our Directors to occupy it. In the great spheres in the Plains our Missions were very weak, and needed reinforcement. Our path was clear. Benares was our sphere, and was needing our return. Mr. Watt was free, but he esteemed it his duty to go back with us.

We returned by a different route from that which we had followed in going. We returned by Nainee Tal, Meerut, and Delhi, and on from Delhi by the Great Trunk Road to Cawnpore, where we entered on our former route. Nainee Tal, for many years the seat of government for the North-West Provinces, and their main Hill Sanitarium, had been discovered only two or three years previously by an officer on leave, when, in the course of his wanderings through forest and over hills without human inhabitant, he came suddenly on a beautiful little lake embosomed in the mountains. I have by me now the book he published, entitled "The Wanderings of a Pilgrim," in which he describes his surprise and delight in finding out, at only some sixteen miles from the region immediately under the mountains, a spot possessing every advantage for the summer residence of Europeans. It was said that only a few hill people knew anything about it, and that the English officials of the province were not aware of its existence; but at that time the policy of the authorities was to prevent the inroad of Europeans, and the more likely supposition is that the knowledge possessed was purposely withheld. Soon a number of our enterprising countrymen made their way to it, and a road was opened up for foot-passengers and ponies from the foot of the Hills. By the time of our going it was being formed into a station. Several houses had been built, and a good road was made round a part of the lake.

We had our first view of Nainee Tal coming from Almora on our suddenly coming to the top of a hill overlooking the lake, lying half a mile below us. Towards its eastern end, from which there was the outflow of its waters, we looked over a wide opening towards the Plains. The day was fine, the sun was shining brightly, the lake was still, the hills and trees were casting their shadow over it. The scene was so beautiful that we stood for a time in silence looking all around with admiration. The *tout ensemble* was to us one of the most pleasing and impressive sights of the kind we ever saw.

We were very kindly entertained by two residents to whom we had introductions, and were happy to stay for four or five days. In the solitude for miles around of hill and almost impenetrable forest, wild beasts had the tangled wood which suits them, and to them the new growing community of human beings was no doubt very disturbing. They still retained partial possession. One of the first residents, who had built a good house for himself, a retired general, Sir William Richards, told us that a short time previously, in the middle of the day, he saw a tiger walk leisurely a little way above his house, stopping now and then as marking the unwelcome intruders who had come into its domain. Some of the lady residents in their walks had come suddenly on bears, and fled in terror. Bears were very numerous in caves under rocks on one side of the lake, and for years sportsmen found occupation in hunting them. In the course of time the station increased rapidly, and has for many years been too large to be frequented by wild beasts.

Not far from it, however, the country is so wild that they still find the coverts they require. Leopards are numerous, and commit depredations on domestic animals, stealthily making their way at night into some of the compounds of the station.

On the Lord's Day I had the opportunity, which I gladly embraced, of preaching to the residents in Sir William Richards' drawing-room.

The first part of our route down to the Plains we did not find much better than the last part of our route up. The road was in many places very bad; the sand at Gurmaktesar ferry, where we crossed the Ganges, was very heavy; it stretched over a great distance, and it took the greater part of a day to get over it. It was far on in the day, from early morning, before we got any food, and night was coming down, when the first cart with a little tent arrived. Unwilling to be detained, instead of erecting it, I succeeded in getting a native shop, all open to the road, to shelter Mrs. Kennedy and the two boys for the night. To turn it into a room, we tried to tie up in front some of the tent-cloths, but, when all looked complete, down they came to our discomfiture. How we got over the night I do not remember, except that it was a night of little rest and great discomfort. Early next morning we started, and after a toilsome day we found ourselves at night in a very desolate spot, without any shelter, none of our carts having come up, though a man had come with a basket of provisions. There was a little grass hut close by, into which Mrs. Kennedy got with the children. Mr. Watt and myself had a stone for our seat. The night was cold, but the cold was a small trouble compared with jackal-doings in our neighbourhood. Within a few yards of us was a dead bullock,

and jackals in great numbers gathered round the prey.
The whole night long they kept up a hideous howl, whilst
partaking of their horrible repast.   Again and again we
shouted and drove them away, but back they were in a
few minutes.   Before dawn Mr. Watt set out, and very
early in the morning we were happily able to move.   This
was by no means the end of our trouble, but I must
restrain myself from recording our adventures—rather mis-
adventures—at too great length.   Enough has been said to
show that in those days travelling in India had its inconveniences—I will not say perils—very bearable for persons
with any degree of hardness.   Those who remember my
dear wife, and many remember her well, need not be told
that where difficulties occurred she did not grumble, did
not fret, did not become disconcerted, was sure we would
get on, and did all she could to provide for our obtaining
necessary food.

At Meerut, then the greatest military station in the
North-West, we stopped only to recruit our stores.   From
it we went on to Delhi, the grand old imperial city of India.

At Delhi we remained for a few days, and saw its most
notable sights—the great mosque, the finest building of
the kind in India, some say in the world, and the Kutub
Minar, a very lofty pillar with inside stair, erected
many centuries ago.   These buildings have been often
described, and it is out of my way to say more than that
we saw them with deep interest.   The Chandni Chowk,
the great wide market-street, with a stream of water
from the Jumna flowing through it, is one of the most
notable objects for the seeing and admiration of travellers.
Within the great fort was the ancient imperial palace,
where the Mogul Emperors resided, and then the abode
of their representatives, bearing the title of the, King of

Delhi, whose rule did not extend beyond the fort, with
the crowd of their descendants, relatives, wives, and attendants, to the number it was said of a thousand. Such
was the misrule within, such were the dreadful acts committed, that we were told the magistrate of Delhi, always
an Englishman, was obliged to interfere.

As is known to every one acquainted with the history
of India, Delhi has been taken and sacked again and
again, its inhabitants massacred, its palaces and houses
burned and demolished, its site changed, so that round
the Delhi of to-day are miles of ruin so broken down, that
the foundations only are seen. The present city is largely
built from the stones supplied by those ruins, but still so
much remained, that when we were first there large pieces
of marble were being excavated.

During the short time we were at Delhi our tent was
erected near the Baptist Mission-House, where an East
Indian, Mr. Thompson, had laboured indefatigably for
many years. He seemed a very devoted servant of the
Lord Jesus Christ. His converts were very few. We
joined with them several times in worship, and with this
good man and his family we had pleasant intercourse. He
died some years afterwards. When the mutineers from
Meerut, on 11th May 1857, made their way into Delhi,
they, led by their rabble followers, went to the Mission-
House, and foully murdered Mr. Thompson's widow and
two daughters, who had up to that time continued to be
the occupants of the house. On the same day they got
hold of the Mission catechist, Wilayat Ali, a convert from
Islam, a man of excellent character, dragged him to the
Chandni Chowk, and there offered him a choice, Islam or
death. We have been told by one who was present that,
surrounded by a furious mob, who shouted, "Repeat the

E

Kalima," the Muhammadan confession of faith, "There is no God but God, and Muhammad is the prophet of God," he calmly replied, almost in the words of Polycarp, "How can I deny my Lord and Saviour Jesus Christ, to whom I owe my all?" No sooner did he utter the words than his head was cut off, he thus joining the noble army of martyrs.

From Delhi to Benares we had a long journey of about five hundred miles. Our rate of progress, with our tentage, beds and bedding, and provisions, was rather more than twelve miles a day for the six working days of the week—the Sabbath rest was very welcome. Mr. Watt and myself visited villages and towns near the spots where our tents were pitched, but such continuous travelling is very unfavourable for the efficient prosecution of evangelistic work. We had a good road all the way, and yet we were very wearied by the time we reached our home. We were very thankful to find ourselves again in the place so dear to us, and to be heartily welcomed by our brethren, European and native.

BENARES.

CHAPTER VI.

LIFE AT BENARES.

1847–1850.

MRS. KENNEDY, on her return from the Hills, took her former position in the Mission, and resumed the duties she had discharged in previous years. Domestic duties, as I have observed, had always with her a primary place. Her growing boys required growing attention to their mental and spiritual training. They were taught to read in such a manner that, while learning their letters, they were more amused than tasked. The "Pilgrim's Progress," "Robinson Crusoe," and other books of the same kind, were read to them with the requisite simplification, and the pictures in our illustrated copies gave great additional interest in the perusal. Paine's "Poetry for Children" was a very favourite book. The boys, especially the oldest, were so fond of being read to, that they would leave their play at once on being told their mother was ready and the book in her hand. Bible-stories from the Old and New Testament gave them great delight. We had an illustrated Bible with many pictures. It was to me a source of intense pleasure to see how eagerly their young minds took in the lessons and information so wisely and lovingly imparted. While the very young mind can see little of the underlying meaning in Bunyan's Pilgrim, its persons and scenes become marvellously vivid and real,

and furnish a kind of picture-gallery on which the little
ones delight to gaze.

Like every true Christian mother, Mrs. Kennedy's
supreme ambition was to draw her loved ones to the
Saviour; but remembering her own early training, its
want of adaptation to the youthful mind, its tendency
to give religion an austere, forbidding aspect, her aim
was, while giving it the highest place, to present it in
the winning form which most truly becomes it, and is
most fitted to win the young heart for Christ. With her
deep conviction of the sacredness of the Sabbath, and of
the great importance of children distinguishing it from
other days, she strove to mark the difference by such
ingenious contrivances as only a mother can invent. The
best Noah's ark was produced, flowers were got to stick
in the cane-chairs to make a sort of Garden of Eden, the
best pictures of Scripture scenes were shown, and formed
the lessons for the day, and constant effort was made to
avoid everything which, while marking the day, tended
to restraint and gloom. The aim was, I think, largely
secured. The difference from other days was easily felt;
but so far as I am aware, the day was never anticipated
with dislike.

Towards the end of 1848 we were called to bear the
great trial of parting with our eldest son, then six and
a half years old, for England. During the previous hot
weather and rains his health and strength had visibly
declined. Our friend Mr. Watt found the climate so
hurtful to him that he had made up his mind to leave
India. He very kindly consented to take charge of our
boy, and to have him made over to our relatives in Scotland. The opportunity seemed so providential that for
the good of our boy we felt bound to embrace it, thus

making our natural desire to keep him bend to what we
deemed his welfare. This was the first of those partings
through which we afterwards passed again and again, as the
necessary and very painful trial of European parents with
an Indian career. To loving mothers like Mrs. Kennedy
the trial is peculiarly severe.

During the three years of which I am now speaking,
the most remarkable event out of our own family was
Mrs. Kennedy's being charged for a time with the training of a daughter of the Raja of Coorg, then a state
prisoner in Benares. Coorg is a principality in the
Deccan, in the south of India. This prince, like others
of his class in India, had full authority within his state,
but by treaty with the British Government, the suzerain
power, he was bound to act justly to his subjects. So
far from thus acting, he was charged with gross tyranny,
with trampling on the rights of his people, and especially
with cruelty to members of his own household. He paid
no heed to remonstrance, and when forcible interference
was threatened he resolved to fight. In the conflict which
ensued he speedily succumbed, was made a prisoner, and
was sent to Benares with a large following.

Dr. George Smith, in his "Geography of India," thus
describes Coorg, its princes, and people: "Coorg is a
picturesque mountain region on the western side of the
Deccan. . . . From the top of the Brahma Giri, near the
source of the Kavari, of a November morning, the eye
may take in the most widely beautiful view in all India,
stretching from the Indian Ocean and Malabar coast inter-
sected with broad rivers to the distant Neelgiri Hills. . . .
The Coorgs are a manly, patriotic people. The Raja of
his day co-operated with the British against Tippoo. In
1790 he became a British feudatory, his annual tribute

being one tame elephant.　Two brothers in succession were so insanely cruel, that the last was declared a public enemy by Lord William Bentinck, and sent to Benares after a short war.　Since his departure the country has increased in prosperity.　Coffee is largely grown.　The people so proved their active loyalty in 1857 that they were specially exempted from the Disarming Act."

At that time we had several deposed princes at Benares. When deprived of their principalities for what the British Government of the day deemed good reason, they were taken, often a very long way, from their homes, to the Sacred City, so that if deprived of their earthly rule they might have the highest religious advantage Hinduism can give.　The deposed kings were allowed a handsome income, had large houses given them for their accommodation, and had a host of attendants.　They had a large measure of freedom.　They had carriages and horses, drove about in all directions, with the one restraint that they were not permitted to go beyond the neighbourhood of the city.　They were under the charge of a high English official, called the Governor-General's Political Agent, who had to see to their affairs and conduct.

This ex-king of Coorg conceived the idea of having a favourite daughter brought up as a Christian.　His object was plain.　He was, so far as I saw him, and I saw a good deal of him, as far from desiring to become a follower of Christ as any one I have ever known.　He hoped, if he made the great sacrifice of giving over his favourite daughter to be trained as a Christian and adopt Christian habits, the British Government would relent and restore him to his kingdom.　This strange notion showed how little he understood our rulers and people. He consulted the Political Agent, who threw no obstacle in his way, and also the Chief Magistrate of Benares, then Mr. Donald MacLeod, afterwards Sir Donald MacLeod, so widely known for his Christian character. We know only a little of what passed between them, but we are sure Mr. MacLeod did not say a word to encourage the hope that he would be reinstated as the Raja of Coorg. He had heard of us, and especially of Mrs. Kennedy, as kind to young people. We were told he asked Mr. MacLeod if I was a gentleman, if I dined with him and the judge. On that point he got an answer which fully satisfied him. He was also told that if he was to have his daughter brought up as a Christian, she might be well entrusted to us. He called, stated his proposal, and was promised an early answer. We felt the responsibility to be great, but we saw our way to accept it in dependence on God's blessing for the right discharge of this very unexpected duty.

The most promising arrangement for success would have been to have his child made over entirely to us, to be in our house day and night. This did not, however, suit the Raja's views. His plan was for her to be taken to our house every morning, and to be taken back to his own mansion in the evening. We felt our opportunity for training the child would be limited by this arrangement, and be indeed marred by it, but we submitted.

Early every morning the Raja drove to our house in a buggy, a covered gig, followed by a close carriage, in which was the little Princess and an attendant. We were told that, when setting out from the Raja's mansion, Brahmins were at his gate performing certain ceremonies to save her from harm when in the hands of Christians. The Raja took her in, and I remember was generally desirous to have a glass of wine for his refreshment before setting out on his return journey.

This dear, beautiful little girl was wonderfully fair for a native girl, and took most kindly to us, especially to Mrs. Kennedy and our children. She was taught with them; the lessons were never hard or tiresome, and she played with them the whole long day. We were surprised at her feeling so quickly at home with us, and with her confidence in us. The child's intellect was very quick, and she took up readily everything she was taught.

After a time a change was proposed. The Raja said it would be a great favour if we would allow two ladies of his household to accompany his daughter to our house, to occupy another room while the little Princess was with us, as she would then feel she was not wholly taken away from her own people. The proposal was very unwelcome, but it was so earnestly made, that we yielded, Mrs. Kennedy hoping, while teaching the girl, to obtain some influence over the ladies. The daily coming of the cavalcade, the Raja's buggy and two carriages behind with attendants, created quite a stir in our quiet establishment. The Raja came first, begged that all the males should disappear, that I would be so good as to keep myself to my room till the ladies were in, and got the privacy to which they were accustomed. The ladies were got into a room, the doorway separating it from that in which we took our food heavily curtained. When they were in hiding I was allowed to come out of my room, and our servants were no longer under restraint.

In a very few days we found that this new arrangement must come to an end. The ladies could not speak a word of English, or a word of our North-Western languages. Mrs. Kennedy could hold no communication with them.

She showed them some fine specimens of needlework, but they looked at them with utter indifference. Their whole manner was that of grown-up children. They tried by raising up a little bit of the corner of the curtain to see what we were doing with our protégé. The little girl became restless. She naturally liked to run in to them, and she was rapidly losing her inclination to learn. We saw this state of things must come to an end.

One morning after the ladies were in for the day, we told the Raja we had made up our mind to part with his daughter. He was surprised and asked the reason. We told him—the ladies. By their coming his daughter had ceased to receive any benefit from us, and as he attached so much importance to their coming, the arrangement must end. He asked if we were willing to continue it on the first footing. We said yes, and seeing we would continue it on no other, he yielded.

Afterwards all went smoothly till the end of 1849, when the state of my health, after nearly twelve years in India, necessitated our leaving for England. The Raja had a considerable time previously applied through the Political Agent for leave to visit England, with the view of presenting to the English Government his claim for restoration. There was evidently much hesitation about granting him the desired leave, and delay in consequence. By the time of our leaving the desired permission had not come. If it had come, he told us he would gladly entrust his daughter to us to be taken to England, but he could not think of her going till his fate was decided.

We parted with the little Princess with great regret, for we had become much attached to her, and she to us, and with the Raja we parted on friendly terms. The evening previous to our departure he called on us with another little daughter, dressed in most gorgeous costume, who was destined to marry into a great family of his own race. On that occasion he thanked us in strong terms for our kindness to his daughter.

I think it right to mention that we resolved to take nothing from the Raja for what we had done. He was willing to pay us a handsome sum. The additional expense to us was inappreciable. As Brahmin priests commonly make no pretence of acting from disinterested. motives, as their purpose to make their services gainful to themselves is most frankly avowed, Mrs. Kennedy was strongly of opinion that here an opportunity was given to us of showing how Christians rose above mercenary considerations when anxious to do good to others. It was ever near her heart to act so that her Lord and Saviour might be glorified. I agreed with her in thinking it would be honouring to the Gospel to take nothing from the Raja, and thus give to him and his people an illustration of Christian disinterestedness.

After parting with the little Princess we never saw her again, but were informed of her future career. She was taken to England, if I remember rightly, by Sir John and Lady Logan. The Queen took an interest in her. She was baptized by the Archbishop of Canterbury, the Queen acting as sponsor and giving her the name of Victoria Gauramna, her own name and the child's original name. She grew up to womanhood with beautiful form and features, and with a tinge so slightly dark that she might be taken as a native of Southern Europe. The Raja hoped that she would be married into one of the great families of England, but this hope was not realised. She was married to a military officer of rank, and died a year afterwards on giving birth to a child. We heard very

little about her education in England and about the
character she developed; but if the information we got
was correct, her last years were far from being happy.
In her grave the Raja's hopes of restoration through her
were buried. The Raja himself got leave to visit England,
and proceeded thither with a small retinue. On my
visiting London some time after my return home, I heard
that he was in one of the great hotels in the west of the
city. I sought an interview with him and obtained it. I
inquired about his daughter, and was told that she was well.
He asked me two questions. "Have you seen the Lord
Bishop, the Lord Bishop of London, since your arrival?"
and I said "no." "Have you seen the Queen?" and
again I was obliged to confess "no." I observed how I at
once fell in his estimation as a man of no rank. He seemed
quite bewildered, as if entirely removed from his usual
surroundings. He resided for years in England and died
in it, utterly foiled as to the object which had led him to
leave India. We heard of his death some time after our
return to Benares. We were told by the civil surgeon of
the city (he had left behind a large harem) that some of
his wives on hearing of his death had poisoned themselves;
but the poisoning ceased on the doctor declaring that
he would dissect the very next woman that committed
suicide!

I am now years beyond the time when the dear little
Princess was with us; but before getting back to the period
when this episode in our missionary life occurred I had
better mention the little which remains for me to say about
the Coorg household.

We had occasional visits from the eldest son of the
Raja, who was supplied by Government with means to
support his large following. The father had a manly frank

bearing, which the son had not. His look and entire
manner testified to the low sensual life he was leading,
with no aim but vicious self-indulgence. It was difficult
to elicit from him an intelligent remark. As he and his
people had been long at Benares, and servants of the place,
male and female, had been engaged, we thought it just
possible Mrs. Kennedy might get into the female department, and might find some who could speak Hindustance.
Mrs. Kennedy asked for permission to go to his house, and
his consent was given with apparent readiness. The day
and hour were appointed, and our part of the engagement
was punctually fulfilled. I went with Mrs. Kennedy, to
remain in an ante-room while she was within. We were
kept a long time in a very dirty verandah, and then the
young man, who clung to the title of Raja, which I believe
was not given him by Government, appeared, and told us
the ladies were at their ceremonies, and we must come
another day. We saw the attempt was useless, and thus
ended our connection with that household.

After coming from Kumaon the Female Orphanage was
increased. Several girls were entrusted to us, and this
increased number imposed new work on Mrs. Kennedy.
We got a new greatly improved house erected for their
accommodation close to the Mission-House. Much attention
was given to their training and education. They were
constantly under Mrs. Kennedy's eye, coming in and going
out at all hours of the day. The aim was with a plain,
useful education to teach them sewing, household work,
and everything which could fit them for their future life.
Between her family, her housekeeping, native Christian
women, native heathen women, and also arrangements for
the orphan boys, Mrs. Kennedy's time and energies had
abundant employment. Two children were born—one

early in 1848 and the other towards the end of 1849. Her general health was far better than it had been, and notwithstanding domestic hindrances much work was done.

As I have already mentioned, towards the end of 1849 my health so failed that, by medical advice, I was compelled to leave for England. We left the sphere of our labour for years with much regret, and parted with the native Christian community with the full hope and desire to return, which they cordially reciprocated.

For us with our family and luggage, we decided the most economical and the easiest plan was to engage a boat and boatmen, and thus to sail down the Ganges. The voyage took us a month, far more than twice the time it now takes to cross the Atlantic to and from America. We had several adventures. The greatest and most trying of all was a severe accident which befell Mrs. Kennedy, from the effect of which she did not fully recover till we were some time at sea. In addition to our own family we had in our charge a boy and a girl, the children of a high official in the Education Department.

Arrangements for the voyage kept us some three weeks in Calcutta. We embarked on a first-class sailing ship, the *Monarch*, well on in January, and after a voyage of three months and a half round the Cape of Good Hope we reached England in May. We touched at St. Helena, but we were not allowed to land, as there was measles on board. We had a large number of passengers, quite a number of whom were children, as was always the case in those days. The weather was varied, fair and foul, as there almost always is on a long voyage through the Indian and Atlantic Oceans, but never any storm of startling severity. Passengers in the voyages of the present day, whose longest is short compared with the voyages of

former times, and broken, when comparatively long, by
calls at different ports, know how peculiar the society on
shipboard is. Persons utterly unknown to each other,
of various, often opposite, characters and conditions, are
penned up within a little space, are brought into close
contact, cannot escape from each other's view, and are
sure either to be repelled or attracted. On short voyages,
especially when there are many passengers, this weighing
of each other is very partial. When the voyage extends
over months and the number of passengers is small, when
disembarking they must carry away a very vivid impression
of their fellow-voyagers, often favourable, perhaps oftener
unfavourable, as the inconveniences of their unnatural
life do much in eliciting character. We had on this
voyage no special cause of complaint, though there was
enough to show we were a motley set.

A Christian can never be brought close to his fellow-
creatures without obtaining opportunities of usefulness
if he has the heart to embrace them. On the Lord's Day
we had generally two public services when the weather
permitted—in the morning on the deck with the crew
assembled, and in the saloon in the evening. These
services were attended by nearly all the passengers, and
were conducted alternately by an English clergyman
and myself. On Sunday, when I got permission from
the captain, I went to the forecastle to the sailors with
tracts, and spoke to those who were off duty. The opportunities granted were very restricted. As to the passengers,
all we could do was to strive to indicate by our words,
and still more by our conduct, that we were the followers
of Jesus. Experience had taught us to beware of entering
into controversy, which so often ends in irritation instead
of conviction.

Mrs. Kennedy had much to do with her own children and those of our friend, but on the Sunday she invited all the children on board to our cabin to teach them by a quiet talk suited to their years. A number came, and at the close something in the way of fruit or sweetmeats from our stores was given to each.

I must not close this account of our home voyage without mentioning one great discomfort, which drew other discomforts after it. In those days passengers got empty cabins, to be furnished by themselves according to their liking and means. Nothing, not even towelling, was supplied to us. We had a well-sized cabin—we needed it, as it was the home of eight, six children and ourselves, for three months and a half. We had bedsteads fastened in by a native upholsterer in Calcutta, but to our horror we found the wood was full of bugs. We got rid of them by breaking all up and throwing it into the sea, and by much scouring and washing we got rid of the plague. For the rest of the voyage we all slept on the floor on such mattresses as we had—rather a hard bed; but after a time we became somewhat reconciled to the only sleeping arrangement we could make in our circumstances —I cannot say we became so reconciled that we sent forward no wistful look to the time when we should get the comfort of a good bedstead. When the wind was high and the ship was tossed by the waves, we felt the night long and dreary; our sleep was light and broken, and we longed for the dawn. The children, on the whole, bore the discomfort well, and we were all in health and high spirits when, to our delight, we saw the English coast. Only those who have been long at sea know the exquisite pleasure of planting foot on *terra firma*, and needing no longer to guard against falling at every step. On landing from sea, we eat and drink with fresh pleasure, for tea and food have quite a different and better taste than what they had on board. The greatest pleasure of all is to find ourselves once more in our own dear native land, dearer than ever by long absence, and to be heartily welcomed by loved relatives and friends. Such was our happiness on reaching England in May 1850.

CHAPTER VII.

LIFE IN BRITAIN.

1850–1853.

DURING this period Mrs. Kennedy led a very domestic life—for a time at Inverness, but during the greater part of the period in Elgin, on account of what was deemed the greater salubrity of the climate. We had two additions to our family—a son born in July 1851, and a daughter in August 1853. Like every good mother, Mrs. Kennedy devoted herself assiduously and lovingly to the training and nurture of our children, the eldest of the six being eight years of age, and the youngest born a few weeks before our departure for India. She felt this period of our family life, with our children all about her, peculiarly precious, and she gave all her heart to turning it to the highest account. She attempted no school work, or, indeed, public work of any kind, as she felt her hands full for the home work devolving on her. With those children who were sufficiently advanced in years she made it her constant aim, as she had formerly done, to labour for their mental and spiritual improvement, as well as for their bodily comfort and welfare.

Along with myself, she formed an acquaintance beyond the circle of our own relatives with a number of excellent persons of different Churches, which ripened in several cases into close Christian friendship. There was one family at Elgin of a retired Indian Doctor, with whom we had been intimate years before in Benares, and between his wife and Mrs. Kennedy there was as warm a friendship and as constant an intercourse as there could well be between sisters, to their mutual satisfaction and benefit—a friendship maintained by letter and intercourse during subsequent years, and now only interrupted by death.

Beside Dr. and Mrs. Morice, we had at this period most frequent and close intimacy with the late Rev. Neil M'Neil, the Congregational minister, and his wife, and the late Rev. John Pringle of the United Presbyterian Church, and his family.

So far as circumstances permitted, occasional visits were paid to relatives and friends in different parts of Scotland, which gave Mrs. Kennedy the great pleasure of renewed personal intercourse. Two visits were paid to Aberfeldy, my native village in Perthshire, and a strong attachment to the place was formed, strengthened by frequent visits in long after years, which remained in all its freshness to the end of her life. She became well acquainted with a number of the people, and got a high place in their esteem and affection. When in the village last autumn, several spoke of her to me in terms which touched my heart.

In her early years she saw a little of the Highlands of Aberdeenshire, and throughout life she had an intense liking for mountain scenery. We had late in the autumn of 1851 a trip in steamer by the Caledonian Canal up Loch Ness to the lakes which lead to the open sea. From Fort William we went by coach through Glencoe, a narrow defile rather than a glen, the scene of the perfidious massacre which brought so much disgrace on King William and his government, through Glenfalloch, the

Black Forest, on to Loch Lomond, where we embarked on a
steamer, which brought us to the end of the loch, where we
got the railway to take us on to Glasgow. The weather was
fine, and when the weather is fine, which at that season
it often is not on the west coast of Scotland, the combination of water and mountain, of grandeur and beauty,
ever changing as the tour proceeds, presents to the eye
of the traveller peculiarly attractive scenery, of which he
retains a vivid and pleasurable recollection for many a
day. Mrs. Kennedy often referred in subsequent years
to this tour as having left on her mind an indelible impression, which retained its vividness, notwithstanding
the grandeur of much which she saw afterwards in India
and on the European continent.

Among the very few letters of that period which have
been preserved, I find one of Mrs. Kennedy's, dated
Elgin, November 22, 1851, addressed to me when absent
on deputation work for the London Missionary Society.
It was written some two months after our tour on the
western coast. She says—

"I am glad you had a fine day to enjoy the view from
Stirling Castle. These dear wild Bens! How much of beauty
has God left in the world, notwithstanding man's sin! It is
a lovely world, but for the moral evil which so pollutes
and blinds its inhabitants. What do we owe, dearest, for
having the eyes of our understanding in some measure en-
lightened to perceive the beauty of holiness, and to taste the
preciousness and sufficiency of the Gospel! The world knows
not its precious truths, and it is sad that, knowing them in
some degree, we should look at things seen and temporal as
we do! Heaven is a place as well as a state, and I cannot
help indulging in the thought that there will be Gagurs,
Kotghars (a hill range and a hill-top in Kumaon), Loch

Lomonds, and Glencoes there. What am I writing? It is well it's to you, who know I am not quite daft, as the last sentence might seem to indicate."

Great though our domestic happiness was at this time, we could not forget, we did not forget, our happiness in that form could not continue. We were well aware it was a stage in our pilgrimage life, and that the time was coming when we must strike our tent and set out afresh on our journey. We had trials before us which we did not anticipate, but which, when they came, we were assured were sent by our Heavenly Father for our good.

The first marked trial was the uncertainty about our future, caused by the failure of my health, owing in a great measure to excessive fatigue in deputation work for the London Missionary Society. Returned missionaries often find still that deputation work is beyond their strength, but it is far easier now than it was formerly, as the facilities for travelling are much greater, and the tours extend over a much shorter period.

The result was uncertainty about our return to India. We had come home for a furlough of two years. The two years had passed. I went up to London to arrange for our going back to Benares. I was sent to Sir Ronald Martin, a physician to whom the East India Company sent their officers for medical examination. He said I was suffering from no acute disease, but that my system was so low, nature was performing its functions so sluggishly, that I was quite unfit to return to India. This medical decision was accepted by the Society. I felt my experience of the twelve years I had spent in the mission-field gave me much more fitness for the work than I previously had, and I was set on returning, if not peremptorily prevented by the providence of God.

During the third year of our home-life I had much less deputation work than I previously had. I was generally with my family, and I had the happiness of giving help to the old excellent pastor of the Congregational Church at Elgin, Mr. M'Neil, as well as preaching occasionally for other friends. In early autumn I went to London, saw again the physician I had formerly consulted, as well as our Society's physician, and was pronounced so improved in health, I might safely go back. Our path was thus plain before us.

We had now in the near future to meet two trials. One was parting with the children we were to leave behind—a trial which we knew must be borne as well as parting with loved relatives—and the other, a very heavy one, which came on us with painful suddenness, which we could not anticipate—the death of two loved and most engaging children—the elder a girl aged four years and a half, and the other a boy above three. Scarlatina was prevailing in a virulent form; both were seized with it, and within a week, commenced in perfect health, both were carried to the grave.

The girl, very beautiful in form, very precocious and loving, had in a special manner won our heart. She had at her mother's knee learned to read so quickly and so well, that for some time she read her verse at family worship with the elder children. She had a singular love for many of the Bible stories, and now and then made remarks which startled us, and led some of our friends to say, " That child will not be long with you." She was, I fear, becoming an idol, and she was taken from us. She was the first of the two who was taken ill and after more than two days of suffering and restlessness, she " fell asleep "—I can surely say—" In Jesus."

We had been greatly perplexed what we were to do with this darling child.   Were we to take her with us ? In that case, for her good she must be sent to England in a couple of years, and we might find it impossible to get one to whom she could be entrusted for the passage. After much prayerful consideration, we resolved to leave her in England, and we made an arrangement which promised love and tender care.   She was taken to the home of perfect love and joy.

She had taken a strong liking to a verse in the Scotch metrical version of Psalm xlv.—

> " They shall be brought, with gladness great
> And mirth on every side,
> Into the palace of the King,
> And there they shall abide."

As her eye was becoming glazed in death, the first three lines were repeated, and we paused.   She looked at us with a faint smile, and said, "And there they shall abide."   And there she does abide—with her mother now, who loved her so fondly, and with us both in God's good time—with Him who has loved and redeemed us.   Her little brother followed her in twenty-four hours.

Writing from Edinburgh on 7th September 1858, her mother said—

"This night five years—what a night was that ! Our precious Maggie, you remember, repeatedly said, ' I want to go home—I want to go to worship at home !' Sweet child ! She was indeed a joy to our hearts, as was her darling brother, joyous happy children, gladdening for a while our earthly lot, but soon transplanted to a better world. Let us not say too soon, sad as has been the blank made by their departure. Oh, for more meetness for that blessed world, where our loved children are ! "

The trial was more acutely felt that only a month had elapsed between the birth of another daughter and the death of these loved children—a much loved daughter spared to us.

Mrs. Kennedy often wondered in after days how she lived through that period of bereavement, when her health and strength were so low. The first pangs of sorrow happily ceased, time had its curing effects, but to the end the impression made was never effaced. Her heart was touched afresh by every anniversary of these bereavements. In the tin box in which she kept her most precious treasures, I find Maggie's New Testament, her " Hymns for Children," the "Children of the Bible," all showing how much they were used by the child. and other things only prized by a mother's heart.

The letter to which I now give place was written by Mr. Aitken on hearing of the death of our children. It will be observed he was from home when it was written. It shows the bloom of his love to the member of his Church in her early youth was not taken off by her change of Church position.

If any parents, especially any mother, read this narrative, I am sure it will excite their sympathy, especially those who have known the pang of bereavement.

" COUPAR-ANGUS, *September 12th*, 1853.

"My DEAR MRS. KENNEDY,—I am truly sorry to learn by a letter from Aberdeen this morning of the severe trial with which God in His holy providence has seen meet to visit your family by the sudden removal of two of your beloved children. We were happy in the prospect of seeing you all on Friday last; but, oh! how shortsighted are all our plans and arrangements! You have been called to pass through a different scene. From the affectionate tenderness of your heart, I know this must be a very painful bereavement; but at the same time, I believe that you will be enabled submissively to bear it. Your Heavenly Father has indeed seen meet to touch you in a very tender part. I know something of your feelings by experience, but we are sure that He who inflicted the wound cannot err. He has doubtless important ends to gain by this dispensation. Some of these you may not now be able to perceive, but one thing is certain, He intends to draw you in this way into closer intercourse with Himself, and I trust by His grace you are now saying, though with a bleeding heart, 'It is well.' 'The cup which my Father hath given me, shall I not drink it?' 'This also cometh forth from the Lord of Hosts, who is wonderful in counsel, and excellent in working,' and more fully in due time, 'It has been good for me that I was afflicted.'

"I could have wished to have written you more largely, yet I was unwilling to delay expressing my sincere and heartfelt sympathy with you and Mr. Kennedy on this very trying occasion."

Our passage had been taken for September, but it was impossible for us to leave England at that time. The passage was cancelled, and a passage secured for October in the *Indiana*, one of a very fine class of steamers built for going to India round the Cape of Good Hope. Then came the parting with our two boys for school, with our beloved parents, with the likelihood of our never meeting them again on earth, with relatives and friends. The two born in Elgin we took with us.

The voyage was clouded by the trials of our departure, but there was much to cheer and reanimate us. The weather all through was remarkably favourable. We had a stiff breeze opposite the Mozambique Channel, a capful of wind, in sailor talk; but with that exception, if that can be called an exception, we had only slight gentle winds, ruffling the surface of the sea. Instead of having our view confined to sea and sky for successive weeks or rather months, as on former voyages, the voyage was broken by our touching at St. Vincent, Ascension, the Cape of Good Hope, the Mauritius, Point de Galle, and Madras. Those have an abnormal love of the sea to whom such breaks in a long voyage, giving a glimpse of our mother earth, are not very welcome. We were some five days detained at Cape Town, which gave us the opportunity of going to the top of Table Mountain and of seeing the vineyards in the neighbourhood. We were hospitably entertained by Mr. Thompson, the agent at the Cape for the London Missionary Society. At the Mauritius we had the pleasure of meeting Mr. Ellis and Mr. Le Brun, the missionary, and seeing a number of the Malagasy refugees. After eleven weeks from the time of embarkation we had the joy of finding ourselves once more on the shore of India.

CHAPTER VIII.

MISSIONARY LIFE.

1854-1857.

A VERY short time was spent with our Calcutta brethren while making preparations for our upward journey. We bought a conveyance which would be of use to us in Benares, and we travelled on it drawn by coolies, whom we found at every sixth or seventh mile, delighted to have the work and the pay. An agent in Calcutta had arranged to have these relays in waiting for us. We often travelled hours in the night and rested on the Day of Rest. The weather at that season, the beginning of the year, was charming. The road was good, most of the streams had been bridged, there were staging bungalows at which we halted for hours, and after twelve days of such travelling, in many respects pleasant, and yet fatiguing, we were happy to find ourselves in our dear old sphere, welcomed by our brethren, European and Indian. On this journey, as on all our journeys, Mrs. Kennedy made it her special duty to make all the preparation in her power by the laying in of stores to supply us with necessary food. She bore with more than patience the inconveniences and fatigue necessarily connected with such travelling, and so managed the little ones that they were kept in health and good-humour.

We entered on this new term of missionary work

chastened in spirit by what we had recently passed
through, and bent, by Divine grace, on bringing to
account the experience of previous years spent in Christ's
service among the heathen.

There is no part of one's life to which a disciple of
Christ can look back with unalloyed satisfaction. Judged
by the standard set before us in God's Word, by the
claims our Master has on us, and by the opportunities of
service given to us, we see how much nearer to God we
might have lived, to how much higher conformity to
Christ's image we might have attained, how much more
dependent for success we might have been on the Spirit's
aid, how much more wisely, zealously, and lovingly we
might have acted. I cannot conceive any child of God to
be an entire stranger to such reflections in review of the
past.

With all this deep sense of imperfection, of shortcoming,
there are seasons on which one can look back, I will not
say with complacency, but with more satisfaction than on
others, and with deep thankfulness for guiding and sustain-
ing grace. Such were the three years succeeding the
resumption of our work in Benares. We must have been
very unteachable if we had not become more efficient
labourers than in our first years. We felt that we had
acquired a firmer grasp of the native languages, that we
spoke them more idiomatically, with greater ease, with
more correct pronunciation, and with better intonation
than at an early period. Missionaries are delighted at
first when they obtain some command of words and can
speak with a degree of fluency, but as years go on they
become more and more impressed with their deficiency,
and are stirred up to strive for something far higher than
fluency. Then we know the people far better than we

had done. We see more clearly what is estimable in their
character and conduct, and while far better acquainted
with their darker aspect, so far as the Christian temper
grows in us, our hearts are more drawn out to them, and
we increasingly long to bring them into the fold of the
Great Shepherd. Many illusions have been scattered.
Past failure and disappointment tend to make us less
sanguine, but we are led to depend more and more, if
grace is doing its work in us, on God's blessing for
success.

Such were the feelings which were stirring in us and
which we strove to cherish when we resumed work in
January 1854. We were agreeably surprised to find that
our unexpectedly long stay in England had not deprived
us of our linguistic attainments or even blurred them.
We felt ourselves so breathing the atmosphere of our
surroundings, that everything retained for us its former
familiarity.

There was much to cheer us in the Mission at that time.
We had a larger native Christian community than at any
previous period — larger than it has been ever since.
There were about twenty Christian households in the
Mission Compound, and several Christian families came
to the Lord's Day services from a little distance. There
was a printing-press, which gave employment to a number,
and in various ways our people got work.

Between the superintendence of our central school for
a part of the time, ministering to the native Christian
congregation, and preaching in the city, my hands were
more than full. To city work I gave much of my time
and strength—more, I believe, than at any other period.
I was often grieved by the fierce opposition I met with,
but also not seldom encouraged by the impression which

seemed to be made. I think I can most truly say I had great delight in the work.

This was a most active and useful period of my dear wife's life. By the number of Christians about us, by the greater number of heathen women who came to her on Saturday, by persons coming to her for medicine, and by the orphan girls and day girls' school, her sphere of influence was greatly enlarged. We were by no means alone during this period. We had other fellow-labourers, Messrs. Buyers and Shurman, though not continuously, working along with us. In Mrs. Buyers my wife had a true, most affectionate sister, who by her whole bearing did honour to the Gospel. During a part of this period, how long I cannot remember, Mr. and Mrs. Buyers occupied what we called the Mission-House, while we lived at a short distance, sufficiently near to enable us constantly to come to the Mission Compound.

While engaged in work which made constant demand on our energies, while seeking the good of all around us, like others of our countrymen who had children at home, our hearts were continually turned towards the loved ones we had left behind. Never did a mail for England go out without letters to our two boys prosecuting their education, and then and always the greater part of this domestic correspondence devolved on Mrs. Kennedy. She had a facile and a happy pen, and it was her delight to write to the loved ones, with whom alone in this way she could communicate. For years there had been only a monthly mail from England, which, owing to the bad roads in India, and the imperfect arrangements of the Indian post-office, took many days from the port to remote places inland. By this time there were two mails in the month, one to Calcutta and the other to Bombay. Owing to Bombay being far more distant from us than Calcutta, the two often reached us about the same time. The Benares post-office officials knew how eager the English residents were to get their letters as quickly as possible; and on the arrival of the mail, at whatever hour of the night, the packet was at once opened, and the letter-carriers were sent out with their precious treasure. Often at midnight, or past it, at a very early hour in the morning, we were awakened by the welcome words " Vilayiti-chitthi "—" foreign letters," and we quickly got up to ascertain what news our letters brought us, opened often with trembling hearts, but generally, on being read, found to contain news which cheered us.

Two events of great interest to us occurred at the end of 1856 and the beginning of 1857.

The Commissioner of the Benares province, Mr. Tucker, a very zealous friend of Christian missions, arranged for an examination at Benares of all the schools in the province to test their knowledge of the Bible. Valuable money prizes were promised to successful competitors, the most of the money having being contributed by Mr. Tucker himself. On the scheme being promulgated, a number of boys and lads, who were entire strangers to the Book, set to its study. The money prizes were the great attraction. The pupils of Mission Schools had a great advantage over their fellow-competitors, and I believe nearly all the prizes of value fell to them. Our own Central School was very successful in carrying off some of the highest prizes. I am quite unprepared to say how far this examination told on the increased study of God's Word.

The other event was the General Missionary Conference, held at the beginning of 1857, the first of the kind ever held in Northern India. The railway and other travelling arrangements were not what they are now, but they were so sufficiently advanced that they gave facilities which enabled missionaries to come from remote parts of the great Indian continent. The Conference was deemed a great success. Most pleasant, cheering, and stimulating was the intercourse we had for nearly a week with brethren whom we had never seen before, and many of whom we never saw afterwards. Very few survive up to this time.

When this Conference was held, all was quiet on the surface of Indian life. Not one of our number was aware that we were on the verge of a tempest which threatened the destruction of us all. Before the end of January there were in different places indications of coming trouble, and we ourselves were startled at signs of unrest which we were not prepared to see.

When the Conference was over, and our missionary friends had retired to their respective spheres, we set out on a tour eastward on the Calcutta Road for about a hundred miles. The country through which we travelled is well cultivated and densely peopled. We travelled *en famille*, as I have already mentioned we often did, from both health and economical considerations. When near Susseram, a large town, we left the Trunk Road and got into a very rough country road. We learned, as we had done before from experience, how much our comfort and ease were dependent on our having a good road to travel over.

We made our way towards the Soane, and found ourselves close to a hill on which some three hundred years before one of the Muhammadan rulers of India had his stronghold and kept his court. We had a visit from an indigo planter in the neighbourhood, who told us of a wonderful deserted fort on the top, and said we should lose a sight well worth seeing if we returned to Benares without ascending this hill. He told us he had a road cut through the dense forest, and that the ascent, though steep, was quite practicable. In the night a severe storm came on, and we were afraid our tent would come down on our heads. As the night advanced the storm abated, and as the morning dawned, we hesitated what to do. Curiosity gained the day; men were procured to carry Mrs. Kennedy and the children up the mile of steep ascent, while I walked. We gained the top and were rewarded. It was a city of the dead, but the stables and many of the buildings were in a state of wonderful preservation. We looked down from a great height on the Soane in its many channels, meandering to join the Ganges. Over that precipice, we were told, many had been thrown who had offended the former occupants of the fort. The view of the country all around was magnificent — the widely extended plains, with their villages and hamlets, stretching away before us, the river below us, and behind forest and mountain.

We had intended to return to our tent in the afternoon, but the day was fine, and we were loath to leave. There was no difficulty in finding shelter. In the principal building—I suppose the palace—we found magnificent halls, in one of which, with some clothing brought to us, we slept for the night. The people with us brought necessary food, and next forenoon we made our way down, delighted with our excursion. We were told by our indigo planter acquaintance that till he made a path up, for many years no one had gone to the fort, and traces were found of tigers having made it their occasional haunt. A few months afterwards, during the Mutiny, a rebel chief, Kower Sing, with his followers, had for a time his headquarters in this ruined fort.

Again we set our face homewards. Both in going and returning, I had visited villages on the way, and talked with the people. I was generally well received, as missionaries commonly are on such occasions, without any special interest shown in my message. So accustomed was I to courteous treatment, I was unprepared for the rude and threatening conduct I encountered in the villages I visited on my return journey to Benares. The people assailed me with opprobrious terms. "You have taken our country, dispossessed our rulers, and you are now bent on destroying our religion. Your day is well-nigh over. You will be soon swept out of our country." This was the substance of their words, but the terms they used were fierce and insulting. In one village they spoke in such hot anger and with such a threatening look, that I expected their words would be followed by blows. I was alone, I had nothing but a walking-stick in my hand; but even then, surrounded by that angry crowd, the English prestige was such that no hand was raised to touch me. I felt the absolute necessity of remaining calm and cool. I tried to speak earnestly and firmly, so far as the clamour would allow me to speak. In words as fitting as I could command, I set forth the claims of Him whose servant I was, whose message of love I brought to them, and told them the day would come when they would repent of the treatment I was then as Christ's servant receiving at their hands. They became a little quieter, and as night was closing in, I walked slowly to my tent, very wearied and chafed in spirit, yet thankful that I had been able to stand up for my Lord and Saviour.

I remember well saying to Mrs. Kennedy, "What can

G

have come over the people ?   What can have caused such
an ebullition ?   What does it mean ? "   We both felt
there was a spirit coming over a portion of the community to which we had been utterly unaccustomed, and
which presaged our entrance into a dark period.   Only a
few weeks passed, when the whole of the English community were roused to anticipate stormy times, some
hoping the excitement would soon cease, while others
dreaded disaster, but the reality exceeded the fears of the
most fearful.

CHAPTER IX.

THE MUTINY OF 1857-58.

In these memorials of my beloved wife there is no need of my repeating the details about the Mutiny given in my book, "Life and Work in Benares and Kumaon." My desire now is by additional information to show how Mrs. Kennedy bore herself during that period of great peril and sore perplexity. I refer to what I have already said only so far as to make my new details intelligible.

I shall never forget May 10, 1857. It was a very quiet day at Benares, though very hot. Every inhabitant of Northern India knows well that May is there a fiery month. In our country the month is most cheering, nature decking itself in its most beautiful garb. Trees and bushes are covered with foliage, crops and fruit are ripening, birds give out their sweetest notes, and the air breathes a refreshing balm. This is the normal though not exactly always the real May. In Northern India May gets us into a warmth which increases as it advances, and makes us pant for the rains of June to moderate the glowing heat.

On that day — the Lord's Day — we had our usual services. On returning from the afternoon service, accompanied by a highly esteemed native Christian friend, with the sun down we had a slow stroll in the garden before coming into the house for tea. We talked about the state of affairs, about the incendiary fires, the revolt of the native troops in different places, the disbanding of some regiments, and the ferment throughout the native army of Northern India. It was plain to us, as to others, we had entered a perilous period, but whatever might befall us and our people, we felt assured we were under the shield of our Heavenly Father, that whatever might come, He would make all to work together for our good. Mrs. Kennedy entered with great interest into the conversation.

We both were greatly pleased with the calm and trustful tone of our native brother. He had come from a town in the province to prosecute his studies at Benares, and had won our esteem and love in a peculiar degree. Natives of his class secured Mrs. Kennedy's special regard, and she showed it in a way to which they warmly responded. This native brother had made his way into the kingdom of God through opposition which only Divine grace could enable any one to overcome. As I am speaking of him, I may mention that he left Benares a short time afterwards, got, through the kindness of an English official, a Christian man, into Government service, bore all through, as we have learned, a high Christian character, and is now retired on a pension in his old age in total blindness. A short time before Mrs. Kennedy's death we received a letter dictated by him, in which he thanked us for our kindness to him in the Mutiny, and gave special thanks to the English lady for her motherly treatment.

To return from this deviation, to which no reader will object. On that quiet Sabbath evening, the moon shining brightly, all so still with us, we little thought of the terrible doings at that hour in Meerut. It was on the following Tuesday the news reached Benares, but we heard nothing of it till Thursday afternoon. I had gone daily to the city. On that afternoon I had gone to one of our preaching stations. On my coming home Mrs. Kennedy met me at the door with a very grave face. Dr. Butter, to whom we were indebted for kindness during many years, then Superintending Surgeon of the province, had called when I was out, and had given the Meerut news. He told Mrs. Kennedy that the large body of Sepoys at Benares, with a mere handful of European artillerymen to check them, were ready to revolt, and that their rising might occur at once, or might be deferred for days. Dr. Butter kindly invited us to his house, which was close to the artillery barracks, and close to the Mint, the only place of refuge. Talking over the matter, looking at it on every side, we thought it best to remain in our own house and await events.

From May 10th to June 4th we were kept in painful suspense. Every succeeding day brought us alarming tidings. If there was a lull for a little, it was quickly followed by a storm. There was no actual rising at Benares, but the old officers of the Sepoys alone had any confidence in their professions of loyalty. They were only waiting their opportunity. Mrs. Kennedy felt this period of suspense most trying. The very thought of falling into the hands of Sepoys, and still worse the ruffians of the city and the jail, filled her with horror. She shuddered as she heard of the atrocities committed on women and children—very dreadful, but no doubt exaggerated in recital. Her faith did not fail. She fell back on God's promises. She felt assured we were His, and whatever might come on us, He would not forsake us. She told me afterwards that she was pleased I slept nearest the door of our bedroom, as a sort of protection from those who at night might burst into the room— a poor shield, indeed, in that case. The thought, half serious, half playful, was often mentioned by her in after days, as giving her at the time some rest of spirit.

On the afternoon of June 4th suspense at Benares came to an end. In my book I have mentioned the events of that day, and of those which followed; how, on being told that the Sepoys had mutinied, and hearing the boom of the cannon and the rattle of the musketry, along with all the Europeans in our vicinity, we made our way to the Ganges; how, after some hours in the house of a friend there, with others, we were escorted to the Mint, the rendezvous; how, after some days spent there, sleeping with a crowd on the roof, we were glad to escape from its heat, and noise, and great discomfort, and return to our own house. We went back with some misgiving, but we thought the outlook was sufficiently calm to justify us in the measure.

I better mention here that, when making our way on June 4th to the Ganges in our little conveyance as fast as we could, our little girl so realised danger that she looked up to her mother and said, "Mamma, God will take care of us." I better mention also, what I have mentioned in my book, that our servants remained most faithful to us, watching over our property, and bringing us food when we could not go to our house. As an illustration of the effect of the mind on the body, I may mention that when we left our house, which we did in great haste, Mrs. Kennedy put a brooch into her stocking. For days she was not able to take off her stocking, and forgot the brooch was there. On her stocking being taken off, she found a deep dark mark where the brooch was, but she had not felt the pressure in the least degree.

Dreary days passed, bringing us tidings which the most hopeful could not construct into an omen of coming security. One of the greatest trials was the absence of reliable news. We could get no sure information of what was passing at places fifty or sixty miles distant from us, and we were thus left to disquieting rumours.

The partial quiet we were enjoying came to an end on Sunday, July 5th. On the evening of that day a buggy drove up to our door. We were so unaccustomed to visits on a Sunday evening, and yet so sensitive to the state of things around us, we hastened to the door to put the question to our visitor, " What news ?" The visitor was a nephew, who came to tell us we must leave at once for the Mint. He had seen an indigo planter, whose house was four or five miles distant, who had come in in hot haste to inform the authorities, and through them the English community, that a little beyond his place there was a great crowd, he supposed three or four thousand, composed of Sepoys and a rabble with them, many armed, with the avowed purpose of attacking the jail, releasing the prisoners, and raising the city. Our nephew urged us to resort at once to the Mint, as our house was in a very exposed condition, between the jail and the city, and would be among the first attacked. There was a refugee family with us. We were very unwilling to leave, but the danger seemed so imminent that we concluded it would be foolhardy to remain. To the Mint we went. Many had gone before us. The rooms were crowded, rain had begun to fall, and it was impossible to spend the night on the roof. The only place for us was a wide, open, dirty passage, and there, on some bedding brought to us, with our backs to the wall, the little ones sleeping soundly at our side, the night was spent. With the expectation of a battle in the course of the night between the rebel force and all the force we could collect, and the extreme discomfort of our position, an occasional doze was all the rest we had. The night wore slowly away, and the morning dawned in perfect quiet.

We resolved to go to our house, rather out of temper with what we thought an unnecessary departure from it the previous night. Oddly enough, as I mention in my book, I had to celebrate a marriage of a native couple that morning. The marriage was soon over, and we made for our home. With breakfast and worship over, we got to our respective rooms to get much-needed rest. The rest had only begun when our watchman, who had warned us on June 4th, rushed into my room, exclaiming, " Fly, fly, or you will all be killed ! " To my question, " What is the matter ? " the only reply I got was " Fly, fly ! " The lady of the refugee family cried, " Mr. Kennedy, don't leave us, don't leave us ! " I assured her that whatever might happen she and hers would not be left. Very quickly we were all ready, and in a sadly over-weighted vehicle we drove to the Mint.

We then learned, as we could not have otherwise learned, how much more easily panic is caused by some unknown, unseen danger than by a fight with a seen and perhaps very formidable enemy. Not only Europeans but natives were seen fleeing as if murderers were at their heels. On reaching the gate of the Mint, we met a friend and asked him what was the meaning of this turmoil. We then learned that, most happily for us, the large rebel force in our neighbourhood had made up their mind to delay their attack till the morning—that all capable of bearing arms had set out with guns to oppose their entrance—that a rumour which spread like wildfire had arisen that they were at Burna Bridge close to us, and hence the panic.

In the course of the day the battle came off, sufficiently near for us to hear the rattle of the musketry as well as the booming of the cannon. Soon we were relieved by persons galloping into the Mint compound to tell us that our enemies could not stand our fire and had betaken themselves to flight. It was deemed prudent for us to remain in the Mint for the night. A number of us in a room, all necessarily on the floor, lay so close to each other on a very sultry night, that I wonder we were not suffocated. The rain would not allow us to be outside.

The question, from the first dreaded by us, could no longer be postponed, What ought we to do? It was plain we could not all remain together at Benares. On July 7th I wrote a letter to the Brigade-major to ask him if he thought we could safely remain in our house. I got the reply that we should immediately leave, as it was one of the most exposed houses in the station. Then the question came, Are we to take another house and remain at Benares? On July 8th a circular reached us, with an order from the General, that as soon as possible all European women and children should leave for Calcutta, and only those men should remain who, if necessary, could bear arms. That threw on us the necessity of deciding without delay what we ought to do.

Our position differed from that of some of our friends. A few ladies, among whom was Mrs. Buyers, who had no children of tender age to care for, resolved to remain with their husbands, and nothing was done to compel their departure. We had four children, the eldest six years

old, the youngest three months. They in charge of
their mother must depart. Should I accompany them?
We had never before in our lifetime so trying and perplexing a question to answer. Some friends said to me,
"You ought to go. How can you let your wife go with
such a charge with so much danger and difficulty to
encounter?" Others thought public duty required me
to remain. We were sorely perplexed as to our path of
duty, and earnestly prayed for direction. We could
scarcely for a little speak about it, but time pressed and
we must decide. Our personal feeling, that of my wife
and myself, was strongly on one side, but there was
another side prompting to a different course. The wives
and children of some officers whom we knew were going,
while their husbands necessarily remained. Was I to
deviate from their course, and give up for a time my
position as a Christian missionary at Benares?

So strong were the claims on each side that for a short
time I hesitated. I stated reasons for and against my
departure. My hesitation was brought to an end by my
dear wife saying to me that, while her heart clung to me
and she knew not how she could part with me, it was
borne in upon her my going away at such a time from
my colleague and the native Christians, and abandonment
of mission work, would be death to my influence, and
would not be approved by the Master. This conviction of
hers nerved us both for separation. Had natural feeling
prevailed and led her to plead for my accompanying her, I
do not know how I could have resisted. I thought at the
time this was a most heroic decision on her part, and
the more I have thought of it since, it has appeared to
me a signal illustration of the triumph of Christian
principle.

CHAPTER X.

MRS. KENNEDY'S DEPARTURE FOR CALCUTTA AND ENGLAND.

MEASURES were at once adopted to carry out the decision. The Calcutta Road was blocked, but armed steamers were passing up and down the Ganges. A few days afterwards, hearing a steamer from Allahabad was expected, I went with my family to await its arrival to the Baptist missionary, whose house on the Ganges was opposite the place where steamers came to anchor. On the steamer's arrival I made my way on board, and saw at once how crowded it was with refugees from the North-West. I went to the captain and asked him if he could give a passage to my wife and children to Calcutta. He replied, "I cannot give them even a deck passage. We are already over-full."

There was nothing for us to do but to return to the station, not to our own house, which we were warned against occupying, but to the house of Mr. and Mrs. Buyers, who were always ready to welcome us. One of our children had been ill during the previous night, and on our way back, while the babe was in Mrs. Kennedy's arms, he was in mine. He was so convulsed that when we reached Mr. Buyers' house, my impression was that he was dead. I was mistaken. He soon revived, to our great comfort.

I wrote immediately to a gentleman at Allahabad whom I knew, begging him to try to secure a passage for my family by the next steamer. The mail to Allahabad was very irregular, but still it came and went at intervals. My friend succeeded, and wrote to me a passage was engaged. About a fortnight passed, and again we went to our port, Raj Ghat, to be in readiness for the steamer. Like the previous steamer, it was very full, but a small, a very small cabin had been reserved for my wife and children. They with their luggage, containing necessary things for their contemplated voyage to England, were got on board. Just as the anchor was being taken up, and I was getting into a small boat to be taken to the shore, I was startled to hear the Sepoys at Dinapore had risen, a place the steamer would reach in two or three days. A person near me said it was a rumour, and probably nothing more. I will not venture to say what our parting was. Those who consider our circumstances can in some degree realise it.

The rumour about Dinapore turned out true. The Sepoys had mutinied, and in a body left the place, doing, for them, very little damage. On the steamer reaching Dinapore, all the passengers were ordered on shore, as a party of English soldiers, joined by volunteers, some of whom were officers of the steamer, were to be taken up on it to a spot nearest a house which had been turned into a fort, occupied by a few determined Europeans, who were holding out, but could not be expected to hold out long against a great host of armed assailants. This relieving party was badly led, fell into an ambuscade, the majority were killed, and the survivors, most of them wounded, made their way to the steamer, which went back with them to Dinapore.

In the meantime those who had disembarked were in
the greatest discomfort and alarm at Dinapore, accommo-
dated as best they could be in the station Church and
the Baptist Chapel, where families were screened so far
as possible from each other. By the few residents they
were treated with all kindness. This well-known military
station was left almost defenceless; a number of Sepoys
were said to be in the neighbourhood; night after night
an attack was feared, and to the extreme discomfort of
the situation was added extreme peril.

At length the detained passengers re-embarked, and
without any further misadventure reached Calcutta, where
arrangements had been made for their reception along
with that of other refugees from the North-West.

Many of these refugees remained in Calcutta, and, when
a measure of peace was restored, returned to their former
homes. There were very urgent reasons for those who
had children to take their passage to England. My wife's
path was plain. There was no place for doubt, but the
time was most unfavourable for departure from India.
There were many English ships lying off Calcutta, but not
one of them had been fitted out for passengers. The
earliest time for these was nearly three months distant.
After some four or five weeks had passed, a passage was
secured in a cargo-ship, on which Mrs. Kennedy and the
children embarked.

Some things connected with her stay at Calcutta must
be mentioned.

Owing to exposure on the steamers, the children were
unwell, and continued to ail till they got to sea. The
infant was suffering from ophthalmia, that most painful
disease, and a distinguished oculist was at once called in.

He said, "The eyes are greatly inflamed. I am glad you sent for me, for I am just in time to save the child's sight."

Friends in Calcutta, missionaries and others, were very kind, but it was, in various respects, a time of great inconvenience and discomfort. Much had to be done to prepare for the long voyage, and the native tradespeople were bent on making more than ordinary profit in their dealings with the many whom the troubles in the North-West had driven to their city. The goods were dear and bad.

A missionary of the Free Church in Calcutta, who had visited Benares a few months previously, rendered to Mrs. Kennedy special help. He called frequently at her quarters, and was ready to serve her in every way in his power. When he had something of special interest to tell, more than once he came to her at midnight.

One of the greatest trials of the period was the want of intelligence. There was no mail running between Calcutta and the North-West, as large portions of the road were in the hands of the mutineers and their associates. The river was in flood, the stream was very strong, and steamers made slow way against it. Disquieting rumours were circulated. It was reported and believed for days that the European residents of Benares had been massacred by an insurrection in the city, thus causing the greatest distress to those who had left loved ones there. Both at Benares and Calcutta letters were posted but could not be forwarded. No message could be sent by telegram, as the wires had been cut. In some places they had been repaired, and word was brought to Mrs. Kennedy the telegraph office was open. She quickly wrote a short message, but she speedily found it could not be sent. We in Benares were as ignorant about affairs in Calcutta as the people there were about us.

When, after a wearying time of anxiety, how long I do not now remember, postal communication was re-opened, the first tidings which reached our party in Calcutta were very sad. Mrs. Buyers' daughter was with Mrs. Kennedy, and they were saddened by the news that after a few days' illness Mrs. Buyers had passed away. I have already referred to her very estimable and lovable character, and to the high place she had secured for herself in the esteem and love of the native Christian community. A tablet to her memory, to which Europeans and natives subscribed, was put up in the Mission Chapel. Her husband and family had the deep sympathy of a large circle. Mrs. Kennedy felt deeply the death of her sister.

All the refugees from Benares, my wife among them, had the great comfort of hearing that their friends there were safe. Plots for our destruction had been discovered and frustrated; assault had been threatened but not executed, and the authorities continued to maintain a firm hold of the city and neighbourhood. For weeks afterwards we were exposed to great peril. The prisoners in the jail made a desperate but happily vain effort to overcome their guards and escape; there was a ferment in the public mind ever threatening mischief, but the greatest danger of all was a threatened raid by a part of the thousands who were besieging the Lucknow Residency. We had no adequate force to resist such a raid, aided as it would certainly be by a host of Benares malcontents. The danger was deemed so great that a mud fort was hastily erected close to the Ganges, to which in the event of a rising we were instructed to repair.

Before Mrs. Kennedy's embarkation she had the comfort of receiving letters from me, assuring her of my safety, though I could not tell her we were living in security. I had also the great joy of receiving letters from her.

CHAPTER XI.

VOYAGE TO ENGLAND—RESIDENCE IN EDINBURGH AND RETURN TO INDIA—CORRESPONDENCE.

1857–1859.

I HAVE mentioned that when Mrs. Kennedy was in Calcutta there were no passenger vessels in the river. The ship on which her passage was taken was a cargo vessel, with accommodation for a very small number, and the accommodation it had was very poor. Besides my family there were only four or five passengers. The captain was a kindly man, and thought he was making ample provision for all on board; but he did not understand the wants of the class of persons he had undertaken to convey to England, and he entirely miscalculated the length of the voyage. He expected to reach Liverpool in three months or a little more, but the voyage actually extended over four months and a half. Very happily they put in at Cape Town, and there got fresh provisions; but the remaining part of the voyage was so prolonged that on entering the Mersey all they had to fall back upon was a very fat pig, hard sea-biscuits, and rice. Happily there was no requisition on the pig, as when they reached the shore all their wants were abundantly met.

The voyage was on various accounts very trying to Mrs. Kennedy. She happily had a native woman, who was very serviceable to her. The most urgent want of all was that of suitable food for the children. All suffered in consequence, and the youngest was brought so low that for a time there was little hope of his recovery. The captain was very kind in his bearing, and the only fault found with him was what between his economy, along with his miscalculation of time, his supplies were too scanty.

The call at the Cape gave Mrs. Kennedy the opportunity of writing to me. I had the great joy of receiving in January a full letter, telling me she was half-way to England. Her actual arrival there was so far beyond the time anticipated, that I had for weeks been looking eagerly and anxiously for tidings, but my anxiety would have been far greater had I not been relieved by the letter from the Cape.

They got into the Mersey, after encountering a gale in the Channel, in the words of my wife, "half drowned and half starved." I had written to my brother and other friends to be on the outlook for them. They most kindly attended to my request. My family met, on their landing, a warm welcome. Everything was done which could be done for their comfort; their most pressing wants, clothing as well as food, were supplied, and after a brief stay in Liverpool they made their way to Edinburgh. It was midwinter, but they were so delighted to get on shore, that the cold was considered a bearable hardship. Such was the effect of the voyage, its privation and its troubles, that Mrs. Kennedy had so fallen off, that every dress she had required to be altered.

Mrs. Kennedy's stay in Edinburgh extended from January to December 1858. Then and always when separate from each other, as is the case with all good husbands and wives, we maintained a full correspondence with each other—a diary on both sides of our outward, and to a great extent our inward, life. Most of these letters have been preserved, and have been looked over by me, the survivor, with feelings I will not attempt to express. Her letters are so characteristic that extracts from them will be given. They serve the purpose of a biography far better than any words of mine can do.

Mrs. Kennedy had the great joy during that period of having all our surviving children with her, our five sons and one daughter, ranging in age from sixteen years to ten months. After a time in lodgings, she secured a small furnished house belonging to the widow of Dr. M'Crie, the biographer of John Knox and the author of valuable works on the Reformation period. The family as it then was remains unbroken up to the present time, with the exception of the loved mother.

To Mrs. Kennedy's motherly heart it was a great joy to have all her children about her. It involved, indeed, much toil and many cares; but love bore all these patiently, and even extracted pleasure from them. Her elder boys were all love and obedience, and in the ways open to them helped her in the management of the younger ones. Then, as always with her, with constant attention to their physical necessities she united effort to promote their mental and spiritual growth. In her letters she often mentions her reading with her elder boys, and with the younger ones such as they could understand. She had special reading with them on the Sunday, suited to the day. She mentions Longfellow, Tennyson, and Shakespeare among the books of which portions were read, so far as school-work and home duties allowed. Her time was necessarily very much occupied all through that period with the ever-recurring work devolving on a mother with such a household, and especially on a mother coming in such peculiar circumstances from a foreign country.

Home-work was not, however, so engrossing as to shut her off from interests outside. Besides relatives and friends of former days, she formed an acquaintance with a number of excellent people, whose society, so far as she was able to avail herself of it, she greatly enjoyed. To the daily prayer-meeting she went as frequently as circumstances permitted. She often mentioned the persons conducting these meetings, the most notable then in the Christian society of Edinburgh, very few of whom now survive. These meetings were refreshing and strengthening to her spirit.

On the Lord's Day she went to Dr. Lindsay Alexander, then worshipping with his people, while Augustine Church was being built, in a hall in Queen Street, and as the distance was too great to go twice, she commonly went in the afternoon to the Rev. James Robertson's church in Newington. She often remarked that the one supplemented the other. Dr. Alexander's exposition of Scripture was very instructive and his preaching weighty and edifying, while in Mr. Robertson's sermons there was less thought, but more pathos, more unction, more simple illustration, which made his ministry very attractive.

In one of her letters she says—

"Dr. Alexander is lecturing on Daniel at present. He has only got to the second chapter. He is a prince among preachers. He and Mr. Robertson pounded together and then made up into two would be a first-rate composition—the one has what the other wants."

Mr. Robertson called on her occasionally, and his kind

genial manner, his simple words to the children, made his visits very welcome. Other ministers she heard occasionally, and what she thought of them will be mentioned presently.

She was able to go occasionally to public meetings. In a letter of November 1858 she gave me an account of a great meeting about the policy of our Indian Government, over which the Duke of Argyle presided. Her remarks on the speakers are not all complimentary. One who has long resided in India, and has seen a good deal of the people, is almost always impressed with the crudeness and inaccuracy of home-speakers, especially when they are at once minute and confident in their statements. Of this meeting she says : " The Duke spoke nearly an hour—very good and sensible on the whole, though one would not like to subscribe to all he said. He speaks exceedingly well, without being at all eloquent. Lord Benholm's short speech was much to my mind—short, Christian, and moderate. Dr. Guthrie made a long, powerful speech— much that was good and much that was true—against our Government, but by far too severe. He made many most unguarded and extravagant statements. I don't think he is at all the man to be trusted for the accuracy of his facts and for fair unbiassed views. Government has much to answer for without being made worse than it is. I left when Thomas Smith, the Calcutta missionary, began to speak. From the report in the papers, he seems to have made a very sensible speech." My wife is too severe on the eloquent Doctor. She gives the impression of the moment.

One Sunday Mrs. Kennedy heard two sermons of a very different order. "Dr. Alexander being from home, we went in the forenoon to Mr. Robertson's. He was from home, and a young man with a great moustache preached. He had a long say-away from the 5th chapter of the Romans; all very good, but so plain from the passage that nine-tenths of what he said was unnecessary. There was not a single salient point or new thought to carry away: delivered, too, with such an air of elaborate reasoning, that I was quite tired." Here, too, I hope she was too severe.

In the afternoon of the same day she heard a very different sermon, and yet, good though it was, she was somewhat disappointed. She writes: "In the afternoon we met your sister by appointment, and went to hear Dr. Guthrie. Of course I liked him; but, as is often the case, when one's expectations are raised too high, disappointment is the consequence. Had I heard nothing of the preacher, I would have been delighted with the sermon, but, from a man of such world-wide celebrity, it seemed nothing so wonderful. The text, to me unspeakably refreshing, was Psalm lxi. 2, ' What time my heart is overwhelmed, lead me to the rock that is higher than I.' Dr. Guthrie's power seems to me to lie in two things—his exhibiting with wonderful clearness the glorious Gospel, and his deep feeling, exerting by that feeling a mighty power over the feelings of his hearers. Your sister says his illustrations are remarkably beautiful and simple. My friend Mr. Robertson is before him, I should say, in this, though one can't judge by one sermon. As to thought, it might have been prepared in half-an-hour."

Mrs. Kennedy had long held Dr. John Brown, of Broughton Place, Edinburgh, in high esteem as an expositor of Scripture, a preacher, and a writer. She had read with great benefit a considerable part of his expository writings, and his smaller works, especially one on

"The Dead in Christ," were special favourites. Writing on 20th September 1858 she says: "This is a solemn day in Edinburgh. Good dear Dr. John Brown's remains are at this hour being committed to the dust. 'Servant of God, well done!' one cannot but say. The shops are closed during the time of procession, the magistrates and other public bodies go collectively. I was to have gone in to accompany your sisters, but the day is wet and damp, and I must not expose myself. How much the precious minister wrote about death and the resurrection! how many bleeding hearts have his writings comforted! All that of which he once thought and wrote so much is now before him. He knows the blessedness of 'The Dead in Christ.' Faith has been turned into sight and hope into fruition."

I have mentioned Mrs. Kennedy's admiration of the Rev. James Robertson. She gives lively expression to it in an account of the sermons she heard him preach on the Sabbath following Dr. Brown's funeral. She says:—

"On Sabbath last the day was wet, and we were twice at Mr. Robertson's. Both services were exquisitely fine and tender. I could not, if I would, tell you much of them. His text in the morning was 'Our friend Lazarus sleepeth.' In the afternoon, 1 Corinthians xv. 4, 'That He was buried,' &c. From the first we had a living picture of the different scenes at Bethany. One seemed to see every countenance and every movement, yet there were few salient points to carry away. The daguerreotype on the mind one can never forget. In the afternoon the sermon was more about the foundation of our faith. Mr. Robertson is a remarkable embodiment of Christ-like character. Every opening of the mouth marks him pre-eminently a man of God. There is no great intellectual power, but, oh! such sweetness—more than Baxterian heavenli-

ness! He seems to know one's every care and sorrow, and
helps one so sweetly to bring all to Jesus. His illustrations,
too, are remarkably beautiful and simple. He is of the same
school as good dear Mr. Aitken, but is greatly his superior over
one's whole emotional nature."

The mere statement of evangelical truth, however
accurate, did not at all meet her views of what preaching
should be. She mentions that on one occasion she was
present at the noon prayer-meeting, when a well-known
Free Church minister of Edinburgh gave the address.
Of it she says: "It was the hard, dry truth, very evangelical, but so hard! nothing mellow or drawing! This is
not, I think, what tells on saints or sinners. It is certainly
not like Him who wept over Jerusalem."

Those who knew Mrs. Kennedy will recognise in these
estimates of preachers characteristics of her mind and
heart.

For residence there was not a place in the United
Kingdom which she deemed superior to Edinburgh. Its
site and surroundings have always secured the admiration
of visitors, and is a source of abiding pleasure to its residents. It has all the advantages of a great city, and yet
it is not so large as to render it difficult to get from the
suburbs to its central places, where most attractive meetings are held. All men of note—travellers, scientists,
distinguished lecturers, great preachers, and great missionaries—are sure to make their way to it, and to be
heartily welcomed. Its spiritual advantages are great in
its ministers, its meetings for the promotion of the highest
objects, its gatherings for prayers, at which persons in
health and any degree of leisure can avail themselves, and
in the general tone of Christ's followers, at once Christian,
and, notwithstanding national ecclesiastical prejudices,

free from sectarian narrowness. The tone of Christian society was specially consonant to Mrs. Kennedy's mind and feeling.

With her children all with her, constant intercourse with relatives, kind attention from friends, and the advantages of Edinburgh to which I have referred, Mrs. Kennedy's stay in that city during nearly the whole of 1858 brought her much enjoyment. And yet, as is always the case in this world, the pleasure was not without its alloy. It was not all sunshine—far from it. There were very serious drawbacks to her rest of spirit.

It was a time of constant occupation, up to the full extent of her time and strength, and not infrequently beyond it. The delight in her domestic work was great, but it was a great strain on her strength, both of body and spirit.

One of her greatest trials was her separation from me, our great distance from each other, and her anxiety about me. For a long time after she left, on to her being for some time in Edinburgh, though the back of the Mutiny and rebellion had been broken, large districts in the North-West and in Central India remained unsubdued, and there was still great unrest in the public mind, which left an unpleasant feeling of insecurity. Then, as the hot weather in India came on, as I shall presently mention, I was obliged to tell her I was very unwell, which led her to look forward to every mail with increased anxiety. There were two mails every week, one from Calcutta and the other from Bombay, but they often reached close on each other.

Her letters at this period bear striking testimony to her great, at times almost overwhelming, struggle between conflicting feelings—her intense desire, on the one

hand, to rejoin me, and take her former part in mission
work, and, on the other hand, the tearing of herself away
from her children, who were dear to her as her own soul.
All along her stay she had to maintain this struggle, and
as the time came for her departure, the painful feeling
became more intense. She gives expression to it in letter
after letter.

I cannot do better, in illustration of Mrs. Kennedy's
character, than, in addition to the quotations already made,
give extracts from her letters. I am sure they will be
read with deep sympathy by those who in any degree
realise her position as she wrote, and who are swayed by
warm domestic feeling. These will not complain that
they are too numerous.

"*February 9th*, 1858.—The house we occupy in Lauriston,
which part of Edinburgh you probably know, is a very respect-
able-looking rather old-fashioned mansion, with a nice garden.
It has no view, for it has walls, walls, on every side. I was
regretting the want of a prospect, and said so to our very kind
doctor, when he smiled, and told me it was just what he con-
gratulated me on, being so well sheltered."

The felt want of a prospect was very characteristic
of Mrs. Kennedy. She removed after a time to Mrs.
M'Crie's house in the south of Edinburgh.

"*February 19th*.—Good Mr. Aitken is gone. At any other
time his death would have affected me very much, but I felt
as if all my emotionary nature were spent. How many of
those we have loved on earth are now in heaven! Surely we
ought to have the pilgrim spirit! In my dear sister Eliza's
(Mrs. Buyers) and Mr. Aitken's death I have lost two of
those I have known best and loved most all my days. They
have met in heaven, I have the confident assurance. Oh, to

be made meet to join them there! I have often felt of late as if near the end of my own journey—so wearied and worn—and such a pressure of anxiety about you, it seemed as if my power of thinking and feeling were exhausted. Now that I am becoming somewhat myself again, the cares of this life are in danger of occupying too large a share of my thoughts.

"You know I have no love for Benares as a place to live in all my days, but you know my affection for you, and I trust my entire willingness to do and go wherever Providence may appoint. To hear of your coming home would be the most joyful news I could receive, and yet I would not for the world turn a straw to bring you home. I have always felt this clearly and strongly to be my duty.

"Last Sabbath we went to Dr. Alexander's. I enjoyed both prayer and sermon very much, and felt unspeakably more at home than in Mr. Pulsford's. He has not so much of the M'Cheyne element about him as I would like, but all things considered, I feel disposed to settle down there. James likes him very much, and this is one strong reason for my going there. Where else should I go? Notwithstanding the liberty you offer me, I 'spect you expect me to act consistently as the wife of an Independent minister."

When embarking for England, Mrs. Kennedy received the tidings of the death of her sister, Mrs. Buyers. Shortly after her arrival in England she got the tidings of the death of another sister.

"My dear sister Anne rests from her sufferings, and is now, I fully believe and trust, among the happy company before the throne. Her death is a new blow, and I was so unprepared for it, I felt it all the more. Most deeply do I lament not having seen her. She had been so long ill, that I suppose my father thought she was to continue so, and then at the last she sank rapidly.

"Two very dear sisters gone in the short space of six

months ! Mr. Aitken gone too ! I cannot tell you how sad
and desolate I have been. All last week I was sadly depressed, but I am again beginning to get a clearer view of the
bright side, and have had some sweet glimpses of the King in
His beauty, and of the land which is afar off. That precious
text has been doubly precious—'Our Saviour Jesus Christ,
who hath *abolished* death, and hath brought life and immor-
tality to light.' Oh, that these repeated strokes may be
abundantly sanctified to us all !

"Sometimes I tremble lest they should pass us without
being improved as they ought to be, and this leads to the
earnest prayer that God would Himself teach us all we ought
to know, and make us all we ought to be. To my poor old
parents this is a great trial.

"When am I to come to you ? I think of you, and feel
inclined to be off by the next mail. When I look at the little
dependent, clinging children, I almost wish I had not come
home. The Lord will, I trust, make our way plain. Past
experience enables me to leave the future more in His hands.
Then, with such bitterly learnt lessons of the shortness and
uncertainty of all here, it is felt to be vexing oneself in vain.
I am afraid I have sometimes been tempted to hard thoughts
of God, and have been frightened at a feeling of indifference
which now and then for a few moments has come over me. I
feel sadly, sadly behind in the best things—feeble, yet I would
be pursuing."

"*April 5th.*—Next mail is eagerly looked for here. There
are large placards, it seems, put up through the town announcing 'Sir Colin Campbell before Lucknow.' It will be a
death-struggle, no doubt, on the part of the rebels, and will
be fearful work for our troops. Oh, the horrors of war ! How
it steels the heart against all the ordinary sympathies of human
nature !

"The idea of your being so solitary, of your having so much
to do, of the possibility of your being ill, &c., I cannot tell you
what a thinking I have had about you. How entirely are we

cast upon God in regard to each other in present circumstances! I do feel Him to be a present help and a sure refuge—blessed be His name—and have been enjoying some quiet seasons of communion with Him, which have strengthened me wonderfully. Where and how He leads we may safely follow. He .is our covenant God and Father, and will never leave nor forsake us. Doubts and cares and gloomy thoughts often come over me, but I look to Him and am lightened. How often are our fears disappointed! I was full of anxiety about your having ventured to Allahabad. That anxiety is removed; another reproof to my unbelief. Again, Benares has been mercifully preserved. 'I shall one day fall by the hand of Saul,' comes up for a lodgment in my mind, but I will rather try to 'thank God and take courage.'

"We have had delightful weather for some weeks back. Oh, the exquisite beauty of spring! How beautifully and impressively does it proclaim a present God! Sometimes one cannot but feel saddened by it, to think of those whose precious dust is quickened to life by no change of season. But then cheering thoughts come to one's help of the glorious awaking which will be theirs in the morning of the Resurrection—no autumn to follow that; death, the last enemy, shall be destroyed.

"We had a beautiful walk one forenoon lately in the Grange Cemetery. You know it is there Dr. Chalmers is buried. Sir A. Agnew, too, a few yards from him. I looked on their graves with deep emotion."

"*April* 10*th.*—Dr. Colestream has just been here, and tells me there is a telegram in this morning announcing that Lucknow is ours, with the loss of 100 men killed and some 300 wounded. I trust this may be correct, but these telegrams are not always to be depended on. How awful the loss of life in this fearful war! One can hardly think it possible that so many fellow-creatures are being shot down from time to time with so little regret; and yet it seems an awful necessity. What a blessed time will be that when each man will recognise in his fellow-man a brother whom he ought to love as himself!

"I like Dr. Alexander's preaching on the whole very much. He is earnest, but there is a want of mellowness and unction about him which I regret — a sarcastic manner in speaking of the views of others, which is anything but dignified and becoming."

"*April* 16*th.*—I often feel as if I ought to be off at once, and I think how much I could do in the Mission in present circumstances; and then when I look at the little ones, so young, and find it so difficult to leave them for half an hour, I know not what to think. I seek daily to commit the matter to God. It is banishment to be away from you, but if that banishment be duty we shall have grace and strength mutually to bear it. It will be a sad trial to leave these little ones, come when it may."

"*April* 30*th.*—On Thursday the four eldest accompanied me to hear Mr. Stoughton. Never did I listen to a more excellent sermon. His text was 'Christ was once offered to put away sin by the sacrifice of Himself.' He dwelt shortly on the sacrifice of Christ, but *the sermon* was about the Christian duty which that involved—the living sacrifice which believers owe to God. What must it be to sit under such a man?"

She was not at all so well pleased with the meeting which followed two days afterwards, as she was with the sermon.

"I went to the meeting of the Scottish Congregational Union. The meeting was as poor an affair as ever I attended. The chief speaker gave one of the longest, stupidest, driest speeches it was ever my lot to hear. It was all about the Fathers of the Union, and if he proved anything, it was how very low the standard of attainment was among the Congregational ministers of Scotland. He talked so much and with such silly vanity, that one could not but remember the old adage that exceptions form the rule. Other speakers followed, but there was much of what is commonly called 'blarney,' and nothing solid."

"*May 22nd.*—Matters are looking dark and gloomy for India. There are some very sad accounts of the state of things in to-day's *Witness*. Your account, too, of the Azimghur affair (sixty miles from Benares) is very distressing. It will be death to our troops to be out in the hot weather. Every mail brings a long letter from Dr. Duff. We are ever thrown back on the great and glorious truth that God reigns, and will make even the wrath of man to praise Him. Each day lately has been the well-remembered anniversary of some new direful news in the progress of the revolt. Sometimes I feel quite over-powered by gloomy forebodings, and then I look to Him and am lightened. May you be kept in the shadow of His wings, and may your labours among our poor soldiers be abundantly owned and blessed! It makes me sad when I think that I cannot be present to do anything to help you.

"One thing I have to ask is this : that you do not think of coming to Calcutta for me, unless on your own account. I feel as I never perhaps felt before the strength of my affection for India. Surely our Heavenly Father, who has given us our children, will not allow them to suffer in any serious way by our absence. Mere feeling shrinks from the trial, but His infinite wisdom knows best what is good for us and them, and He seeks our highest and greatest good by means often painful enough to us. I trust I do simply seek to be led and guided by Him alone."

"*May 31st.*—If spared to meet, I trust I may be a greater help to you than I have ever been, confident in my own consciousness of desiring to be where and doing what our Heavenly Father would have me to be and do. I fear I have spoken too much about your leaving Benares. I suppose I have said nothing I did not feel, but I have expressed one-sided views, and I tremble lest I have done wrong in giving expression to them. When you see your way clearly, be assured your Margaret will be ever ready to fall in with your views. If I know myself, I would not for a thousand worlds take a single step out of that course which Infinite Wisdom and Love have marked out for us, whatever sacrifices that may involve.

"Why do you fancy I object to your writing on Sabbaths? I should write to you often on that day, but it is far the busiest I have."

She then proceeds to show how fully the day is occupied with public services and home-duties, ending with reading at night with the two eldest boys. She proceeds :—

"Many a Sabbath I scarcely get a chapter read in private, much to my own privation, yet no way to my having a bad conscience, for I feel duty requires me to deny myself. I try to make up for it on week-days. I was again at the Union Prayer-Meeting—a very delightful one.

"How you can travel about as you do with the country still so disturbed is to me very surprising. I think it very unwise even if my sage husband dares to do it. I see by the papers how two gentlemen have just been murdered between Agra and Alyghur."

"*August 24th.*—I cannot tell you into what a state of anxiety and uneasiness your letter of July 9th, received this morning, has thrown me. You ill, and me sixteen thousand miles from you (by the long sea-route)! Alas! what poor, feeble creatures we are! Fain would I come to you at once to nurse, cheer, and help you; yet what cause of thankfulness have we for the mercy mixed with this trial, for the assurance that all things shall work together for our good, if, as I trust, we do, though feebly, alas! love God. I am so thankful your fever had abated before the leaving of the mail.

"It is too bad in you to banter me about the ease with which I pass from one subject to another. To you the pen runs on as fast as my fingers can wield it. You have just what comes, and as it comes—all things and subjects jumbled together. Never mind; you and I don't want fine, stiff, well-arranged sentiment, following an orderly announcement of fact. We want free spontaneous talk about subjects mutually interesting.

"Mrs. B—— has been here the last hour, and we have had a sweet talk about our mutual cares and anxieties. These are not few, as you may well know, but I do feel as if God were enabling me to cast my burden on Himself; and not only that, but to leave it more on Him than I have hitherto done. My precious, clinging children! how shall I tear myself from them? It is a bitter, bitter trial, but God will carry me through, I believe and trust. I am not now harassed by those distressing questions as to duty which were so painful. My path seems clearly indicated by God in His providence, and when that is the case, we may, as you say, tread it with a firm step.

"The halo of your dear face seems to come across the water, and I sometimes long to be away. People wonder I can leave my children. One or two have actually said to me, 'Won't you be sorry to leave your children?' I cannot reply to such. I look at them, hardly perhaps intimating there is any difficulty in the matter. I suppose I am sometimes thought stoical. Ah! little do they know the fearful struggle, the soul conflict, which has often threatened to separate it from the body, I have passed through. I now feel as if the worst were over, and almost wonder at myself. I have attained within the last few weeks to a degree of quiet confidence in giving our children entirely to God that I do not remember before.

"What a busy time have I had since I left you! Never before had I so long a time of continuous occupation; not that I have had a great deal to do, but that I have had little time when I could retire for secret prayer and reading for more than a few minutes at a time. I seem to have been living on the strength of former experiences in a great measure, though I have had some sweet moments many a time in reference to family circumstances. Some passages of Scripture have been very sweet to me of late, such as 'They shall never be ashamed that wait for Me;' 'None of them that trust in Him shall be desolate.'"

I

"*May 6th*, 1858.—I fear it will be long before the country is anything like settled. Oh, dear! that lovely place Rhotasgarh! How it enriches the mind to have visited the magnificent scenes in the Himalaya and elsewhere you and I have been privileged to see! A fine summer day here, all nature rejoicing in God's works. What would this world have been had sin not entered it? What would heaven be? No partings, no diminutions there! May all the discipline through which we are called to pass be the means of fitting us for that blessed abode of purity and peace!"

"*September* 12th.—Lately I have been weighed down by anxiety about the children, their spiritual interests especially. How unspeakably precious is the throne of grace! yet I do not seem to get so near to God as I have often done in former years. The 'cares of this life' press so heavily and near, and now that I have fairly commenced to arrange for leaving a thousand new cares and anxieties open up before me. I hope I do try to cast my burden on the Lord, but I ought to leave it with Him, and here is the difficulty. The Monday forenoon prayer-meetings are very precious—more helpful to me than any other means. I never omit them when it is possible for me to be present. I take the four youngest and nurse with me. They remain in the Princes Street Gardens, which are perfectly safe and full of amusement for children."

In autumn Mrs. Kennedy paid a brief visit to Aberdeen, Elgin, and Inverness. She spent a few days with her parents and relatives in Aberdeen, and had much happy, interesting, and yet sad conversation with them about the years which had passed since they had parted. She visited her sister Anne's grave. She called on the widow of her pastor, and was told by her that the last words her husband uttered were, "In Thy presence is fulness of joy." She went to the prayer-meeting in her old church, and heard Mr. Aitken's son give an address "in the good old style." She spent two days at Elgin with very dear friends. She says, "I went alone and walked for some little time in the neighbourhood of the house we occupied. The past five years seemed obliterated, and our lambs in heaven ran and sported in my mind's eye as once they did in reality. I did not shed a tear. Next morning I rose early and went at 7 A.M. to the Cathedral, round which the cemetery lies where our two children are buried. I spent an hour there with my Bible. You know what my thoughts and feelings would be, and to what portions of the blessed Book I would turn. Death is indeed an enemy, but its sting is gone. The bright world beyond sometimes assumes a more dazzling brightness when viewed through the gloom of the grave."

From Elgin she went on to Inverness. "I spent a very pleasant afternoon and evening with the dear old people. Your father would see me on board, for which I was very sorry. Dear old man! he is failing a good deal more than your mother. Still the same genuine character."

Mrs. Kennedy returned by steamer to Edinburgh, and was glad to find herself again with her children, whom she was unwilling to leave for a day. They had been left in the charge of her loved sister-in-law, my sister Eliza.

The letters from which these extracts are taken abound with the information which an affectionate wife far distant from her husband would naturally give him about herself, her children, her society, her circumstances, cares, worries, hopes, fears, and joys. She had from an early period been fond of arithmetic, and one of her temptations was to indulge in figures and calculations, to her own disquietude, as they led her to fear that she would get into debt, of which she had a peculiar dread. She thought herself at times on the verge of that pit, but happily into it she never fell.   In one letter she said, "I have worried myself about money and done no good by it."

In her case, the warmest domestic affections, with all the feelings to which, amidst the vicissitudes of life, they naturally give rise, were modified, regulated, and sanctified by communion with her Heavenly Father and trust in Him. This blending of earthly love with love to Him to whom supreme love is due was in her case by no means perfectly, but in a very happy measure accomplished.   To the mere glib utterance of pious words and phrases she was ever averse.   Her utterances of love, trust, and homage to her Heavenly Father and to her Saviour, who redeemed her, came from her inmost soul.

To make some things intelligible which are mentioned in these letters, it may be well to state that the question of my coming home and giving up my work was mooted, but only mooted.   I suppose, when unwell and depressed, I had written as if my power for working in India was coming to an end.   The thought was soon put aside. This speedily appeared to us both as turning back after having put our hand to the plough.   If I was to remain in India, were we to remain separate—I at Benares and Mrs. Kennedy with the children in Scotland?   After a time of painful perplexity, in which we sought guidance from above, and I trust obtained it, we came to the conclusion arrangements should be made for the children at home, and Mrs. Kennedy should return to me, bringing with her the youngest, who was under two years.   The path for the elder children was plain.   For the one next the youngest, whose being brought out to India we deemed for various reasons very undesirable, after much inquiry and perplexity an arrangement was at last made which proved satisfactory.

Mrs. Kennedy had intended to leave by the overland route on November 20th, but owing to delay on the part of the person to whom the taking of the passage had been entrusted, she did not actually leave till December 20th. Then she was called to the ordeal of parting with her loved ones, and was carried through it.

When in London ready to embark, Mrs. Kennedy got a letter from our eldest son, to which I find her reply among her preserved letters.

" LONDON, *December* 1858.

" I am delighted to hear you say my coming home has been useful to you. I trust, my precious boy, you are beginning to be in earnest about the one great question. How much shall I pray for every one of you individually ! The image of each is ever before me, but I have been wonderfully sustained this week. Well may I say Ebenezer ! Never did I attain to such a sweet confidence that every one of my beloved children will be brought to Christ. I could not have believed that I should be so upheld. Well might the Psalmist say, 'Trust Him at all times, ye people, pour out your heart before Him ; God is a refuge for us.' "

During the whole of 1857 my health was unusually good. The great perils and the intense excitement of the year, instead of doing me harm, braced me to bear the glowing heat of the hot season and the muggy weather of the rains. I do not think I passed any year in India with so little discomfort from the climate.

The reaction came as soon as the hot weather of 1858 set in. Boils, so well known by painful experience by European residents in Northern India, broke out on different parts of my body, causing me intense pain. With the boils came low constant fever, with all its weakening effects. Everything was done which skilful treatment, change of diet, and medicine could do, with no marked benefit. At length my medical attendant said that so soon as the season permitted I should go to Calcutta and take a sea-voyage, as the most likely means to effect a cure. I felt an urgent need for change, and the change proposed was doubly welcome, as my wife was to come out in the cold weather, and by holding down the Bay of Bengal to Ceylon, I could meet her at Galle.

In compliance with medical decision, I left Benares in October for Calcutta by a river steamer, as at once the easiest and the safest. I dreaded the jolting of a land journey, as my boils were still very troublesome. Besides, the river voyage was the safest. The rebellion still flickered in Behar. A rebel chief, Kower Singh, whose headquarters I have already mentioned were at Rhotasgarh, made now and then incursions into the Calcutta road, and some officers in high position narrowly escaped capture. In consequence, other travellers like myself to the Capital were happy to avail themselves of the river steamers. I may quote here a few sentences from my book on Benares and Kumaon—"We had the clear sky and the gentle breeze of that delightful season in Northern India. From morning to night we sat under a thick awning, reading or talking as we were inclined, refreshed by the breeze, and interested in the various objects presented to our view on the river and its banks. The fortnight passed most pleasantly, and I arrived in Calcutta half cured of my ailments. I was happy to find myself in time for the outgoing steamer of the Peninsular and Oriental Company, on which I took passage to Point de Galle."

The voyage down the Bay was stormy and prolonged. No observation could be taken, as the sky was covered with dense cloud, and we passed a port at which we should have called, which required us to go back. The tossing did me no harm—it did me good, and I landed in greatly improved health.

On landing, I saw the last received number of the *Overland News,* and to my great disappointment I found my wife's name in the list of passengers for December instead of November. I had calculated on being a week or a little more in Galle before the arrival of the steamer, and I found that instead I should be detained close on six weeks.

I could not hesitate as to the course I should pursue. I made up my mind to proceed by coach the next day to Colombo, the English Capital of the island, and after a short time there, get into the interior, on to Kandy, the old capital, and Newerellia, under Pedro Talla Galla, now deemed the highest mountain in Ceylon. All this I accomplished, meeting everywhere kindness and hospitality from the coffee-planters, chaplains, missionaries, and officials, and got back to Galle a few days before the arrival of the English steamer. It does not fall within my present object to repeat the account I have given in my book of my travels in Ceylon.

Well on in January, to the joy of other expectants as well as myself who were eagerly on the watch, we saw at some distance the smoke of the coming steamer, and as soon as it came to anchor we were ready to get on board from our boat. The first look of my beloved wife startled me. Her hair was dark when we parted eighteen months previously, but, to my surprise, I found it had become white in the interval. It had rapidly whitened under the hardships and anxieties she had endured. I was very thankful, however, to find she and our little boy were in good health.

We had a pleasant and quick run up the bay, and after a few days in Calcutta with our Calcutta friends, we set out for Benares, travelling a part of the way by train, and then by a four-wheeled conveyance, with a change of horses every sixth or seventh mile. There were then two Companies arranging for forwarding passengers in conveyances to the North-West. "Instead of spending three weeks on the way, as we had done in 1839 when proceeding to Benares in a steamer, and twelve days in 1853 in a conveyance drawn by coolies, we now completed our journey in five days." A few years afterwards the rail was finished, and the journey was completed in some twenty-six hours.

CHAPTER XII.

MISSION LIFE FROM FEBRUARY 1859 TO JANUARY 1862.

WE were glad to find ourselves again in our old sphere of labour, the city where we had toiled much, endured much, and enjoyed much, doubly dear to us by all we had passed through since we first entered it, Mrs. Kennedy returning to it after an absence of eighteen months, and I after an absence of some three months.

The decreasing number of the native Christians connected with us was discouraging. After the Mutiny there was increasing difficulty in getting employment, and in consequence the Christian community was reduced in number. On the other hand, there was a very great increase in the number of Europeans, chiefly soldiers. We were no longer left to be guarded by a company or two of European artillerymen. The Government, taught by the terrible experience of the Mutiny, garrisoned Benares with a large body of English soldiers, to show the futility of attempts to throw off our rule.

The presence of so many of our countrymen suggested the obvious duty of giving more of our attention to English work than we had previously done. For many years a weekly English service had been held in the largest room of the Mission-House, and on the Lord's Day evening the Baptists had always an English service in their chapel. A number of our countrymen, chiefly members of the

Church of England, had gladly availed themselves of this
opportunity of worshipping with us, as not infrequently
the ministry of the English chaplains wo had in succession was not such as to meet their spiritual wants. For
a considerable time, however, these services were inter-
mitted on account of the weakness of our Mission and
the small number of Europeans at the station.   Those
who wished for a service conducted in the Nonconformist
fashion found their want supplied by going to the Baptist
chapel on Sunday evening.

From the Mutiny onwards the members of our Mission
felt that a sphere of usefulness opened up to us among
our countrymen which it would be wrong to neglect.   In
1859 the late Rev. William Moody Blake joined the
Mission.   The superintendence of our Central School was
made over to him, and as he was unacquainted with the
native language, the greater part of the English work
devolved on him, thus leaving me to give my strength
to ministering to the native Christians and to the prosecution of evangelistic work in the city and neighbourhood.
I generally preached in English once in the month. I had
great and increasing delight in work among the people
from day to day, in telling them in the language in which
they were born of the crucified and glorious Redeemer,
and entreating them to betake themselves to Him for
salvation.   Mr. Blake's ministrations were very acceptable
to our countrymen, and proved spiritually profitable to
many.   In the Central School at the time the head-master
under the superintendent was Baboo Ram Chundar Bose,
a highly qualified and very efficient teacher.   Many years
have passed since his connection with our Mission ended,
but in all the intervening years we have by letters maintained with him most friendly intercourse.   We have

occasionally met for a few days, but we have generally been far distant from each other.

Mrs. Kennedy on her return from England resumed her work in the orphanage, the girls' day-school, the native Christian women, and, so far as she could draw them, the native women from the outside. There was besides a school for East Indian girls. She found abundant and useful occupation in the sphere for which her past experience had increasingly fitted her.

Mrs. Kennedy every now and then visited the barracks, and tried to exercise a good influence on the wives and children of the soldiers. She returned from these visits gratified by the reception she had met and trustful she had done some good.

There was one class of natives—a very small but a very choice one—in whom she took a special interest. Connected with the Church Mission and our own there were some five native Christians, differing from the others by their knowledge of the English language, and differing still more by their culture, their general intelligence, and their large Scriptural knowledge. It would have been very wrong in us to look down on others because they had not been favoured with a liberal education and their knowledge was limited. We felt at home with them, took a deep interest in everything that concerned them, and held a number of them in high esteem. Those of a superior class I have just mentioned had much in their history, their character, and attainments which had claims on our regard. Every one of them had pressed into the Kingdom through obstacles which only Divine grace in lively exercise could have overcome. They had each made great sacrifices by avowing themselves the followers of Jesus. They were always ready to enter into conversation on the

highest subjects.   These subjects had been profoundly
thought over by them, and their remarks were in consequence the outcome of much reflection.

Mrs. Kennedy on several occasions invited these young
men to tea and spend the evenings with us.   They readily
and thankfully accepted her invitation.   These evenings
were much enjoyed by them, and not less by us.   Mrs.
Kennedy took a lively part in the conversation, and her
remarks were always heard by the young men with
peculiar deference.   Often when they went away—we had
always worship together before we parted—she made the
remark, "What a pleasant evening!   It is not often with
our English brethren our evenings are so profitably
spent."

For a time the postmaster of Benares was a Bengalese
native Christian, who, with his wife, an intelligent and
devoted follower of Jesus, attended our native services.
The office this native brother held was very responsible
and highly paid, and brought him into constant intercourse
with all classes, European and native.   There was quite
a colony of Bengalees in Benares, and among them were
several in official positions who had been educated in the
great schools of Calcutta.   The postmaster knew them
well, and maintained a friendly bearing towards them.   He
was very desirous to exercise Christian influence over them.
With that view he had asked my friend and colleague,
Mr. Sherring, to meet them at his house, and Mr. Sherring
gladly complied with his request.   After Mr. Sherring's
departure the same request was made to me, and with no
ordinary pleasure and thankfulness I made my way to his
house one evening every week..   The subject these educated
Bengalees professed themselves eager to discuss was religion.   What did Christianity inculcate?   What were its

claims? Was there any good reason for accepting it at the cost of abandonment of the religion of their fathers? These men had eager minds and were keen disputants. For the first few evenings I was with them the conversation was animated, but thorough good temper was maintained; it was too desultory to be satisfactory. I proposed to them we should proceed more regularly to the consideration of our great subject, if our intercourse were to issue in good. One of them said that he understood Paul's Epistle to the Romans gave the most systematic and logical exposition of the Gospel ever given. Would I make its study our occupation at our weekly meeting? I most readily assented.

I have often looked back with deep interest to the successive week evenings I spent with these "searchers after truth," as they called themselves, while together, with our Bibles before us—each of them had a Bible— we pondered the teaching of the great Apostle of the Gentiles. I prepared for that class with as great care as I ever did for preaching to our own countrymen. Many were the pertinent remarks they made—many were the difficulties they suggested—many were the hard questions they put, some of them, I had often occasion to remark, beyond human solution. Once and again I felt myself unable on the spur of the moment to say what I felt ought to be said, and I asked them to allow me to ponder the right reply and bring it to our next meeting, to which they readily agreed. Again and again, in prospect of our meeting, I wrote in my study a deliberate reply to their objections, and these little essays were received with peculiar favour, as giving my calmly thought-out opinion. What I felt all through, as I often did with persons of this class, was that their intellectual interest in these

high subjects went far beyond their moral interest, and
still further beyond their spiritual. This led me to put
special emphasis on the thought that the subject of our
study had a transcendent spiritual bearing, and could
never lead us to success if we merely plied our intellect.
With this view I aimed at bringing our Lord Himself
before them in His glorious person, His teaching, His
life, His redemptive work. Again and again it was
acknowledged that Christianity had many claims to preference over all others, but before embracing it their
difficulties must be solved. I was often thanked for my
zeal in teaching them.

Before the breaking up of the class by several being
removed from Benares to other places, I said to them one
evening when leaving, " It gives me great pleasure to
meet you and converse with you, but owing to your anti-
social customs we cannot take even a cup of tea together."
One of them said, " Try us, sir." Knowing well how
readily Mrs. Kennedy would approve of what I did, I said,
"Will you, then, come to my house and take tea with us?"
They all assented, the day being fixed, and they all came.
Mrs. Kennedy, as I knew she would, was much pleased
with the proposal, and these Bengalee friends were evidently much gratified by her attention to them. She
entered into free conversation with them, and I was
hopeful her gentle words might tell more powerfully than
my stronger and more urgent words had done. Some
time afterwards the postmaster retired on his well-won
pension after many years of Government service, and
went to enjoy it in his own native land, Bengal. I lost
sight of the members of his interesting class, but have
often hoped the seed sown had not been altogether lost.
Again and again I have heard in India in a few cases

in my own experience, of seed sown and long buried having been found germinating after many days.

In the cold weather of 1859-60 we made a trip to Allahabad, Cawnpore, and Lucknow. We had been several times at Allahabad and Cawnpore, but now we saw them with peculiar feelings, bearing as they did so manifestly the traces of the desolating storm which had swept over them. Allahabad was rapidly assuming its former appearance, though here and there ruined houses told that it had been for a time in the hands of the enemy. English people who know anything of the Mutiny of 1857—surely there are no English persons entirely ignorant—have read with horror of the fearful events which occurred in Cawnpore in July 1857. These events have got a place in the history of the English in India which can never be effaced. When we were there in January 1860, the ruins of the houses along the banks of the Ganges, the desolate ruins and the stained walls of the house in which so many of our countrywomen and children were so cruelly massacred; the well, then covered up, into which their bodies had been thrown; the remains of the mud wall, the poor rampart within which our people were crowded when assailed by a savage host bent on their destruction; the way to the Ghat, the ferry on the Ganges, truly to our people a *via dolorosa,* by which they were hoping for escape according to the pledged word of their captors, but, as the event speedily proved, to the immediate death of many, and to the death of the rest a short time after—all these we saw with saddened hearts. We had personally known some of the victims, and everything we saw gave new and painful reality to all we had read about that sad suffering company.

From Cawnpore we went on to Lucknow. All along

the forty intervening miles we saw traces of the fierce conflict which our English force under Havelock had to maintain on their way to the relief of the besieged Lucknow Residency. The mud walls were still partly standing of the defences thrown up by our soldiers where they halted, and the loopholed houses of the villages close to the road through which their enemies poured on them a deadly fire. Every mile of the way was keenly contested, and the fiercest opposition of all was encountered when they reached the outskirts of the city. Taking a detour, for which the enemy were not prepared, they pushed on, the foe hastening to arrest and overthrow them. The bullet-marks on the walls, which I observed walking over the ground, showed how fierce the contest had been.

During the few days we remained in Lucknow we were very hospitably entertained by a Church missionary and his wife, occupying a house which had belonged to a rebel leader, and had been partly battered by fire from the Residency. It had been sufficiently repaired to make it fit for occupation, but the traces of its exposure to bombs had not been effaced. I went out several times with this missionary to speak to the people, and a number gathered round us, who quietly heard our message. On the Lord's Day I was requested to preach to the native Christians in their own language, and I had much pleasure in discoursing on Romans xvi. 5, "First-fruits of Asia unto Christ," to point out to them their high privileges and great responsibility as the first-fruit in this land of a glorious harvest which would yet be gathered to the salvation of their people and the glory of the Redeemer. On the same day we attended an English service held in an Imambara, a name given to a building where Muhammadans of the Shiah sect worship.

We returned to Cawnpore by night. The moon was full, the sky was cloudless, and we reached the Ganges about four in the morning. When waiting for a boat to cross over, in the stillness of the morning, from a little hut close by, to our great delight and no small surprise, we heard—we concluded a man from the voice—a person chanting the praises of the Redeemer of mankind. The words were those of a well-known hymn in native metre. We listened with intense pleasure, and wished we could get into the cluster of huts to see the singer, thank him, and congratulate him. A short time previously the mention of that name with honour in that place would have exposed him who uttered it to a violent death. The incident was very cheering as an omen of the dawn to benighted India, when, through the tender mercy of our God, Jesus the Light of the World shall shine into the hearts of its teeming population, and raise them into the sunshine of heaven.

In Benares we continued our work till March 1861, when, through the kindness of our Directors, we obtained a much needed retreat to the Hills for a few months. We travelled by Allahabad, Cawnpore, and Delhi. We stayed a few days in the grand old imperial city, and saw more of it and of the neighbourhood than we had seen on our former visit in 1847. A military friend, who kindly entertained us, took us to the heights a short distance from the city, where an army was encamped in 1857, where it maintained for very life a fierce conflict, and from which at last it issued for the assault on the city, which was taken after a most severe and bloody contest lasting over days. The different objects of interest in that life and death struggle were pointed out to us—the Cashmere Gate, and the spots where the battle was hottest, where besiegers and besieged wrestled with each other in deadly fight. Those would be strangely stolid who could look unmoved on places associated with such events. In 1847 we saw only the walls of the fort, within which were the palace and the principal buildings of the Mogul court. Now it was thrown open to the public, at least the English public. We walked all over it. The palace with its magnificent halls, on which vast sums had been spent, and where the Emperors of India had lived and ruled in royal state, had been turned into barracks and an arsenal for soldiers of a people who three hundred years before had made humble application for trading facilities. To how many of the great empires of the West, that looked so stable that no power could overthrow them, are the oft-quoted words applicable—*Sic transit gloria mundi !* There is one Kingdom which will survive them all, and endure for ever.

On going to Almora in the spring of 1861, we were glad to find ourselves the fellow-occupants of the Mission-House with our dear friend and colleague Mr. Buyers, who had been there for some time, and, in the absence of Mr. Budden, was in charge of the Mission. When we were in Almora in 1847, there was no Mission in the province. Through the deep interest of Captain Ramsay, for many years Sir Henry Ramsay, and by his munificent liberality, the Mission was established in 1850. For years it was wholly supported by local contributors, of whom Captain Ramsay was the chief. On this our second visit to the province we found it taking root. It was from the beginning in charge of Mr. Budden, whose health forbad his remaining in the Plains, and under his charge it remained till his death, with occasional assistance from his brethren of Benares and Mirzapore. During his furloughs to England his place was supplied by them. Among the Missions in the province it holds, and for many years has held, the highest place. Mr. Budden was in many respects one of the most able, active, and competent missionaries our Society ever sent to India.

Mrs. Kennedy and our little boy had good health during the months of 1861 we spent in Almora, but I was an invalid a great part of the time, and under medical treatment. I was quite incapacitated for active mission work, but I did a little, so far as my strength permitted. I took part with Mr. Buyers in conducting the English service, and also in preaching to the small native Christian community. The Leper Asylum had been established a short time previously, and was under charge of a competent native Christian. I visited it occasionally with Mrs. Kennedy. To both of us the visits were very trying. Owing, I suppose, to my health having become impaired, I almost fainted on one occasion on seeing some of the poor sufferers, and was obliged to leave suddenly without saying anything to them. Mrs. Kennedy and myself, as I shall have occasion to show, got entirely over this feeling, and in after years took our part in ministering to their spiritual need.

Medical opinion decided strongly against my returning to labour in the Plains. Furlough to England was declared to be indispensable to the establishment of my health. A medical certificate to that effect was sent to our Board in London, and ready consent was given to my acting in accordance with it.

Before leaving Almora, my health having greatly improved with the bracing weather which set in after the rains, we made up our mind to make a trip into the interior. We had heard much about the Pindaree Valley,

leading up to the Pindaree Glacier. We were told that
the journey was fatiguing, that the traveller should be
prepared for hardship, but that the sight of the valley
would be ample compensation. Our doctor gave his consent to my going. He thought it might benefit Mrs.
Kennedy and myself. One doctor said, " Don't take that
little boy." Another doctor then at Almora said, "Take
him. He can stand it well." Mrs. Kennedy would not
go without him, and I certainly would not think of going
without her. Like others, we like the advice which pleases
us, and are ready to follow it. Indeed, but for Mrs.
Kennedy I believe this trip would not have been attempted
at all. I have already said she was extremely fond of
mountain scenery, and had to put restraint on herself to
keep this liking within bounds. Her strong sense of
duty, her deep abiding concern for the health of those
dearest to her, ever checked her from wishing to do
anything which could be hurtful to them ; but when
thus unchecked, she was eager to go forward. Thus the
trip to the Pindaree Glacier was undertaken and accomplished.

The journey was fatiguing, and to none was it more so
than Mrs. Kennedy herself, but she bore it and its inconveniences not only patiently but joyfully. She was carried
sideways, as I have already described, on a piece of carpet
attached to a pole borne on men's shoulders. Our little
boy was carried in a somewhat similar manner. I had a
pony, but the path was often so steep, and the precipice
close to which it led so threatening, that I deemed it wise
to part with the pony half-way and keep on foot, getting
now and then help in the steepest places with a belt round
my waist, which, attached to a rope in the hand of a
strong highlander, enabled me to descend and ascend

more easily. When we got to the valley, with its roaring torrent of yellow snow-melted water hastening down, and the lofty grand rocks rising sheer upon both sides, we were rewarded by the sight of the most impressive and awe-inspiring view of the kind we had ever witnessed. As we were looking up, gazing with admiration on the scene before us, a man from the Plains was walking behind, and I heard him muttering to himself, "Such a horrible (wicked) place I never saw in all my life." We got to within six miles of the glacier, close to a rock with openings under it, and there put up for the night—those with us under the rock, and we in our little tent. Early next morning we set out; got on the glacier; on our way saw and heard an avalanche, which made the mountains resound as with the loudest thunder; got breakfast, a man with us with a basket preparing it, and a highlander carrying a little wood, and soon made our way back to the tent. The following morning we were glad to make our way down as quickly as we could, and after some twelve days reached our Almora abode, feeling we had seen what would by its memory enrich us for life.

The two nights we spent near the glacier were intensely cold, but they did us no harm. We reached Almora in better health than when we left it. We tried, as we travelled in these high regions, to have intercourse with those we met. They are a stronger, more stalwart people than their brethren in the country farther down. Judging by the little we saw, we thought them very simple and unsophisticated. I suppose many had been sometime or other in Almora, the capital of the province, but their dialect was somewhat different, and we found it difficult to understand each other. I tried to speak to them about the Saviour, but with the subject so utterly strange to them, the opportunity so slight, and the barrier of the language making understanding so difficult, there could be little hope of an impression being made. There might be that slight awakening of curiosity which in many a case has led to greater readiness to hear when a preacher has come with fuller opportunity to make known the truth.

We were by no means the first visitors to the Pindaree Valley, but we were told no lady had gone previously. When we found ourselves, on reaching our halting-place for the day, close to a hamlet or village, which was generally early in the afternoon, we tried to make an acquaintance with the inhabitants. The men received us very frankly, but the women and children fled when they saw us. Often, however, they got over their fears, especially where we stopped a couple of days. Mrs. Kennedy spoke to them in her own kind way, though I am afraid with little intelligibility, and the women seemed so pleased to see her, saying they had never previously seen a white lady. Our little boy, then more than four years of age, was an object of very special attraction. There had never been previously any such visitor to the valley. They took his hand and praised his beauty, as if he had come from the bright world beyond. They did not, however, set their heart on keeping him, as once occurred to a missionary brother of mine, who had made his way to a wild tribe in India, taking his little boy with him. The people he met said, "This is the king whose rule over us has been predicted by our wise men. You must leave him with us. We shall take all care of him, and he will grow up to be our ruler. Then we shall have a very prosperous time." They were urgent in their demand, and seemed determined to keep him by force. My friend got alarmed, and at last got his boy away by promising to return to them as soon as he could, and then telling them what he thought about it. No such demand was made on us by our mountaineers.

After a short stay in Almora we set out for the Plains. We spent a few weeks very happily with our brethren, European and native, at Benares, and, accompanied by two boys, the sons of an officer, entrusted to us to be taken to England, made our way to Calcutta, travelling the first part of the way by such a staging coach as I have already described, and then by rail.

We had a few very pleasant days with our friends in Calcutta, and late in January 1862 embarked on a ship for England *vid* the Cape of Good Hope, reaching London in April, after a pleasant and prosperous voyage.

Mrs. Kennedy's Letters to her Children.

During the period of this chapter, from 1859 to 1862, Mrs. Kennedy, as she always did when absent from her children, wrote constantly to them. Many of these letters have been preserved. They are so characteristic of her devout, loving, and intelligent spirit, that the extracts from them I now proceed to give will, I am sure, be welcome to the readers of her biography. The five children to whom these letters were addressed ranged from our eldest, eighteen years of age, to the youngest, above six years, with the exception of the youngest of all, under two years, whom she took out with her. I do not give in these extracts the names of the children, nor the endearing terms with which her letters both to myself and her children abound. The difference in style gives a clue to the age of those to whom the letters were sent.

The first letter before me was to the three youngest, and is dated Calcutta, February 7, 1859:—

"Here Alick and I are in Calcutta with dear Papa, after a rough and disagreeable voyage for the most part. I had hoped to have written many letters on the way, but was so sick and had so much to do with dear little Alick that I could not. You are continually in my thoughts, my own precious children, and many times every day do I pray for each one of you. I hope you are all well, good, and happy. You know there is no being truly happy without being truly good, and the way to be good is to love God. . . . It seems a long, long time since I heard of you, and sometimes this makes me very sad; but then the promises of God's blessed Word come to my help, and I am enabled to commit you all to Him. I met Papa at Ceylon, and was very, very thankful to find him so much better. He had been travelling about in that island for nearly two months, and had seen a great many wonderful things. He says Ceylon is very beautiful. There are some hills 8000 feet high, and he climbed to the top of one of them. There are also cascades and waterfalls finer than any he has seen elsewhere. Large coffee plantations are very numerous. Wild elephants are common, too, and I daresay you would hardly like to meet one of them. There is one very disagreeable thing in some parts of Ceylon, and that is the leech—a great annoyance. Papa says he has taken half-a-dozen off his legs in one day. They spring upon the shoe or boot till they find the bare skin, and then fix for a draught. They will often find their way up to one's neck. I am sure my children would not like to have such neighbours.

"I did not see much of Ceylon, as the steamer remained only one day there. I saw the Pyramids of Egypt, however, and Mount Sinai, and sailed down the Red Sea, where you know God opened a way for the Israelites to pass over when they were followed by the Egyptians. We also travelled over part of the great desert of Egypt, which is just loose sand, in which we sank to our ankles when we went to the refreshment tents. Is it not very wonderful that they have managed to make a railway in such a country? We had a little distance to walk now and then, and I got an Arab to carry Alick, and managed to carry our basket and hats myself. Alick did not like his Arab bearer, but there was no help for that. We got plenty of oranges, figs, and dates in Egypt; and at one o'clock in the morning we came to the tent where our dinner was laid out. I cannot say it was very nice, except the fruit part of it. There was meat which some of our passengers called roast-kite, and another kind which seemed like stewed-camel."

"Benares, *February* 26, 1859.

"Your very nice and very welcome letter of 3rd January reached us about a week ago. I cannot tell how very glad we were to receive it. It seemed an age since 'voice or sound' had reached me from any of you.

"Nearly two months, you know, had elapsed, and my thoughts being ever with you and of you made the time seem much longer. Now, I wonder if I'll manage to write to you as I used to do to Papa—that is, sit down and talk as fast as the pen will run. I think I shall. Last year's intercourse has enabled me to realise somewhat your present character and attainments. I say somewhat, for you are now far ahead of Mamma in many things. You can read books which I hardly know even by name, are a profound mathematician, &c., &c. Well, I suppose the more we know, we feel our deficiencies the more. I am sure I do, and I trust my dearest boys may do so too. May it be given to us to know Him whom to know is eternal life, and in the enjoyment of whose favour alone we can be happy either in this world or in that to come.

" In coming out I read the memoir of Mr. Hewitson, a young minister of the Free Kirk, who was for a short time in Madeira, and afterwards settled in a country part of Ayrshire. It is a book I should like you to read. Mr. Hewitson was a first-rate scholar, dazzled by the fictitious glare of literary ambition.

He studied beyond his strength, and found it a phantom after all. Then when he, as Pollock beautifully expresses it, 'As some sere leaf of autumn, which the wolfish winds chase far from its fallen sisters, God passed in mercy by.' Ah! dearest J——, your father's and mother's ambition for you all is, not that you may be learned and great in this world, though these things in their own place are good, but that you may be the children and servants of God. . . .

"We have now been in Benares a fortnight, and during that time have been as busy as possible. The girls' school has been kept up, but it is sadly in want of more efficient management. I have begun my Saturday's Bible-class with the native Christian women. There were fifteen present to-day. I wish much to try and do something among the families of European soldiers here, but there is so much to do in the compound that I fear it will hardly be possible. We have been getting the house into something like order."

Letter to our Second Son.

"We are both very busy, and would need to do a great deal more than we can manage to get through. There are an immense number of European women and children here now in the barracks, and I should be very glad to give a portion of my time to them. They are much neglected and exposed to many temptations and hurtful influences.

"How thankful ought you and I to be for early religious instruction! Papa has been reading to me for half an hour after tea lately by way of a little relaxation.

"The life of Chatterton, the mad boy poet of Bristol, has been our last subject. A more tragic or harrowing account of any human being I have never listened to. What a fearful overturn has sin made in God's fair creation! We know that the Judge of all the earth will do right, and often and often we are thrown back on this great first truth. One's heart bleeds to think of the number of 'Roland Leighs' there are in the world—poor, neglected, untaught or ill-taught children. Chatterton did not belong to this class, yet he seems to have had no one to lead him to Him who is rest to the weary and heavy laden.[1] Try, my dearest boy, to live not for yourself only; let the world be the better for your having been in it. You may never be able to accomplish anything great or grand in the cause of philanthropy, but every day will afford you opportunity of doing good on a small scale, opportunities of denying yourself for the good of others, and of lessening, if it be only by units, the aggregate of human suffering and misery. There are few things Papa and I have remarked more than the deformities of character in some well-known public benefactors —persons who do an immense amount of good in a certain way, but who seem so carried away by flattery, that it is positively disagreeable to have anything to do with them. The unknown and unacknowledged effort to deny oneself; the patient endurance of an unjust insinuation, may require far higher Christian attainment than the most glaring acts of charity. I have lately read 'English Hearts and Hands,' and do not like it at all. To do the work recorded in the book was well, but to publish it to the world is, in my humble opinion, alike inconsistent with the spirit of the Gospel and feminine propriety. In a man it would be bad, in a woman it is worse.

"I did not mean to speak of this, but you see I do not now think of you as a little boy, but as a sensible companion as you are. The boy has given place to the lad. How old you and James make us appear!"

"BENARES, March 3, 1859.

" . . . We hope you try to be good children, and seek to do exactly as Miss and Mrs. Jack tell you. It is very good in them and others, is it not, to be so very kind to you? Well, you know that it is God who makes people kind, and you must try and love Him best of all.

---

[1] I well remember when I approached the end of Chatterton's Life, Mrs. Kennedy said, "Stop, stop! I cannot bear it—so dreadful."

" We are glad Aunt Donaldson took you to see the wild beasts. It was very kind in her to do so. I wonder what kind of animals they were. We have no wild beasts in Benares, but there are plenty of them running wild in the woods all over the country. Once when we were in the hills a poor woman was killed by a tiger quite close to us. Another night a cow was torn in pieces by a leopard. Many children, too, have been carried away and devoured by wolves. I daresay you would rather not meet them loose in the open country. Though we have no wild beasts here, we have some tame beasts which you do not often see at home. There are hundreds of camels and a great many elephants on the parade ground behind our house. You have both been on the back of an elephant, though you do not remember it.

" We had lately a dreadful storm of thunder, lightning, and hailstones. It was on the very night we reached Benares. Six people were killed by the lightning, the hailstones were as large as eggs and broke the tiles of a great many houses. One gentleman's drawing-room furniture was nearly all broken after the hailstones had broken through the tiles. People were walking through their houses with umbrellas over their heads."

" Benares, *April* 28, 1859.

" . . . You wish to come to India. Well, I would like you to be here just now for twenty-four hours, at any rate. India would then, I expect, be at a discount. I am sitting in the mouth of a thermantidote, which is being kept in use by two coolies, one throwing water on the tatties (scented grass screens), and another turning the wheel. Still the heat is very trying, and the slightest relaxation on the part of the coolies makes it unbearable. When I look at the poor creatures, and yet must keep them close at their work, Southey's lines sometimes come to me —

' Who turn for him the mazy wheel,
  Who grind for him the mill.'

I seem to myself for a moment the personification of all that is hard-hearted and cruel. The coolies have of course only a proper amount of work, for all that. I think it was not in the way of blessing altogether that it was prophesied of the children of Japheth that they were to dwell in the tents of Shem. Shem should have all his tents to himself for me, so far as personal liking is concerned—unless, indeed, I could get to his hills, and then all would be right.

"The very recollection of what spring is at home makes me unspeakably glad, and increases the desolate, scorched-up appearance and feeling of everything here by way of contrast. Yet I would not for the world leave Benares one hour sooner than our Heavenly Father appoints. I never was more fully engaged in the Mission, and never felt more happy in the work than now. We know that the path of duty is the only path of safety and happiness, and even on that low ground this is our sphere at present. God will make your way plain, too, my dearest boy. Seek Him as your portion, acknowledge Him in all your ways, and be assured He will direct your paths. You are approaching a very interesting period of your life, the termination of your school-days. Youth is a joyous time, and there is nothing in religion to check that joyousness, but there is much to sanctify and guide it. Religion has a wonderful power in putting everything in its own place, which I trust you may in some measure realise."

"BENARES (*no date*).

"We are so glad to learn from Mrs. Jack that you are getting on so well, that you are learning to read a little, and that you like to hear her read to you from the Bible, the 'Peep of Day,' your 'Pilgrim's Progress,' and other good books. She tells us, too, that you are a very good little boy, and like to help her whenever you can. The cold weather will be soon going away, and you will be able to get out for nice long walks. The pretty little flowers will be putting out their little buds as if to say, 'May we come?' I wonder whether you know the 'snowdrop' and the 'crocus.' I am sure you are sometimes taken to walk in the Princes Street Gardens, and I hope when

you go there you will not only like to run about and amuse
yourself, but that you will try to make acquaintances among
the daisies and buttercups. God's works are all very beautiful;
flowers are particularly so, far more beautiful than gold and pearls.
I like to think of them, and of the joy I had when as young as
you in becoming acquainted with the world we live in, especially with flowers. The world is very beautiful even now, and
the more we know of God's works, the more we feel this. Then
what must it have been before Adam and Eve sinned? I often
think flowers are something left to us of Eden. What beautiful
things they are! such a variety of colour and form, and every
month having its own peculiar kind!

"Then they teach us so much. You know, my darling, our
bodies must die and be laid in the cold dark grave; but Jesus
has promised to raise these bodies again far more beautiful and
glorious than they are now, if we believe in Him. We cannot
understand how this is possible, but it helps us very much
when we see lovely little flowers coming out of the cold dark
earth. They teach many lessons besides, which I hope you will
learn when you are older. Meantime, always try and look well
at flowers when you have an opportunity. . . . You used to be
at times a very passionate little boy. Now you are a big boy,
and can understand how foolish and naughty that was. Do the
naughty heart and temper ever speak now? I fear they try now
and then. I am sure they are not quite still in older people.
Now, if we would always say, 'Naughty heart, be quiet till I
think about what you are going to say,' it would be the first
step to victory.

"How I wish I could join you in your walks sometimes! I
dreamed the other night that I was walking with all my children
in a beautiful hilly country, and when I awoke and found it
was only a dream, there was a great pain on my chest. My
dearest boy, you know Papa and Mamma love you and your
brothers and sister very much, and would not choose to go
away and leave you. I am sure dear Mrs. Jack tells you
why it is that we are in India. It is to teach the poor heathen

about Jesus Christ, God's dear Son, who came down from
heaven to die for us. The people here do not know God, but
pray to ugly figures made of wood, stone, and brass. Some of
these gods are even made of mud. I have seen a man plastering
the cheeks of a great ugly idol with handfuls of mud, and then
he would begin to worship. The Hindoos think that when
they die they will be changed into animals. In Benares there
are many hundreds of temples, and every evening you may
hear the priests of these temples calling the people to idol-
worship by the ringing of bells, blowing horns, and beating of
drums. Some of the Hindoos have left off praying to idols
and have become Christians. I know some of them very, very
well, and love them very, very much. Papa preaches every
Sabbath to a congregation of native Christians, and if you
only saw how attentive they are, I am sure you would be very
glad. I teach the children, and they learn their lessons quite
as well as English children do.

"We have been away from Benares for some weeks, and in
one place where we spent a few days there were a great many
wolves, so many that they used to come at night and walk
round the house. One night they walked round and round
the house for nearly half an hour, howling in a frightful way.
These wolves often carry away children, but they seldom attack
grown-up people. You may be sure that night we took very
good care of Alick. A little black child was found in the garden
of a gentleman close by lately, and nobody ever came to claim
it, but the gentleman took care of it, and has arranged for its
being brought up. There was a beautiful place near to which
we went several times where a Brahmin lived, and spent a long
time every morning in saying his prayers. Papa tried to teach
him about Jesus Christ, but though he listened respectfully, it
was evident the truth made no impression on him. Perhaps
the seed may afterwards bring forth fruit."

"BENARES, 1860.

"In your last letter you say you often think of the evils con-
sequent on our separation as a family. I am sure if I had not

faith in an over-ruling and directing Providence I should go
distracted in thinking of them. Even if we were to go home
now, we could hardly hope to have both you and John with us
as a permanent arrangement. Nature often rebels sadly against
this, but better thoughts come and quiet the tumult within.
Your dear father has all along had a strong conviction that this
was his post. We have the consciousness of having sought to
commit our way to God. We could not have kept our children
here without sacrificing their interests to our own feelings.

"We have the assurance that God can far more than make
up to our beloved children what they lose by our absence.
These and similar considerations come to our help, and we feel
confident that our trust will not be disappointed.

"We were much affected two evenings ago to hear of the
death of poor Mrs. L.'s son. She hastened home, but found he
had been buried ten days. He was the only son of his mother,
and she was a widow. My heart bleeds for her, but I believe
she has much comfort from the confident hope that he had
chosen the better part."

"BENARES, *April* 2, 1860.

"You see I date this April, a month of beauty with you, the
mention of which suggests the recollection of buttercups and
daisies and a host of exquisite garden flowers. With us it
brings the idea of dust and hot winds, punkahs, tatties, and
troublesome coolies, all preparing us for the frying-pan heat of
May, and the still more literal fire of June. How we get
through without being cinderised I cannot tell. I have had
the punkah for the last week. Papa has not yet begun, but
sits in comfortable dishabile in his study-room.

"We are nearly done with our preparations for the hot
weather, and it will be no small relief when we are."

"BENARES, *April* 26, 1860.

"The heat has been to me quite dreadful, as Dr. Naismith
forbade Alick's having either punkah, tatty, or thermantidote—
(he was suffering from measles at the time)—I think of May at

home, with its lilies and laburnums, its polyanthuses and other spring flowers, and contrast it with May in Benares, the thermometer at 90° and above it, night and day, in our coolest room, the wind blowing a flame, and seeming to make the very earth movable in one dense cloud of dry, blinding dust. Vegetation has gone to other climes, except in the larger trees, whose roots are nourished from below."

"Benares, *June* 14, 1860.

"You see this is dated 14th June. We ought to have had rain a week ago. We had one slight shower then, and heavy clouds have been hanging about ever since, but no rain.

"The heat has been and is dreadful. Anything like active exertion is out of the question, except in the mornings. All schools have a month's holiday, and everybody is panting for rain, man and beast."

Written apparently two days later :—

"To-day and yesterday we have had great masses of cloud, and are hourly looking for a fall of rain. Meantime, we keep grumbling and growling about the heat, as if that would do us any good. The fact of our existing through it almost surprises us. It does one good to think of Scotland."

"Benares, *October* 18, 1860.

"We have had, as you know, a long, weary, hot season, the thermometer seldom below 90°—no relief, no coolness, night or day. The rains were deficient, and brought little change. At last this has come to an end. Since the beginning of this month the weather has been gradually getting cooler. We have the punkah only at meals, and in a few days we hope to dispense with it altogether. It is an unspeakable relief to feel that we can move about without a living machine in the shape of a fellow-creature to pull, pull, pull, from morn till night—from night to morn. The rains have been so far below the average this year that great fears of famine were entertained.

L

These fears are now mercifully relieved, but it is feared things may continue at their present high rates. What a blessing will railways be to India! The Punjaub, it is said, could supply grain for the whole country, and when the means of transit are available, famine can hardly be possible, unless by special judgment. Next week we go over (D.V.) to Mirzapore and Ushtbhooja for a little change, of which we are all much in need. I hope much from the change to Ushtbhooja, as well as from the rest and quiet. We have always very regular work here, and there is no getting rid of it but by going away."

" BENARES, *December* 12, 1860.

" If you be spared a few years, we are likely to see you fairly afloat. I think about you all till I make myself ill, and just begin the same rôle day after day. I know it is wrong to be so anxious, and I try and struggle against it, and believe that in God's good time our many prayers on your behalf will be more than answered.

" Here we are all going on as usual. The weather is delightful, and we are enjoying it amazingly. Papa has been going into the city much as he used to do in former times. It is the heat, the dreadful heat of Benares, that is so enervating. The prospect of escaping it next hot weather is very delightful, though it would have been more so had we been going to England, and not to the Hills."

" *January* 2, 1861.

" I hope we shall be able to give some introductions for you to some of the really good people in Berlin. I have a great horror of the baptized infidelity of the Continent, the more so that the poison is presented in so many forms, and is so unlabelled."

" ALMORA, *August* 28, 1861.

" We are glad to see that you are getting on so well in the German capital, and that your companionship is so much among Free Kirk students.

"Professor Smeaton and his wife were friends of my cousin Mrs. Grant, and when in Aberdeen three years ago she spoke of them with much regard. I trust, however, that our James is to be among the leaders in society. You know it is said that we all take our place very decidedly in one of two parties— those who act on others by their moral influence and example, or those who are acted upon. We no doubt occupy both places to a certain extent, but the proposition is true in the main. By this time you will be thinking of your journey through the Black Forest and trip down the Rhine. We are glad to think of your having such a delightful prospect, and I am sure you must be in want of a holiday. Take care of over-working yourself. . . .

"What an unsettled life we have had for many years! When the Pillar of Cloud and Fire go before us all is well. We have the bright and blessed hope of travelling to the City which hath foundations. This alone is worth living for."

"BENARES, *October* 1860.

"The Ushtbhooja Hill is covered with temples, and everywhere there one is met by the sadly debasing effects of superstition and idolatry.

"At Mirzapore we had a series of interesting meetings. About fifty of our native Christians went over, and at the evening soirée we had English, Scotch, Welsh, Portuguese, Armenians, Bengalese, and Hindustanis; one man said he was of Irish extraction. It was very pleasant to see so many from different countries professing to be one in Christ. Oh, that the blessed work now going on at home may extend to this dark land! We hope and pray it may. We hear of many wishing to be baptized, but so far as we have been able to learn, there is nothing like a general awakening in any portion of this community."

I conclude these extracts from Mrs. Kennedy's letters by a few remarks on their contents.

Very strong expression is given to the suffering caused by the extreme heat of Benares, I may say of the North-Western Provinces, during some months of the year.[1] Some suffer from the heat far more than do others, but to all it is trying. Very few felt it more than my dear wife did, but her love to the people and her deep sense of duty sustained her spirit and enabled her to hold on. Had she not been upheld by the sense of her Saviour's presence and the assurance that He had sent her to Benares, she would have broken down. What some cold-weather travellers have called "soft indulgences" she now and then truly said were simply "alleviations of misery." I have often wished that those who condemn missionaries as wanting in self-denial would be so good as to stay over the whole year in Northern India. Their testimony would then be of some value. There are abnormal persons who can do and bear what others cannot, but as a rule those who expose themselves to the severity of the climate are praised by many for their self-denial and endurance, with the result that they either die or give up the work before they have well commenced it, while not a few, who take due precaution, and at the same time work assiduously, are spared and able to labour on for years.

As in the hot weather outdoor work is carried on in the early hours of the morning, the long hours of the day are spent in the shut-up house in a half-darkened room. The hours are not spent in idleness. It is often surprising how much indoor work, bearing directly on the object of our going to India, is carried on in the hottest season of the year—work for which there is more leisure than during the active outdoor season. And then, except

---

[1] I may mention that the heat was often for weeks, day and night, at 90°, and above it, in our coolest rooms.

for the few hottest days of the year, there is evening work.

From the extracts given, it is evident Mrs. Kennedy's mind was the scene of contendings between different feelings, drawing her in different directions. Her strong, tender, domestic feelings strove with her love to Mission work, and her abiding sense of duty to do only what the Master would approve. She dreaded taking a step or expressing a feeling which would interfere with consecration to Christ and the promotion of His kingdom. It was very difficult for her to bring conflicting feelings into thorough harmony, but she succeeded in a large and satisfactory degree, by the exercise of Christian principle, in reconciling them in her mind and heart.

In one of her letters Mrs. Kennedy gives to one of her sons an account of a *fête* given to English soldiers at Benares. I find in another letter a long account of a *fête* at Almora on occasion of the presentation of colours to a Goorkha regiment—a dinner, with the games that followed. She was not one of those Christians who deemed themselves bound by the command, "Come out from among them and be ye separate," to keep aloof from all gatherings for amusement and recreation. She with a good conscience not only now and then was present, but felt interested in what interested others. There is no hard-and-fast line laid down in Scripture on these subjects, but we find clearly set before us views of the Christian life which, if firmly held and habitually acted on, give guidance to Christ's followers as to the things they may rightly allow, and the things from which they should abstain. No one could hold more firmly than Mrs. Kennedy did, that living to God is entirely inconsistent with the giving of oneself to the pursuit of some pleasures in which people of the world have great delight, and the manifest effect of which is the strengthening of a worldliness which takes them away still farther from God.

Mention is made of visits to Ushtbhooja. This is a place a few miles out from Mirzapore, about thirty miles from Benares. It is a plateau some two or three hundred feet above the level of the plain, and behind are low hills, which gradually rise till they join the Vindhya range. A wealthy native of Mirzapore built many years ago a large beautiful bungalow on the brow of this plateau, which has a commanding view of the Ganges below and of the country beyond. This house was built for the special benefit of Europeans, who by application can obtain its occupancy for a few days without charge. It is a most pleasant residence in the cold weather, and is occupied by families in succession. The name is one of Kali's titles —that gloomy, fierce goddess, the Eight-Armed, to whom many temples have been erected over these hills. There is a famous temple at a place called Vindhyachal, a few miles distant, where goats are continually offered, and blood flows in streams. I have often been at this temple. In former times Thugs, professional murderers, were in the habit of frequenting it and presenting their offerings, to secure the favour of the goddess in their plundering and murdering expeditions.

CHAPTER XIII.

VISIT TO ENGLAND—RETURN TO INDIA—MISSION WORK IN BENARES AND ALMORA.

1862–1869.

WE remained in England from 1862 to September 1865. Our place of abode during nearly the whole of that period was Blackheath, that our younger boys might attend the Mission School. My time was much occupied with deputation work for the London Missionary Society and preaching. The Rev. J. Beazley was at that time pastor of the Congregational church. I was only occasionally present at his Sunday services, but Mrs. Kennedy attended regularly with our children, and was greatly benefited by his spiritual and experimental preaching. In after years she often referred with deep thankfulness to her enjoyment and profit under Mr. Beazley's ministrations.

When my two years' furlough came to an end, the former difficulty of return to India presented itself. Medical opinion was opposed to my return. My own impression was that I could not labour long in the Plains, but if the way was open to my going to the Hills, I might go back with a reasonable hope of efficient service. The following year was one of great perplexity and trial. I was very desirous to return, but the way seemed blocked. At length the Directors consented to my going back to Benares, and Mrs. Kennedy and myself, in company with

Messrs. Lambert and Hutton, appointed to Northern India, embarked for Calcutta in September 1865 by a ship round the Cape of Good Hope.

Our eldest son had preceded us. In 1862 he had been an accepted candidate of the Indian Civil Service, and had in 1863, after passing his final examination, gone to India. It was a great trial to part with our other children, but as they were now more advanced in life, and we had made satisfactory arrangements for them, the trial was not so great as it had previously been.

How Mrs. Kennedy felt at this time of perplexity, when it looked as if our return to India was effectually blocked, is indicated by a note she wrote me during a temporary absence :—

"I think I have long felt attached to the missionary cause, but it never seemed so attractive as now. Many a time do I try to school myself into the thought, How deeply did I feel separation from my children ! Should I not accept this as a kind arrangement of my Heavenly Father for our mutual comfort and happiness ?   I dare say I shall be able to come to that by-and-by."

As I have already said, our perplexity was brought to an end by the decision of the Directors that we should return, precarious though my health was.

I must acknowledge we were very unwilling to undertake the long sea-voyage, as the Suez Canal had been opened, and most Indian passengers went by it. The long sea-route was still the most economical, and as two young missionaries were to accompany us, it was deemed best we should make the voyage as we had formerly done.

Early in the voyage, along with my young brethren and

some young officers who joined us, we set to the study of the Hindustani language, giving to it about three hours daily. In addition to the grammar, we read a Hindustani novel, which, from its idiomatic style, is deemed a classic, the *Bagh-o-Bahar—The Garden of Delight.* The story is thoroughly Eastern, is very lively, has many surprises, but in parts is decidedly objectionable in a moral aspect. I had previously, on account of its style, read it more than once carefully, and was familiar with it. We managed to get through it before the end of the voyage along with the grammar, and thus my young brethren got an entrance into the language they had to learn in order to the fulfilment of their great aim in going to India.

We reached Calcutta before the end of December, glad with the hope that we should require no more to traverse the Atlantic and Indian Oceans. The overland route was becoming more and more established, and the most conservative for former ways, were being shut up to the abandonment of the old route. The first news we got on our arrival was the announcement of the death of our friend, colleague, and relative, Mr. Buyers.

After a brief stay in Calcutta we proceded to Benares, which we reached on January 4th by rail in twenty-six hours—by far the quickest journey we had made between the two cities.

During 1866 our Benares Mission was strong in number, composed of Messrs Blake, Lambert, Hutton, and myself; and yet, as often happens, our efficient strength was not great. The two younger brethren gave help in English preaching, but of course could do no Mission work. Mr. Blake was in charge of the central school, and I was left to minister to the native Christians and to carry on evangelistic work so far as my strength enabled me—Mrs.

Kennedy attending to the women and girls as she had formerly done, Mrs. Blake taking part with her in this work.

On getting into the hot season of 1866, my fear of inability to stand the climate was too surely realised. Till the middle of April I prosecuted my work with pleasure, finding, however, after the middle of March the heat of every day increasingly oppressive, but after that date, in spite of my struggling against it, I was prostrated. During the next three or four months I attended with great difficulty to the most pressing duties, and the greater part of every day was spent on my couch. Mrs. Kennedy was also much oppressed by the heat; all along it had been to her a great trial. She often playfully called Benares "that dear Pandemonium;" but she was more flexible than I was, and could bear up better than I did. People speak of being acclimatised. Some no doubt are, perhaps many, but I think quite as many, like myself, have felt that the longer their stay in India the more unequal they are to the bearing of its heat. Their strength has gone down under the severity of the climate, and every successive year the heat has been felt more trying.

In November 1866 Mr. Hewlett returned to Benares from Almora, where he had done excellent service. The way seemed open to our escaping the heat of 1867. I applied for transference to Almora for the six trying months of that year, stating in my application I should be well-nigh useless if during these months I remained in the Plains. The Directors kindly consented to my request. In the beginning of April we left Benares, and reached Almora on the 13th of that month, by far the quickest journey to the Hills we had made. Our stay at Almora extended from April to the end of October.

The Mission had made marked progress since our former visit, in its schools, its buildings, its extended missionary work, and in the bringing of many of the lepers within the Christian pale. The first marked drawing to Christ of these poor sufferers was under Mr. Hewlett's ministrations. He baptized a number, and since his time the good work has been carried on with great success. Mr. Budden had a year previously returned from England, and Mrs. Kennedy and myself had great pleasure in uniting with him and his daughters in carrying on the work of the Mission. I took part with Mr. Budden in preaching to the native Christian congregation, and every alternate Sunday in preaching to the English congregation.

I have mentioned how repulsive the look of the lepers was to us when we were in Almora in 1861. We now succeeded in rising above it, and took an active part in ministering to them. Mr. Budden requested Mrs. Kennedy and myself to conduct service with them every Sunday morning, to instruct them afterwards, and visit them occasionally during the week. We most willingly assented to his request.

There are few periods of our missionary life to which Mrs. Kennedy and myself look back with greater thankfulness and pleasure than to the period of our work in the Leper Asylum. All who knew her are aware how extremely, I may say how painfully, sensitive she was to sights forbidding to the eye and heart—to repulsive forms of disease and suffering. When Christian principle required her not to yield to this feeling, instead of yielding to contend against it, she successfully strove to master it, so as to enable her to do the work assigned her. She at once, as she believed, was required by the Master, accepted the call to minister to the leper women. From Sunday to Sunday we went together to the Asylum. I conducted a brief service of prayer and preaching. After it I took the men on one side of their chapel, and Mrs. Kennedy the women on the other side, to examine them on the sermon, to make it more intelligible to them, and to impress its lessons on them. Often we took some passage from the Gospels, or from other narrative portions of Scripture, every now and then a simple catechism in the Hindu language, so that by every means we might by God's blessing convey into their very limited minds the saving truth of God. In this work Mrs. Kennedy took intense interest, and seemed often more successful in securing the attention of the women than I was with the men. At first she put on coloured spectacles, but she thought her influence was thereby lessened, that the spectacles kept the poor creatures at a greater distance from her, and she discarded them. After a few Sundays she got over her repugnance, and felt herself highly privileged in being called to so Christ-like a work.

The majority of the lepers had been baptized, and from the unbaptized there were frequent applicants for the rite. The baptized were limited in knowledge and weak in faith, but none were admitted into the Church who did not give us the impression by their character that they were coming into the fold of the Good Shepherd. Special attention was given to the instruction of applicants for baptism. The women were for this purpose entrusted to Mrs. Kennedy, and we acted on her report.

We commonly spent about two hours on Sunday morning in the Asylum, and Mrs. Kennedy went to it once during the week, while I was engaged in evangelistic work.

These six months in Almora in 1867 were to Mrs. Kennedy and myself a great contrast to the same period in Benares in 1866. The escape from the heat was to us both an invaluable boon. We had an elasticity of spirit and a vigour of body which made life a joy, and fitted us for active service. Mrs. Kennedy took a part with Mr. Budden's daughters in conducting girls' classes. I tried to get into intercourse with the people, and especially with a large section called Doms, on whom the caste people looked down as a class immeasurably below them. They are generally regarded as the descendants of the inhabitants of that region before the arrival of the Hindus. They are the artisans of Kumaon, and are engaged in a variety of useful occupations. Even they, in imitation of their betters, try to divide themselves into classes resembling castes, but their social ties are very lax. The caste people are dependent on them for many indispensable services, from which they themselves shrink with utter disgust.

I was much among these people in the part of Almora which they occupied, separate from the rest of the town, and visited also their villages in the neighbourhood. I was always courteously received, but I found it very difficult to excite in them the slightest interest in Divine things. They were profoundly ignorant, very stolid, and quite satisfied to remain as they were. Their fathers were just as they were, and so their descendents would be after them. This was their prevailing tone. I saw much of the same class in after years, as I shall have occasion to state.

In October we left Almora for Benares, and reached it in November. At the close of the month we had a conference of all the missionaries of our Society in the North-

West, and of several from Bengal, European and native.
It extended over six days, and was very refreshing and
stimulating to us all. Our work was considered in its
various bearings, and full and free expression was given
to our respective views. There was perfect unity of spirit,
but a difference of opinion on several subjects brought up
for discussion. The discussion was often lively and animated, but good temper was thoroughly maintained. The
native brethren took a prominent part in our deliberations.
Their earnestness, good sense, and intelligence were very
gratifying to us, their European brethren. The private
intercourse was perhaps still more refreshing than our
public meetings. In these the ladies took their part. The
entertaining of so many was a labour, but a labour of
love, which was borne by the ladies, among whom I may
say Mrs. Kennedy took her full share and something
more.

Early in 1868 we had the great privilege of entertaining
Drs. M'Leod and Watson, I attending to their seeing the
nost notable objects in the sacred city, and Mrs. Kennedy
attending to their comfort. Our only regret was their visit
was so brief and hurried.

On our reaching Benares early in November we resumed
our former work, and continued in it until March, when
again, to our great relief, the way was open to our going
back to the Hills. We reached Almora in April 1868, and
re-entered our work of 1867 among the lepers and the
people, Mrs. Kennedy giving herself to her department of
work, and I to mine. We remained in Almora during
the winter of 1868–69, which enabled me to visit places in
the province some distance from Almora. I went for the
first time to the great Mela, the annual gathering for
worship and business held at Bageswar, some thirty miles

north of Almora. Vast numbers of Hill people, people from the Plains, the inhabitants of the country, chiefly traders, who live in valleys close to the Snowy Range, and Tibetans from the region beyond, attend that great annual fair. It presents peculiar opportunities for asserting before great crowds the claims of the Saviour of the world, the Supreme Lord of all, of which missionaries and their assistants avail themselves. On this occasion I accompanied Mr. Budden, and for a few days, from forenoon till evening, so far as our strength enabled us, we went from one part of the fair to another, bent on declaring our message. We met with the reception we expected. Many stared on us, wondering what our object could be, and heard as if they heard us not. Here and there individuals stoutly opposed us, plying us with objections and questions. Some assented, saying all we said was true, but it was not the time yet to accept a new religion.

A number of Europeans were present, officers on leave from the Plains, Kumaon officials, tea-planters, and others. We dined together in a hall in a staging bungalow, each arranging for himself. Among them there were some who thoroughly sympathised with us, and others who frankly declared they disapproved missionary doings. There were no angry words, but there was earnest talk, which I believe did good.

We had little tents with us, pitched close to the Mela ground. The singing, dancing, and merriment of the fair people, carried on well into the early morning hours, and the howling of the Mongolian dogs, allowed us little sleep; but after the first night the fatigue of the day enabled us to get a good deal of rest in spite of the din.

In the spring of 1869 I received the decision of the Directors of the London Missionary Society, dissolving

my connection with the Benares Mission, and directing
me to commence a new mission at Ranee Khet, twenty
miles north-west of Almora, where an engineer was, by
direction of Government, constructing roads with a view
to the formation of a military sanitarium.

Here it may be proper to mention an opinion often
expressed by Mrs. Kennedy, with which I thoroughly
agreed. Like myself, to her the climate, especially in
our later years, was a great trial, and she thought that if
for two or three of the most trying months missionaries
could in turn get away to the Hills, their health would be
benefited, their spirits refreshed, and their missionary
efficiency increased. For missionaries in former years
this plan would have been utterly impracticable, as the
distance from the Hills of such places as Benares and
Mirzapore was great, and no facilities for travelling
existed. Very different has the case been since the
railway has been established. During the months in
the Hills they might be most actively and usefully
employed.

Another thought may be mentioned, When missionaries can no longer work in the Plains, ought they
to return to the country of their birth? To this question one answer cannot be given. Health considerations
and family circumstances may make it a duty to return
to England, while in some cases there is no special
call homeward, and in a Hill station there may be a
reasonable hope of health being maintained. Indeed, to
some the climate of our Indian sanitarium is decidedly
more favourable to health than that of our own land.
Of late years several old missionaries of different Societies
have remained to spend their last days in these retreats,
and, so far as strength has permitted, have availed

themselves of opportunities of usefulness. Their acquaintance with the native language and their large experience has enabled them to render excellent service among the many natives, servants, and traders, who, with Europeans, spend the hot and rainy months in the Hills.

CHAPTER XIV.

RANEE KHET MISSION.

1869–1877.

In my book "Benares and Kumaon," to which I have frequently referred, I have given four chapters to Kumaon, its history, products, people, and missions. I do not repeat what I have said in these chapters, except so far as they bear on this biography. Much will be now omitted which these chapters contain, and yet there must be frequent reference to events there related, if the narrative I am now giving is to be intelligible. Our lives as missionary agents have been so intertwined, that it is only in their connection that either of us can be understood.

Ranee Khet may be described as a rough tableland, with an elevation of from 6000 to 7000 feet above the sea-level. With the exception of a little land cleared on one side, the country for miles around was covered with a forest of pine, oak, and rhododendron, over which the people of the valleys around pastured their cattle at some seasons of the year. On it and all around there was abundant covert for wild beasts, leopards, bears, and tigers, over which they roamed, and from which they went forth on their predatory excursions. They began to be scared when roads were being opened up, but after a considerable population took up their abode in it, night visits, and even occasional day visits, were paid by leopards.

Well up on the plateau there is a temple, a small roughly-built structure, with an image of Kalee, the bloody goddess to whom many such buildings are dedicated all over this province, often in the most solitary spots. No priest is attached to these temples, but in Ranee Khet and in many other places a yearly festival is held in honour of Kalee. The meaning of the word Ranee Khet is the "Field of the Queen"—the goddess being no doubt the queen honoured.

In accordance with instructions received from home to commence a new mission in the north-west of the province of Kumaon, early in spring I paid visits to Ranee Khet to reconnoitre its fitness for missionary purposes. The only Europeans then at the place were Captain Birney, now Lieutenant-Colonel Birney, R.E., an assistant engineer, and a sergeant of the Works Department. No house had been erected by that time, those I have named having put up temporary structures for their accommodation. In the immediate neighbourhood was Mr. Robert Troup, a retired military officer, a tea-planter, who had purchased the ground from Government when it had no intention of turning it into a sanitarium. A short time afterwards the attention of Government was drawn to it, and the report given by military experts was so favourable, that Government resolved to make it a hot weather resort for English soldiers. Captain Birney was instructed to open up roads and prepare for the accommodation of a military party from the Plains. His great kindness and very efficient help I shall have frequent occasion to mention.

The prospect of Ranee Khet as a European station, where soon a large population was sure to gather, was one reason for regarding it as a good sphere for a new mission.

The chief reason, however, for the choice was the fact that within twelve miles, on the sides of the hills and the valleys around, there was a large accessible population, furnishing a wide sphere for missionary effort.

I had my little tent, which I got pitched in a central place, and from day to day I traversed the neighbourhood, visiting the villages and conversing with all I met either in the villages or on the road. The inhabitants had frequent occasion to go to Almora, the Capital, for court and business purposes. They were familiar with English faces, and knew as much of their character and habits as could be obtained by the little they saw of them, but they could not comprehend what my object could be when I told them I was not a Government official, no tea-planter, no trader, no mere visitor from the Plains; but I wished to settle among them to teach them and their children about the Living God and the Saviour of the world. I put emphasis on the education of their children—on giving *vidiya*—knowledge to them. Meeting one morning a party of wood-cutters, one of their number, after slowly discovering what I meant, said, lifting his axe, "This is my *vidiya*, this is my knowledge; I got it from my ancestors, and it is enough for my children, as it is for me." In some of the villages, however, I met persons who expressed a strong desire for the establishment of schools, of which there was not one for many miles around. A very few had learned to read at Almora and elsewhere, but with these rare exceptions the people were entirely illiterate.

Early in May 1869 Mrs. Kennedy and myself left Almora to enter on a life in many respects very different from that of our previous years in India. We had formerly carried on a work commenced long before our time. We had much to do in building, both materially and spiritually, but we had built on foundations firmly laid before our connection with the missions had begun. We were now going to a place where there was no house to receive us, where no preparatory work had been done, where the foundation, both material and spiritual, had to be laid. We had sent a tent before us, and had taken with us the most necessary things in the way of furniture and food, if we were to live with some degree of the conveniences to which we had been habituated all our days.

The journey was only about eighteen miles, but in our mode of travelling it was fatiguing and slow, and afternoon was well advanced when we got to our tent. Ranee Khet was in view some time before our reaching it, and in coming to it we felt somewhat like Abraham when he had his first view of the promised land. He was assured that God was with him, and would be with him to sustain and prosper him. I think we had somewhat of the same feeling, for we knew that, so far as we were Abraham's children, the blessing of Abraham's God would overshadow us. We had on the night of our arrival in a very lively degree the feeling of pilgrims, a feeling in which the sadness of loneliness and the inspiration of hope are strangely combined, and that night with no ordinary earnestness we united in the prayer that God would make our way prosperous.

Our first days at Ranee Khet were very trying. It was midsummer. The sun was strong, and the tent in the daytime was intolerably hot. The pine-trees near us with their spike leaves gave no shelter. There was a small oak close by, but it afforded shade for only a part of the day. For two or three days Mrs. Kennedy was so unwell, that I feared she would be obliged to go to Almora

or Nynee Tal till better arrangements could be made for
our accommodation, I remaining behind. We quickly
got a booth erected, and in it we took refuge during the
hottest part of the day. Mrs. Kennedy happily got better,
and all thought of her going away was abandoned. Mr.
Troup had kindly promised to erect a temporary wooden
house for us, but it was only commenced by the time of
our arrival, and more than two months elapsed before it
was ready for occupation.

It is no part of my plan in this biography to follow our
Ranee Khet course from year to year. My aim is to give
as faithful a picture as I can of my dear wife's life during
that period, when she had new and till then unknown
duties to perform, new privations to endure, new difficulties
to overcome, and I can most truly say new enjoyment to
receive. Our position was widely different from that of
pioneers among a wild barbarous people, exposed to constant peril, but in some degree we shared their pioneering
experience. For food, for accommodation, for the conveniences of life, we had with no small difficulty to make
arrangements unknown by those who have ' close to
them facilities for supplying their wants. As missionary
pioneers we had no fear of violence, we had no fear that
the people around would rob and murder us, but we had
to encounter crass ignorance, inveterate prejudice, and
gross superstition.

In a life like that on which we were then entering, husband and wife have different duties to perform—the main
weight and care of domestic arrangements resting on the
wife, while the weight of the work beyond the home rests
on the husband. The cleavage is not, cannot be, complete.
The husband's comfort, and even life, are dependent on
the wife's success in her department, and she is deeply

concerned and interested in his success. This is very
specially the case in missionary life. Their work, though
in many respects separate, is largely intertwined, and cannot be accomplished without united feeling, and, in some
respects, united action. I must therefore in this narrative
give a good deal of space to my special work, in which
Mrs. Kennedy took the warmest interest, and constantly
helped me; but I wish to give special prominence to the
work in which the main weight rested on her.

As to accommodation—for about two months we had
our tent and booth for our abode. The booth gave us
very welcome shelter during the hottest part of the day,
but often towards afternoon we had severe thunderstorms,
with rain, which drove us out of it into the tent, which,
when the wind was high, threatened to come down on our
heads. What added to our difficulty at this time was a
visit from our eldest son, whose sight had been seriously
affected by his work in the Plains, and required far better
accommodation than we could give.

We were glad when our wooden house was ready for our
reception. It was made of timber, roughly sawn, of un-
seasoned wood, and roughly put together, divided into
compartments by wooden partitions. Into it we got some
very necessary articles of furniture we had left at Almora,
and soon by arrangements which only a lady can make
the rooms got a presentable appearance. The roof was
open, and the whole aspect of the rooms was what might
be expected from pioneers struggling to retain the habits
of settled civilised life. We were very thankful to get
into this rough wooden house, but we speedily found
trouble awaiting us. With great difficulty we succeeded
in screening off a corner sufficiently darkened for our son
who was suffering much from his eyes. No sooner did

the rain set in, as it does in torrents in July, August, and
September in the Hills of Northern India, than it came
down on us, not in drops, but in a constant heavy drizzle.
Mrs. Kennedy one night, after doing all she could to
dodge the rain, spread over the bed her waterproof cloak,
and thus managed to get some sleep. The slope had not
been steep enough, and the thatch, mainly of pine spikes,
had not been put on with sufficient skill. This house was
our abode for two years and a half. Many were our attempts
to cure the leakage, with partial success. At last it was
thoroughly cured when we were preparing to leave it.

Leakage was not our greatest trial. Rats abound in
the fields, I suppose all over the province, at least they do
where we have been, and they speedily made their way to
our house as if they came to take full possession. They
were an awful nuisance. They got into the roof, and a
great part of the night played all sorts of gambols, often
visiting us below, and when we stirred scampering away.
Every now and then a new-born rat came down upon us.
Like others, I had a great dislike to rats as fellow-occupants
of a house, but they were a horror to Mrs. Kennedy. To
leakage she became tolerably reconciled, but her horror at
rats continued unabated, and their invasion was a great
trial to her.

As to servants—here I must shorten a long grievous
story. For them we got at once huts erected, and everything was done which we could think of to suit their habits,
but we had great difficulty in getting any to remain with
us. The place was strange and wild to them; they were
away from their friends. The bazaar arrangements for
supplies were at the time very defective, and one after
another came, saying, "My heart does not sit here. I
must leave." We arranged for the food they were accus-

tomed to, but they were bent on going back to Almora.
We ourselves could with difficulty obtain the necessaries
of life, and it looked as if we were to be left to struggle
on unaided the best way we could. After a few months
the severe pressure relaxed, but all through our years at
Ranee Khet the servant difficulty remained in some degree.
This was to Mrs. Kennedy often a severe trial, a great
perplexity, and often she was at her wits' end; but she
held on, and not infrequently help came when she was
most tried.

How dependent we were on servants will appear when
I mention, as I now do, the difficulty we had *in getting
supplies.* The Government had instructed the engineer
to open up roads and arrange for the arrival of soldiers
from the Plains. On the roads and on the barracks which
were being built a great crowd of labourers were employed.
These were without their families, and easily managed
with their primitive habits to obtain shelter for themselves.
Grain was by Government arrangement brought into the
place to feed the labourers, but once and again the supply
fell short of the need, and Captain Birney, his assistants,
and ourselves were left to make our own arrangements.
At times there was difficulty in obtaining the bare necessaries of life, and still greater difficulty in obtaining the
food to which we had been accustomed. We had to send
a special messenger a number of miles to get potatoes.
We got bread, sometimes from Almora, twenty miles off,
sometimes from Nynee Tal, thirty miles off, which required
to serve us for a week. We had no facility for baking.
Fowls were sent to us from these places, but owing to
want of proper care they reached us either dead or dying.
Beef and mutton were not to be thought of. A peasant
proprietor on the side of the Ranee Khet Hill, called *Zam-*

indar, landlord, as all such are called, with great ado was induced to supply us daily with a little milk for a consideration, but we had to pay dearly for it, not only in money, which we gladly gave, but in the enduring of pestering which we found it hard to bear. How vividly I remember how the little man came to us constantly with "*Ek aur arz*,"—"*One request more*"—request after request with which it was impossible to comply. When he came to us, there was no escape his requesting, but he gave us fairly good milk, and for its sake we bore with his persistency. We had to get out of our wooden structure before we were able to make arrangements for supplying ourselves with milk. ·Captain Birney was most kind to us, and helped us greatly, but we were very unwilling to be a burden on him.

A few months after our proceeding to Ranee Khet two Companies of soldiers came from the Plains, and their coming gave us great relief. Through the kindness of the commanding officer the commissariat officer was instructed to sell us whatever we needed in the way of bread, flour, and other things. Tame fowls are an abomination to caste Hindus in the Plains and the Hills, but low-caste people keep them, and both from the Hills and Plains fowls were brought to Ranee Khet for sale. Thus our larder lost its lean estate. We had not seen eatable beef for a long time. One Sunday a butcher from Nynee came to our door with beef, which Mrs. Kennedy recognised as good. Notwithstanding her strict Sabbatarian notions, she at once bargained for a large piece. I told her that if she were to do such a thing in Aberdeen she would be at once summoned to the session to account for her conduct. She said she had never in her lifetime done anything with a better conscience.

We at once got a piece of ground cleared close to our house, and there grew vegetables, which formed an important part of our food. My wife had such aptitude for work of this kind, and had such delight in it, that I found it best to stand aside, approve and commend, and thankfully accept the benefit.

How dependent we were on servant help may be inferred from the arrangements we required to make after getting away from the wooden structure, which I have already mentioned was our abode for two years and a half. I shall have presently to speak about the erection of the Mission-House. While it was being built, we entered on arrangements which in the main held good during our remaining residence in Rance Khet. We set up as gardeners and farmers on a small scale. On the slope, in front of the Mission-House, we got the pine-trees cut down, the land cleared, terraces made, and a garden laid out, in which were grown peas, carrots, cabbages, and other useful vegetables, and also rhubarb and strawberries. We bought a buffalo and a cow, the one to give us milk to be churned into butter, and the other milk for daily use. In our garden we sowed barley, to give to our animals something better than the poor grass of the forest. We bought a few small sheep to supply us with mutton. All along I had my pony, without which it was impossible for me to do the work assigned me.

For our farm and ourselves we required a formidable host of servants and labourers, each having very moderate wages, but taken together costing a large sum. We had a gardener, a cow-keeper, and a groom outside the house. We had four men to carry Mrs. Kennedy when she went out in her darbie. The roads were so steep that without them she could not go any distance, but the carrying of

Mrs. Kennedy was by far the least and easiest part of their work. One had to bring the water required for the house from a considerable distance. Another went to the forest for wood and brought it to the kitchen. A third had to cut grass for the horse and our cow and buffalo. A fourth was chiefly engaged about the house, cleaning the furniture and doing the work of a house-servant.

All these were Hill people, with their homes a few miles off. We required to be diplomats on a small scale to keep them in humour, to prevent a revolt, and to get from them the work for which they were paid. They were very combustible material. A spark, a word of dissatisfaction, a suggestion that work might be done in a different way, was ready to burst out in a flame of insurrection. In many a case no incitement from us, direct or indirect, was required. One after another would come saying, "There is sickness in my house," or "My fields require me and I must go." "When?" "To-morrow morning." "Who is to do your work?" "I don't know, but I must go." If wages were due, they would at times rather lose them than remain.

One evening the cow-man came weeping bitterly and threw himself at my feet, sobbing out the words, "I have lost five hundred rupees; I have lost five hundred rupees." I asked "How?" After a little he sobbed out, "A person has come from my village to tell me that my wife is dead. She cost me five hundred rupees. What shall I do?" Mrs. Kennedy happened to be out at the time. On her coming in I told her, and she said, "Surely you are mistaken." While I was speaking to her, the man came, threw himself down at her feet, with the same piteous cry. It was the loss of the rupees, not the loss of the wife, which had so gone to the poor man's heart. He could no doubt get another wife, but at a ruinous cost. We, of course, let the poor man go, paid him his wages, and never saw him again. The house-servant engaged to look after the animals till the cow-man's place could be supplied.

Occasionally of an evening, on coming in, we found the whole band in the verandah, with their respective implements, hatchet, shearing-hook, ropes, &c., all laid out, to tell us that they must resign their offices, as their homes required them. They must leave the next morning. We had to exercise all our persuasive powers to prevent them from decamping. As time went on things got more and more settled, and these threatened insurrections became less and less frequent. When travelling the difficulty was sometimes greater. We must pitch our tent just where they wished it to be pitched, and do other things which we did not approve. There was one man we called "The leader of the opposition," ever ready to oppose, and well supplied with plausible reasons for opposing. As the Government party we had hard work to maintain our place. The man gave us some amusement but more annoyance. He did not succeed in ousting us.

These details of our domestic life are given to show the work which devolved on Mrs. Kennedy. I of course gave such help as I could, but the brunt of the work and the anxiety it caused came on her. She never lost heart, though sometimes much perplexed, and met every fresh difficulty, thankful we had got on so far, and hopeful we should still get on. Those who knew her well give her credit for administrative talent and for tact, and our circumstances required their exercise. Her management conferred signal benefit on us both, and greatly helped us in accomplishing the object for which we had gone to

Ranee Khet. I might here most appropriately mention as a trial, and for some months at the commencement a heavy trial, the great difficulty we had in getting servants to cook our food and do the most necessary house-work. Some had turned out utterly incompetent, and when we got a good servant we could not keep him, so great was his dislike to a place so unlike the places where he had previously been.

In after years Mrs. Kennedy often remarked we could make a doleful story about our first year in Ranee Khet, but that it would be very wrong to do so, for we were not doleful at all. The climate, in its coolness so great a contrast to that of the Plains, was itself an inestimable boon. Then there was the grand scenery around, the source of perennial enjoyment. There was a degree of pleasure in the very demand for thought and planning to overcome our difficulties and meet unexpected contingencies, and special pleasure when difficulties were overcome and our path opened before us.

It is time for me to turn to another subject. After great delay and much correspondence, largely through the kind help of Sir William Muir, then Lieutenant-Governor of the North-West Provinces, and Captain Birney, the Engineer officer at Ranee Khet, excellent sites were granted for the erection of the Mission-House and a school-house on the side of the hill on which a native town was sure to rise. Previously a site had been obtained for the erection of a place of worship for Europeans close to the site chosen for cantonments. This building was the first erected by the Mission, and was opened for worship some time before our leaving the wooden hut. The opening services were very successful. Mr. Budden and myself preached on the occasion in English, and a brother of the

Episcopal Methodist Church preached in Hindustanee.
Sir William Muir, Sir Henry Ramsay, the Commissioner
of the Province, several provincial officers, a large body
of English soldiers with their officers, and several members
of the American Episcopal Methodist Church were present.
All was concluded by the dispensation of the Lord's
Supper. The collection, with previous contributions, went
far to pay for the erection of what we called Union Church.
Along with other friends at Ranee Khet, we had great
pleasure in entertaining the friends who kindly came to
congratulate us on the erection of our place of worship
and to take part with us in its opening. Never previously
had our wooden house so many guests in it.

When the site for the Mission-House was secured, we
at once made arrangements for its erection. We first of
all arranged for the building of suitable houses for our
servants. The past had taught us that it was indispensable for them and us to have them housed. A cook-
house was erected close to the site for the Mission-
House, and to it we had a temporory room attached,
which became our abode till the house should be ready
for our reception. Our only daughter joined us from
England while we were in the hut, and now we had a
tent erected close to us for her accommodation at night,
she bearing cheerfully the inconveniences of our life.
For months this was our habitat while the house was
being built. We entered it long before it was finished,
finding in it rooms which, notwithstanding all the noise of
hammering and dust about us, were more suitable for
occupancy than our cook-room. It was a joyful day
when the workmen went out, and we had the whole
house for our abode. Friends from the Plains joined us,
pleased we could take them in for the hottest months.

I have mentioned that a short time after our arrival at
Ranee Khet English soldiers had been sent to it from the
Plains. They were sent too soon, for accommodation
was not ready. They were chiefly in tents during the
rainy season, and great sickness prevailed. A temporary
hospital was quickly erected, and everything was done
for the sufferers which could be done, but a number
succumbed to disease. Gradually barracks were erected
for the unmarried men, and at a place very accessible
to us the married men and their families were housed
in suitable quarters.

For a considerable time I was the only Christian
minister at the place, and the consequence was much
English work devolved on me. Service was first held
in the open air, then in the canteen, then in the school-
room, which was left for Union Chapel as soon as it was
ready. I preached twice on Sunday—in the forenoon
to the Episcopalians, in the afternoon to the Presbyterians and those who preferred the Nonconformist mode
of worship. During the week, so far as other duties
allowed, I visited the hospital.

Mrs. Kennedy found a large field for usefulness among
our own people. This was to her well-nigh an entirely
new sphere. At Benares she had done a little in this
department, but now on to the end of our residence at
Ranee Khet this was her chief employment beyond her
own household. A Sunday-school was early set up.
Others took part with her. For a time almost every
boy and girl, Protestant and Roman Catholic, of fitting
age attended. The teachers were diligent, had the requisite tact, firmness, and kindness, and the cheerful
and regular attendance of the children was secured.
We had them now and then to our house in the even-

ing, where they were duly entertained. Latterly we found the school-house the better place for an evening gathering. This continued till a Roman Catholic priest came as Chaplain to the Roman Catholic soldiers. He insisted on the withdrawal of the children of his communion. The parents were pleased the children should remain with us, but they could not resist the mandate of the priest. A number of the children were very reluctant to obey, but they were obliged to yield, with the exception of two or three, with the connivance of their parents. We had Church of England Chaplains in succession, but they set up no Sunday-school, and did not interfere with ours.

Mrs. Kennedy visited the barracks of the married people frequently, and was well received by them. This was a work in which she had great delight, and the encouragement she received gave her the hope good was being done. Roman Catholic families received her courteously as well as Protestant.

There were few native families at Ranee Khet, and these were almost entirely of the lowest caste, who, themselves uneducated, were indifferent to the education of their children. We had a school-house with several apartments erected, but we did not succeed in getting many boys. The attempt was made to get up a girls' school, but it was an utter failure. A few of the boys expressed a wish to learn English, and for a considerable time they came daily to Mrs. Kennedy to get lessons from her.

At Ranee Khet, occasionally in the hut, and still more in the Mission-House, we had the privilege of exercising hospitality. This is the lady's special department, and for its duties my dear wife was always ready. A devoted

N

German lady who had laboured faithfully in the Plains was with us for months. She was one with whom Mrs. Kennedy had formed a close intimacy. Our most frequent visitors were members of the American Episcopal Methodist Church, travelling to and from their Mission still farther into the Hills. With them, and with others of their Church travelling in the Hills, we had at Ranee Khet and in other places much pleasant Christian intercourse and co-operation. Reciprocal hospitality is the rule among missionaries, guests at one time being hosts at another. I cannot say that the reciprocal principle is always carried out faithfully, but it is carried out to a large and satisfactory extent.

During the summer and autumn months of 1869 our dear friends Dr. and Mrs. Mather resided in Almora. We had the pleasure of a visit from them. Dr. Mather and myself arranged for a mission tour to the east of the province late in autumn, which occupied us the greater part of a month. We had many opportunities as we travelled of speaking to the people on the greatest subjects. We had travelling difficulties which were patiently borne, but would have been less felt, had we been younger in years and stronger in body.

One great family advantage we had at Ranee Khet was that during the latter part of our stay four of our children were in India, three of them in the North-West Provinces, and the fourth in Bengal. We had the pleasure of having them all with us some time, and three of them frequently, when circumstances allowed them to escape from the heat of the Plains. These family gatherings gave us intense pleasure.

It is no part of my object in this biography to enter into details regarding my own work in the Hills, but I must give some account of it, if the position and work of my wife is to be understood.

I have already mentioned my work among our own countrymen. On the arrival of a Church of England chaplain it was greatly lessened. I preached only once on the Sunday, and visited only the Presbyterian sick in the hospital. Occasionally others expressed a wish to see me, and I gladly complied with the request. When at home I had a weekly Bible-class, when a few attended regularly, who, I trust, were spiritually benefited. In this work Mrs. Kennedy was my fellow-labourer, as I have already mentioned, we working with the same aim in our respective departments.

My main work was among the natives. I went often to the bazaar to speak to those I might meet there. I set up a night-school for the artisans, almost all Doms, who were, as I have already mentioned, very useful to the caste people, but were at the same time despised by them. They set vigorously to learn their letters, and the more diligent and capable learned to read, write, and cipher fairly. On Sunday evening I had a service in the native language, which was attended by most of the day-scholars, the artisan scholars, and a few native Christians. I made special effort to get into intercourse with educated natives, some from the Almora school, others from the Plains, who were employed in the public offices of the place. A room in the school-house was turned into a reading-room, to which they might go every evening, where they would find books, papers, and periodicals supplied by the kindness of friends. One evening every week I went to this room to meet with persons of this class and read with them. A few seemed to value this meeting.

During the greater part of the year my chief work was

in the villages within ten or twelve miles of Ranee Khet.
I had for a time nine schools, one at Ranee Khet, and
eight in villages around.   These I visited as frequently as
I could, generally leaving my house at the earliest dawn,
and returning by noon or afterwards.   A few of the
villagers were sure to gather around me when examining
the boys, and thus I had an opportunity for evangelistic
as well as scholastic work.   I often spent days together
in the neighbourhood of a school, visiting all the villages
and hamlets round, and putting up for the night in a little
tent or in the school-house.   Besides, when I could, I set
out on itineracy for a week or longer to places where we
had no school.

Mrs. Kennedy did not at all like to be left alone at
Ranee Khet, especially while we resided in the hut.   On
one occasion I was away from it close on a fortnight, but
instead of seeking to keep me at home, she always cheered
me, as she had thorough sympathy with the object which
took me away.   I was sure to have from her messengers
with the supplies I needed.   Occasionally she accompanied
me, and when she did she greatly enjoyed the excursion,
her love for mountain scenery being intense; but the expense was far more than doubled when she travelled with
me, and this consideration kept her generally at home.

For nearly three months every year, the winter months,
we were away from Ranee Khet, generally following the
people in their migration with their families and cattle
to the foot of the Hills, and sometimes travelling to
parts of the Kumaon province which we could not visit
at other times.   The people went down to the region
under the mountains called the Bhabur for greater heat
—"in search of sunshine," to use an expression of their
own—and for the good pasture they got for their cattle.

A new and very valuable source of income has been for a number of years opened to them in land made arable by irrigation works planned and carried out by the Commissioner, Sir Henry Ramsay.

Mrs. Kennedy always accompanied me on these visits to the Bhabur. It was much more economical to do so than for her to remain behind at Ranee Khet, and also much more pleasant. We lived in tents during that season, which served us well, except when it rained heavily, or, still more unpleasantly, when it blew hard. One night there was a severe storm, when there was danger of our being buried under our tent. We had a number of small adventures in those tents as we moved from place to place, some of them annoying, which my wife bore very patiently. I tried to set up temporary schools for boys, some of whom had been our pupils in the Hills, but with poor success. We were often in the vicinity of tigers and wild elephants. On one occasion our tent was pitched close to the tents of a party out for tiger-shooting. They held out in the morning on their business, and I on mine. In the evening they returned with a host of followers, who dragged to the spot three tigers that had been killed in the course of the day. On another occasion one morning, in riding about four miles to a school, I found only three or four boys present, and was told that wild elephants had crossed the road and committed depredations in the night-time, spreading terror all around. When returning to my tent I observed traces of the elephants on the road.

Occasionally in the prosecution of my work when away from Ranee Khet I had to leave Mrs. Kennedy in the tent, I may say in the wilderness, for two or three days. She shrank from being alone in such circumstances, but she quickly came to herself, and said, "Dear, your work requires it. Why should I be afraid?" The principle on which she strove to act throughout was to be a help, not a hindrance, to me, however much feeling might plead against my movements.

When we did not go down in winter I went to the great Mela at Bageswar. On one occasion she accompanied me, but we both felt it was a mistake. She could do no service, and stood rather in my way. She went once through the Mela, and was not a little interested in the prayer-wheels of the Mongolians, who perform their devotions by this simple mechanical contrivance.

The last winter of our mission life in India was spent chiefly in a very populous part of the Kumaon province, from which the people do not go down to the Plains. Mrs. Kennedy greatly enjoyed this tour to a part of the country she had not previously seen. She had with her a very favourite book, Dr. M'Millan's "Bible Teachings in Nature," which she had read through twice or thrice. I remember how, one afternoon on the brow of a hill, with a forest of lofty trees before her, she read with exquisite pleasure the chapter, "*The Trees of the Lord.*" We did not move about frequently on that tour. We spent more than three weeks in one place, as there were populous villages all around us, where I had no difficulty in getting an audience. In after years Mrs. Kennedy often referred to this tour—to the fine open valley, beyond which we saw a part of the Snowy Range, and on our way to it terrace rising above terrace from a depth to a height we had not seen elsewhere. Its image impressed on her mind was never effaced.

To go back in time. In the spring of 1874 Mrs. Kennedy was very unwell, and family circumstances

made it very desirable she should visit England. Our
doctor thought a trip home would do her much good.
Our Directors kindly consented. The journey to Bombay
was very long, with various changes on the way. It was
very undesirable for me to be at the time long away from
my Mission work, which I should be if I accompanied her
to Bombay and saw her embark for England. She was
naturally timid, and dreaded travelling alone, but she
most readily agreed to my seeing her away from the
nearest town in Rohilkund, from which I could in twelve
hours get back to my tent, which I had left pitched.
Letters had been sent to friends to help her on, to which
they kindly attended. She was especially indebted for
hospitable treatment to Sir William and Lady Muir at
Allahabad, and to the Rev. J. S. Robertson, Secretary of
the Church Missionary Society at Bombay, and his wife,
two excellent friends, with whom we had afterwards most
friendly intercourse in England, till their removal to the
better land. At Bombay the late Dr. Wilson showed her
special attention.

Her stay in England was brief, but in many respects
satisfactory. Her health was recruited, and within eight
months of her departure she returned to India, accompanied by a son who had succeeded in getting into the
Indian Civil Service. During a great part of her absence
I had the pleasure of having with me at Ranee Khet my
dear friend the late Mr. Sherring, with his wife and little
boy.

From Mrs. Kennedy's return to our final departure
from Ranee Khet at the beginning of 1877, she gave
herself to her former work, often regretting she could not
do more, but gladly doing all within her power.

I have mentioned some of the guests we were honoured

to entertain at Ranee Khet.　Much as we esteemed them, we had a still higher place in our esteem and a still warmer place in our hearts for resident friends.　If I had followed the order of my cordial regard instead of facts referring to my wife as they came to my recollection, these friends would have been first named.　I have already mentioned Captain, now Lieutenant-Colonel Birney, R.E., who treated us so kindly at the beginning, and who all through with his wife acted towards us in the most friendly manner.　A foremost place is due to Colonel Chamberlain, who came to Ranee Khet a few months after us as Cantonment Magistrate, and who with his wife ever onward were very intimate, affectionate, and helpful friends.　Their temporary house was close to ours, and while there, we saw each other daily, till they and we got permanent abodes, when we met frequently.　They left India a short time after our departure, and in this country our intimacy was continued.　Colonel Chamberlain retired as major-general. He was suddenly called away by the Saviour whom he had long faithfully served, leaving his widow to mourn his loss, in which we joined with many others who knew and loved him.　For years he acted as a kind of elder to me, and in many ways greatly helped us.　The very close friendship between Mrs. Chamberlain and Mrs. Kennedy remained till ended by the death of my beloved one, if, in the case of Christians, we ought to speak of friendship as ended by death.

Some time after the formation of the Ranee Khet Mission a Mission Committee was formed, consisting of Captain Birney, Colonel Chamberlain, Mr. Robert Troup, Mr. Ashhurst, an engineer officer, and latterly Captain Crowther. These friends rendered inestimable service to the Mission in the erection of the buildings, the Church, the Mission-

House, the Ranee Khet school-house, and school-houses in the villages, also in liberal contributions and many other ways. This was a part of pioneering work in which I should have felt myself helpless but for this help rendered by these friends. Indeed, without the service they rendered, I do not see how the necessary buildings could have been erected.

Other residents in Ranee Khet, besides those I have named, aided us by sympathy and contributions. Beyond Ranee Khet we had very helpful friends. The Commissioner of the province, Colonel (for years) Sir Henry Ramsay, was the liberal and hearty supporter of every thing done for the good of the people, and he laid us, with others, under lasting obligation. Sir William Muir was, during a considerable part of our term Lieutenant-Governor of the North-Western Provinces, and he and Lady Muir showed great kindness to ourselves, and gave very efficient help to the Mission. For successive years, in autumn, missionary meetings were held in Nynee Tal, in the Mission Chapel of the American Episcopal Methodists, attended by all the missionaries of the province, and by the friends of missions at that season at Nynee Tal. They extended over several days, were well attended, and were very refreshing and stimulating. On these occasions we were generally the guests of Sir William and Lady Muir.

In the summer of 1876 my active work as an Indian missionary came to an end. A sudden and severe illness utterly incapacitated me for the pleasant and yet toiling life of a missionary in a Hill country like Kumaon. Medical opinion decided against my attempting to continue the work in which I had been engaged. The directors of the London Missionary Society accepted this opinion, and gave their ready and kind consent to my retirement. We accordingly left Ranee Khet at the end of 1876, made our way to Bombay, visited all the Mission Stations on our way, were everywhere kindly entertained, saw much which deeply interested us, and embarked for England, which we reached in February 1877.

The Mission at Ranee Khet at the time of our leaving had a promising aspect. The night-school had carried several on to fair ability to read, write, and keep accounts. The native service in the hall of the school-house was unusually well attended, and, so far as we could learn from look and words, a strong impression Christward was made. With little pecuniary help from the Society, by the liberal contributions of friends, not only were all the buildings free of debt, but a considerable sum remained to the credit of the Mission. The place which in 1869 we found a rough table-land covered with forest, without one permanent structure, had risen to a large military station, with many buildings, and is now, 1 suppose, the largest military sanitarium in India. The place had become very endeared to us, and we left it with great reluctance.

What can I say about our departure from India? Our native land had many attractions, there was much to draw us to it; but a great part of our life had been given to India; our best years had been spent in it in the Master's service; we were bound to it by most sacred associations, by ties of no ordinary strength, and we left it with feelings which those only can realise who have passed through a similar experience.

LETTERS FROM MRS. KENNEDY TO A NIECE.

A much-loved niece has supplied me with letters which she had received from her aunt, and I have made extracts from them, which I am sure will be read with pleasure, as illustrations of her character and circumstances when they were written. With the exception of four of an earlier date, they come within the time of the chapter to which they are now appended.

"BENARES, *28th November* 1854.

"How thankful we are to think that you have been led to seek the Lord in the days of your youth! It is such a happy thing to be a Christian. Wisdom's ways are indeed pleasantness, and all her paths are peace; and this, I doubt not, you experience.

"Then the pleasures of religion are so enduring. The path of the just is as the shining light, that shineth more and more unto the perfect day. The way, indeed, may be often rough and difficult, but the end is peace and safety."

This letter was sent to her niece by the pilot as Mrs. Kennedy was leaving India in 1857: —

"OFF KEDGEREE, *September* 1857.

"I go with a sad heart. My thoughts have been much with you, my dear niece, and feel much for you in your present circumstances. Dear, dear Auntie! is she really never, never more to cheer and encourage us by her glad smile? Well, we shall meet ere long in that bright and blessed world, whither her redeemed spirit has flown. To be with Christ is far better. Alas! that we are so slow to realise it!"

The Auntie mentioned in this letter was Mrs. Kennedy's sister, the beloved "Auntie" of our children, and the mother of this niece.

"BENARES, *4th August* 1860.

"We were glad to hear that Mrs. Lacroix was so well. What a change in that household since you were there formerly!

But it is sweet to think of those who sleep in Jesus, and to anticipate the glorious morning of the Resurrection. Even now, how much superior to ours is the state of the departed in knowledge, purity, and happiness! Sometimes, when one is enabled to realise these things, though but feebly, we wonder at our own worldliness and undue care about things seen and temporal. You have the prospect of being on the move for a considerable time, and I have always found that being so was unfavourable to spiritual progress. May you have grace to live near to God, though in the midst of change, and be enabled to act as a decided follower of the Saviour! How much good may one do by a quiet, unostentatious, consistent example; and, on the other hand, how much dishonour may we bring on that blessed name by which we are called by an opposite course! Pray pardon my seeming to preach to you."

This letter was sent to our niece on our receiving the news of the death of her father:—

"BENARES, 24*th January* 1865.

"On receiving your letter containing the news of dear uncle's death, my impulse was to write at once. I felt the news much, and cannot but feel deeply the absence of one more whom I knew and loved most of my own life. Benares has few in it now who were here when we came to it; but so it ever is in this world: everything pointing us to a higher and better state. May we be enabled to occupy more faithfully till the Master come! I could have wished, if it had been possible, the graves of your dear parents were close to each other, but in India circumstances often make this impossible. Their spirits are together before the throne above, and it matters little where the earthly tabernacle rests."

"RANEE KHET, *May* 22, 1869.

"I am all alone to-day in our booth, your uncle having gone down to Seonnee for to-morrow's service. Seonnee is a place where the soldiers' huts are, twelve miles from here. They are, of course, not to remain there, but are meanwhile working on the roads. Our hut progresses very slowly, but we hope to get into it in a week or two; and oh! how glad shall we be to do so, for this tent and booth life even here is very trying at this season. I was afraid it was going to kill me quite, but I am now nearly well again. The place is lovely, and when we get settled, even in our hut, we shall be very comfortable. . . . Scarcely anything is to be got here in the way of supplies. We have to send coolies in all directions. We get fowls dead and dying from neglect on the way, meat too far gone for use, &c. These are, however, only temporary difficulties. In a short time there will be abundance. Your uncle has begun three schools in central localities, which promise well."

"RANEE KHET, *August* 11, 1869.

"At Ranee Khet there is no such thing as a baby, so you see how very barbarous we are. There is just one house for permanent residence, if I except a sergeant's at the station. Our wooden one is, on the whole, pretty good, though it leaks sadly. It is a large long shed, with a verandah, and tolerable doors and windows, very like what one sees at railway stations in the Plains. Whatever the outside atmosphere is, we have it within. Compared with the Plains, it is paradise. We are getting a garden made, and a good summer-house. Your uncle has about a hundred boys in four schools, two of these six and eight miles from here. As yet, nothing can be done for girls. The Bunyahs (grain dealers) are only squatting without their families."

"RANEE KHET, *November* 25, 1869.

"The weather here is charming, beautiful. How I wish you would spend just a day with us, even to see our habitat and its surroundings. We have, of course, a good many drawbacks, especially from not having a proper house to live in, but withal we are most thankful to be here. We had Lord Mayo, the Governor-General, and Lady Mayo here, and had the honour of dining with them. It wasn't much pleasure. Such things are always so stiff, and one knows nobody among the strangers. Lady Mayo is frank and pleasant."

"RANEE KHET, *July* 23, 1870.

"Ranee Khet is a fine open place, not nearly so wet as Nynee Tal; but you will come and see it, and visit us in our hill shanty or kraal. We have done a good deal to it lately, and, with such a climate, would be little disposed to complain if we could only make it water-tight. Happily, it does not always rain, but when it does, there is such a rushing and running for basins of all sorts and sizes, that you would laugh to see us."

On 4th June 1857 the Sepoys mutinied at Benares:—

"RANEE KHET, *June* 8, 1875.

"Your most welcome letter, written on the memorable 4th June, was received this morning, and read with true sympathy of feeling. It is indeed a day to be much remembered by us every year as it comes round, and is so, I am sure, with deep and devout thankfulness. How entirely do I agree with you in every word you say about the past as regards the present life, and the future as regards that to come! We would not retrace life's weary pilgrimage if we might; albeit we have had many happy days, and experienced much of the Lord's goodness to us both in providence and grace. 'Onward and upward' ought certainly to be the Christian's motto.

"You seem just beginning to realise some of the experiences of human life, known long ago, but not felt as now. Your thoughts about heaven are exactly my own. Surely this world is typical of the heavenly. I have often enjoyed the remark of the late Dr. Brown of Edinburgh, 'Religion makes war on nothing in man but his depravity.' Have you ever met with a sermon by Norman M'Leod, preached on the occasion of Dr. Wardlaw's death, from the text 'In Thy presence is fulness of joy?' It met and satisfied many longing and floating thoughts in my mind. He speaks of the vague, ghostly views so many have had about heaven as a place of merely ecstatic unearthly bliss, and then, in his own happy way, shows how there will be ample provision for man's enjoyment as a *moral, intellectual, sentient, social,* and *active* being. He has something of the same kind in his 'Parish Papers,' but in the sermon it seemed to me the thoughts were more fully worked out. You must come up to the Hills, if spared until another year, and then we can talk over all these things.

"I may just say that to me the idea of ever learning in heaven is one of the most delightful."

The following letter was written on hearing of the death of our niece's husband :—

"RANEE KHET, *December* 2, 1875.

"Little did I think, in opening a letter addressed by an unknown hand this morning, what its contents would be. I feel as if, with Job's friends, I could only sit down and weep with you. Your sorrow is far past human help or sympathy. I feel so unnerved that I can scarcely write, and yet I cannot let the mail go without a few words. May He, who alone can, be very near you in this time of sore trouble! May He sustain and comfort you by the consolations of His grace, and may His everlasting arms be under you! It will be long before you can even realise what your loss is—longer still before you can attain the peace which comes after the storm; but it will come, I trust, in God's time. Dear kind man! I can hardly think it possible I shall see him no more on earth. I am so glad of the few days I had with you a year and a half ago *en route* for Bombay. I seemed to get better acquainted with him, and to love him more for his own sake than ever before. He has finished his course, and got, I trust, the palm of victory. But for you and your five fatherless children my heart bleeds. May you experience the truth of the promise that God is the Husband of the widow and the Father of the fatherless! Yet, with all the help the Gospel gives, your life will henceforward be in shade, so far as regards the present life. To myself the spiritual and unseen has seemed more real and tangible since 1853 than the present, and as one and another passes away, I feel they have only gone before, and that I shall soon follow. God will be with you in the depths, and keep you from being overwhelmed, even when passing through the floods of great waters.

"Your uncle is from home, but I expect him in to-morrow. It will be a terrible stroke to him, as it has been to me."

"KOUSANNIE, *December* 28, 1875.

"We were both very thankful to get your letter written from Ulwar. We had been very anxious about you, and learning you had gone to your brother John, I wrote last week to Isabel, requesting her to write and let us know how you were. We are sure they will do all in their power to soothe and help, though many a time you will doubtless feel that vain is the help of man. We rejoice to know you are being upheld and sustained by help from above. He will never leave or forsake those who trust in Him, and you have not to begin to do that now.

"May your path be made smooth, and friends be raised up to help you in every way in their power, solitary though your road must henceforward be! Are there not times when the words, generally felt to be words of warning, 'The time is short,' come as balm to the stricken heart?"

"ALLAHABAD, *February* 16, 1877.

"We are very thankful to know that your way has been so opened up, and thankful also for the abundant occupation your new circumstances must bring. I never knew the value of work till I went to Ranee Khet. Many times does my mind go back to those years when 'my children were about me,' and to you in active middle life occupation must have a double blessing. The mind wearing and hinging on itself is apt to become morbid even in the most spiritual Christians. Have you ever met with a little book called 'The Gates Ajar'? I had often heard of it, but it never came in my way till a few days ago at Mirzapore. There is much that is fanciful in it, but much also that commends itself to one's hopes and spiritual aspirations. Only those who have buried their dead, dearer than their own souls, can understand how the bereaved soul tries to follow and know about the condition of those who are gone. This little book is evidently the production of one who has felt and thought deeply, and the conjectures are pleasing, and I should say probable; but the truth comes back to me that 'like children here we speak and think.' Well, heaven will reveal this to us, as we cannot understand it now; but I indulge in Milton's idea that 'earth is but its shadow.'"

CHAPTER XV.

HOME LIFE.

1877–1891.

On reaching England at the end of March 1877, we made our way to Edinburgh, where, at that time, our youngest son was in an office. We found a house at Portobello to suit us, within three miles of Edinburgh, and there we abode till May 1882.

Till the end of the year, I was much engaged in deputation work for the London Missionary Society and in occasional preaching. During these months there was a change in the pastorate of the Congregational church in Portobello, the pastor having accepted a call to a Church in Edinburgh. His place was speedily supplied, but the new pastor's health very soon broke down, and he left for New Zealand, with the intention of returning if his health was sufficiently restored. I complied with the request to act for him, and on the receipt of his resignation in 1878, at the wish of the Church, I continued to perform the duties of the pastorate. In the summer of 1880 I was laid aside by illness for more than two months, which was the beginning of the end of our work in Portobello. It closed in November 1881.

Throughout the four years of my pastorate, Mrs. Kennedy, by her entire bearing, by her intercourse with the people of my charge, by her kindness to the poor, and

specially by her sympathy with the sick, the sorrowful, and
the bereaved, did much to help me in the discharge of my
duties and to promote my efficiency. We had, during that
period, much pleasure in the society of people of our own
communion, and of many members of other Churches,
both in Portobello and Edinburgh. Mrs. Kennedy went
to the noon-day prayer-meeting in Edinburgh as often as
she could, and also a mothers' prayer-meeting, attended by
a number of the most excellent ladies in the city, with
whom she had warm Christian fellowship. I have already
observed that the Capital of our native land had always
for her peculiar attractions, both social and religious. On
to the end of life she often said that for residence, if
residence alone was to be considered, apart from family
reasons, it would have had the preference.

The previous year our youngest son had gone to India,
and as my work at Portobello had come to an end, we
made up our mind, for domestic reasons, to remove to
London.

Before settling down, we thought it well, on leaving
Portobello in May 1882, to see more of our own country
than we had yet seen, and afterwards to have a long-pro-
jected tour on the Continent. The most of the time, from
May to September, was spent in the Scottish Highlands.
We made our way to the Isle of Skye and the north-
western part of Ross-shire, visiting, as we travelled, places
which interested us greatly, and making ourselves acquainted, so far as we could, with the character and condition of the people. When circumstances permitted, when
duty did not intervene, as I have already mentioned, it
gave Mrs. Kennedy intense enjoyment to see Nature in its
most impressive forms, and on this tour in Braemar,
Aberdeenshire, in the mountains of Skye, in Loch Maree,

Ross-shire, the least known of the great Scotch lakes, but
in the rugged grandeur of the mountains between which
it is embosomed equally worthy of admiration, there was
much to afford her gratification. We visited Aberdeen,
Elgin, and Inverness, which had for us most tender and
sacred associations.

We returned to Edinburgh in September to attend the
marriage of a son, and with this pleasant duty discharged,
we proceeded to London, where we made arrangements for
our Continental tour. The ordinary touring time on the
Continent had come to an end, but the season turned out
unusually favourable, and we succeeded in accomplishing
in good weather all we had intended.

Seven weeks were spent on the Continent, during which,
following a route which thousands of our people have
followed, and which has been very often described, we saw
a little of Belgium, Holland, Germany, Switzerland, and
France. We were deeply interested wherever we were,
but Switzerland, with its scenery and its memorable
associations, got more of our attention and heart than any
other part of our tour. We had one drawback—a very
serious drawback. Mrs. Kennedy was very unwell during
a part of the tour, especially when we were in Switzerland.
We were ten days in Geneva, and during nearly half of
the time she was in bed under medical treatment. This
was a great disappointment to her, but still she managed
to see St. Pierre, the Cathedral Church, the Consistory
Hall, and other spots made for ever memorable by their
association with Calvin, the most illustrious of the Re-
formers. We went to his grave, with its simple head-
stone with his initials, to show where his remains were
laid. When at Geneva, we received kindly attentions from
persons to whom we had notes of introduction.

After a week in Paris, where, after the manner of tourists, we saw, as we best could, places of much interest, we made our way to England, and were happy to find ourselves again with our relatives and friends.

Our wish was to take up our abode in Hampstead, near a son and his wife, but we did not succeed in getting a house to suit us. A friend told us that at Acton, within an easy distance of Hampstead by train, we might get a house to our mind. We were told that the place was healthy, and the result was that, finding a house with the requisite accommodation, we became residents in that town in March 1883.

There we remained for the remaining part of Mrs. Kennedy's life. Our residence in Acton, extending over eight years, was much longer than at any other place in Great Britain since we first went to India. We in some respects perhaps took deeper root there than we had done in any other place of our residence at home. We were alone, the son who had been with us in Edinburgh having gone to India. We met weekly with the members of our family in London and their wives, and had constant intercourse with other relatives and friends. During these years Mrs. Kennedy had the great joy of seeing, for a longer or shorter period, all her children, those with an Indian career having come, some of them, more than once on furlough to this country. Towards the end of our residence, two members of the family took up their abode in London, as their Indian career had closed. Her anxiety about their worldly career had come to an end, all of them occupying honourable positions, and discharging diligently, as she had every reason to believe, the duties of their respective offices.

This family rest, connected with so much family enjoyment, was very gratifying to Mrs. Kennedy, and drew forth her heart-felt thanks to our Heavenly Father, for children fondly attached to their parents, and the children to each other. She knew well she had in no ordinary degree the love and reverence of her loved ones, and those who by marriage had become connected with us. Every sign in them of a heart going Godward was hailed by her with intense satisfaction, and her constant earnest prayer for them was that they, and those nearly related to them, might be wholly and unmistakably the children of God. With the absent members of the family she kept up a constant correspondence.

On going to Acton we became members of the Congregational Church under the pastorate of the Rev. W. F. Adeney, now Professor Adeney of New College. Professor Radford Thomson was at that time resident in Acton—indeed, it was at his suggestion I had gone to look for a house in that town—and with him and his family we had very pleasant intercourse until their departure. We greatly enjoyed Mr. Adeney's very interesting and thoughtful ministrations, and gradually we got into most friendly intercourse with him and many of his people. Mrs. Kennedy was soon seen to be not only an estimable and intelligent Christian, with whom it would be profitable to have frequent intercourse, but one who, though advanced in life, was able and willing to take part in Church work. To such work she was soon introduced, and she entered into it with a zeal which was maintained to the end. With no child resident with us, with the care and anxiety and toil of many previous years having come to an end, she had abundant leisure, and she turned it into activity beyond her strength. Often, especially in later years, she returned from visits to mothers, to the sick, the bereaved, and the poor, some of them at distances too great for her, much exhausted, and I begged her not to undertake what I saw was too trying for her health. She also for a considerable time taught a class of young women on Sunday afternoons, and took part in conducting meetings with them, besides going often to the women's working party in the Mission-Hall in South Acton.

When Mr. Adeney resigned his charge on accepting a professorship, we were brought into closer communion with the Church than we had previously been. The vacancy in the pastorate was unexpectedly long, and I was requested to act as chairman of the Church and to conduct the Thursday evening service till a pastor should be appointed. Mrs. Kennedy strove to do her part in her sphere.

At length, to our great joy, the Rev. William Bolton was called to fill the vacant place, and with him, as with his predecessor, we felt quite at home. It gave us great satisfaction to see the place filled by one who from character and attainments had every promise, by the Divine blessing, of ministerial success—a promise which we have every reason to hope will be amply fulfilled.

The winter of 1890–91, as all remember, was one of great severity. During it I was often unwell, but Mrs. Kennedy went about, I think, more than any previous winter. Several persons expressed their surprise at seeing her out when heavy snow lay on the ground. It looked as if she had regained the strength of her youth, but it was far otherwise. She had the presentiment she had only a short time to live, and she was bent on putting forth all her strength in the Master's service. She often returned much exhausted, which led me to remonstrate with her on going out. She felt so weak that she said to me again and again, "I think, dear, I will slip away from you one of these days." I often hoped that her strength was greater than her felt weakness indicated. We had spoken of going to Scotland in autumn if spared, and she said that much though she would like to go, she was sure she could not stand the fatigue.

Never was her faith stronger nor her hope more assured than during the last few months of her life. So retentive was her memory, that after reading a hymn twice or thrice she could repeat it afterwards without a slip. She put it, as she herself said, "in her pocket." She had for many years peculiar delight in hymns. Latterly she was long awake in the morning before rising, and she spent the time, as she now and then told me, in quietly repeating hymns to herself, generally ending with the *Te Deum*, that noble hymn of Ambrose, which has for ages given utterance to the loftiest feelings of the Christian heart. The *Te Deum* had been a special favourite for many a day. The thought of death, and of her passing immediately after death into the Saviour's presence, seemed continually present to her. She often said she was in the land of Beulah, waiting, in Bunyan's language, for "the post." She had left Doubting Castle far behind. She observed I was distressed by her speaking so much in this strain, and since her death two of her most intimate lady friends have told me she spoke to them in this strain more plainly than she had done to me. Yet so various and so conflicting are the feelings which spring up in the mind, that at times she looked forward to the winter of 1891–92 as if she expected to see it. A son from India was coming home on furlough in the spring of 1891. He was in bad health, and was ordered by his physician to remain in the South of France till summer, and also to reside there in the winter of 1891–92. It was quite a trial to her to think of her not seeing him during a whole winter while he was in Europe, though, if his health required his residing in France, submission was her duty. She spoke of it again and again. She was comforted by his writing to her that he would during the winter come to her as often as he could. In fact, as I shall presently state, she never saw him at all.

During the long winter nights of 1890–91 she spoke much about the state of the world, how sad, how distressed it was, to a large degree how debased, how terrible its prospects. She often put to me questions which I was quite unable to answer. I told her the burden of the world was too heavy for us; if we were to realise it, it would crush us. We should pray for it, hope for it, labour for it, as opportunity was given, and rest our whole soul on the Rock, the immovable foundation of God's righteousness, wisdom, and love for the world's government and destiny. I quoted a remark made many years ago by a thoughtful, excellent man. " Let us thank God we can forget." To know the world as it is, realise and remember it, in all its sadness and sin, would overthrow the strongest mind. Our thinkings and questionings those evenings ended by our casting ourselves anew on our Heavenly Father for ourselves, our children, the Church, and the world. In addition to our family worship, I observed how constantly, when circumstances permitted, at a certain hour she retired to her room for private devotion.

Notwithstanding Mrs. Kennedy's growing impression that she was on the border of the unseen world, the end came suddenly, in a way unexpected by her and by us all. For years she was never in robust health, but notwithstanding occasional and sometimes severe illnesses, her health while at Acton was generally good—so good as to make life a pleasure, and to enable her to go freely about. The spring of 1891 passed pleasantly away in the enjoyment for her of fair health, and we entered on summer with the hope it might be to us what the previous summer had been. We had the very pleasant prospect of seeing soon our son from India and his wife, who had stayed behind in France till summer had fully set in.

On May 13th, 14th, and 15th the meetings of the London Missionary Society were held—the Ladies' Meeting on the 13th, the Annual Meeting of the Society on the 14th, and the Ladies' Annual Breakfast on the 15th. Mrs. Kennedy attended all these meetings, a great and unusual effort for her, and she greatly enjoyed them. The weather on the 13th and 14th was very hot, and she in consequence dressed more lightly for the 15th. On coming home on that day, being Indian mail-day, she wrote a short letter to one of our sons in India, and shortly afterwards complained of being chill. There had been a storm on the 15th, which had lowered the temperature. A fire was lit, but still feeling chilled, she retired early to bed. She was evidently suffering from bronchitis, from which she had often suffered, and from feverishness, to which she was always subject after unusual fatigue. The bronchitis was not severe and the fever was slight. I was hopeful she would speedily get over it, as she had done over more severe attacks. On Saturday the 16th I sent for our medical attendant. He called, prescribed for her complaint, and thought she would soon be herself again. Next day I went out to service in the forenoon, and while I was absent the doctor called, telling her she was getting on well. Her illness did not abate, but it did not seem to increase. I wished to stop with her in the evening, but she begged me to go to the service, as the servant could well attend to her, and we should show a good example. The next day she continued very unwell, and towards the close of that day I began to dread the issue, not from the severity of the illness, but from her strength so failing that she was unable to overcome it. On from Tuesday her state was very critical. The medical attendant called thrice every day, and at my request a London specialist in such diseases was called in. He approved of what was being done, and spoke in a way which we afterwards interpreted as meaning there was scarcely any hope, though, to save our feelings, he did not plainly say what he thought. We had the comfort of knowing that everything was being done which medical skill could do.

From the time the illness assumed a severe form, we had a trained nurse, who did her work with all tenderness and efficiency, and with her, not leaving the bedroom for the few succeeding days, except for an occasional snatch of rest, was our own loved daughter, whose constant presence and loving attendance were very welcome to her mother. She did not seem to suffer much pain, but she was very restless from the difficulty of breathing, begged that the window might be opened, which could not be done, as the weather was cold, and frequently begged to be raised, with which we complied, as it served in a measure to relieve her, though the doctor said she should lie, as the heart was very weak.

At an early period she said to me, "This is no common illness ; I was never so ill before ; " and added, "I am in God's hand. All is well." I expressed the hope that she would be still spared to me. She had been more than

once at death's door, and had recovered. The day afterwards she said to her daughter, "Does the doctor think I
am sick unto death?" But she scarcely attended to the
reply. Her mind wandered, and it was evident she was
so oppressed by sickness that she could not think of anything consecutively. About forty-eight hours before her
death she said, "I feel better. The great burden of
sickness is gone." This she said to me often afterwards,
and several times to her daughter at her side. With this
feeling of relief her mind became clearer, and with it came
the full conviction of approaching death.

About twenty-four hours before her death she said to
her daughter in her natural voice, "Go for your father;
I want to speak to him." I was in the adjoining room,
and was at once at her side. She then requested her
daughter and the nurse to go out of the room, as she
wished us to be alone.

She spoke to me as calmly and quietly, with as much
composure as if she was preparing for a journey to Edinburgh. She told me that in the tin-box, in which she
kept precious memorials of the children taken from us, I
would find papers, some of which she had never previously
mentioned to me, which she was sure our children would
value, as coming from their mother, when taken from
them. She requested me to take special care of some
important business papers which had been entrusted to
us by one of our sons. She then spoke with marvellous
calmness, and at the same time with the warmest love of
our children, making special mention of the two in India.
Then, as ever since she was a mother, she expressed the
deepest interest in their spiritual welfare. She was grieved
to leave me and our loved ones, but it was only for a little
time. The Master was bidding her "come to the glory of

His presence and the gladness of His home." These two lines, sometimes a little varied, she said often during the last forty-eight hours of her life. Where she got them, or if they were her own, I do not know. A letter to Mrs. Kennedy, written by a very dear German zenana teacher, an intimate friend for many years, dated Clarkabad, Punjab, July 28th, 1891, written in ignorance of her having entered the unseen world two months previously, quotes them as coming from her. This lady, Miss Ellwagen, replying to a letter she had received, says: "Yes, dear Mrs. Kennedy, the Master shall bid us come to the glory of His presence and the gladness of His home." During this to me most memorable interview, she was far calmer than I was. I was stunned by the thought she was being taken from me.

A little later a loved daughter-in-law entered the room and asked her how she was. She said, "I am quite well, as well as I can be when I am within the valley of the shadow." Her daughter-in-law said, "Oh, grandmamma, don't speak like that." She answered, quite happily, "But I know it—I know it. I am not afraid to be with Christ, which is far better." She repeated the lines already quoted. In the afternoon of the day she said to her daughter, "I seem to have come back for a little while. I was nearly unconscious, but now I know you all, and I hear every word you say." On afterwards her speaking was so indistinct that we could not make out her words. I heard her once say, "The swellings of Jordan." All along her illness she spoke much of our son and his wife, then in the South of France, whom she had not seen for years. It had been arranged that they were to come to London at the end of May, and to take up their abode with us for a time. She was full of the thought of preparing for their reception. The first indication of her mind wandering was her saying to me on Tuesday, "Joseph is coming to-night, and the room is not ready." In my memorable interview with her she said, "This is a sad coming home for Josèph." On her last night she said, "At last I have found Joe." A telegram was sent to him, but it did not reach him so soon as was intended. On receiving it, he and his wife at once set out for London, travelling day and night, but they did not reach till a few hours after her departure. Within a few hours of her death I asked her if she knew me. She looked at me with a faint smile, and uttered words I could not make out. The nurse, the only other one in the room at the time, said they were words of endearment. Her end came at 9.20 A.M. on the 23rd. It was very calm, very peaceful, as if she were falling into a gentle sleep. Unlike Christian in the "Pilgrim's Progress," a very favourite book of hers, whose passage through Jordan was full of distress and sorrow till he was about to emerge from it, but, like Hopeful, she felt "bottom," and went on cheerily till she got to the shore on the other side, and then, led by the Shining Ones, she entered by the gate into the city of the blessed.

From the commencement of the serious illness to the close, in addition to the nurse, our daughter, and myself, who were always near, our two sons in London and their wives were constantly with us, rendering all the loving assistance in their power. My brother, our pastor, Mr. Bolton, and other friends, came often to show their affectionate concern.

The funeral was on the following Wednesday. Our old warmly-attached friend, the Rev. D. G. Watt, and Professor Adeney were to have taken part in conducting the funeral service, but were prevented from attending by illness. Our intimate friend, the Rev. E. Storrow of Brighton, who had been many years in Calcutta, gave an address, and Mr. Bolton prayed, at the service held in the Congregational Church, which was largely attended. As the funeral procession passed through the town, we were touched by observing the blinds drawn in the shops and houses. On every side were heard expressions of regret at the death of one who had become well known by her kindly acts. The funeral was at the Hampstead Cemetery, where Mr. Bolton prayed. Among those present were Professor Radford Thomson, and Mr. Wardlaw Thompson as the representative of the Society with which we had been so long and happily connected.

Friends at Acton—Mrs. Budden—Mrs. Braden's Memorial.

I have mentioned the friendships formed at Acton. If I may single out one friend from others, I may well name Mrs. Edward Budden for most frequent intercourse, for kindly bearing, for constant readiness to help, from the beginning to the end of our residence in that town. With Mrs. Braden, widow of the late Mr. Braden of the Weigh-House Chapel, Mrs. Kennedy felt in no ordinary degree spiritually congenial, and with her she formed a warm Christian friendship. She has kindly at my request furnished me with the following memorial of her friend, which I am sure will be read with interest :—

"Acton, *May 10th*, 1892.

"I send a few poor memorials, not what I could wish, but ours was so entirely a friendship of feeling, and not of incident, it has been difficult to express its charm.

" You ask me for some little details of the brief but happy friendship of dear Mrs. Kennedy, which it was my honour and privilege to enjoy for a few years. I believe we first became acquainted through a mutual interest in the mothers' meetings connected with the Acton Church.

" Once acquainted, it was impossible to linger long among externals and conventionalities. It always seemed to me that the spirit in Mrs. Kennedy was so fully developed, she lived so closely in communion with the Divine and Eternal, that earthly forms fell away unheeded, and thus every remembrance of her is associated with holy converse, gentle counsels of a wide experience, and intimate revelations of an inner life, too sacred for the general gaze.

" It became an understood thing that when duty allowed I should run in and spend an hour or two with my dear friend. The pleasantest of memories is of the hospitable tea-table to which she welcomed me so often with a ' Come away, come away, my dear Mrs. Braden ;' a special warmth of greeting marking the utterance of my name. I think we both felt the peculiar comfort of being able to speak to each other without reserve on matters of spiritual import.

" I remember entering the familiar drawing-room one summer afternoon to find Mrs. Kennedy leaning back in her easy-chair, evidently languid and weary. She held out her hand to me and said quietly, as I seated myself beside her, ' I am just getting home to my Father again. I have been shopping all the morning, busy here and there ; and I am glad to get back to *conscious* communion again.' Then, guarding the utterance, she went on to explain that while the believer's entire life is lived in God, the voluntary and conscious contact of the soul with Him is essential to its proper nutrition. I look back, too, upon our little monthly Bible reading, which was partly Mrs. Kennedy's arrangement. It was literally a gathering of two or three, often of two only, though intended for a larger circle of the praying women of the Church. Very perseveringly we endeavoured to carry out our first programme, and have a regular Bible study of a given subject. But somehow we never kept to it. There was always some suggestion from the passage read, some new and precious 'find,' that sent us off into long earnest talks upon holy things, and ended in prayer, solemn, believing, and submissive, for our children, the Church, and the great heathen world lying in ignorance and sin. How well I recall the stately ample figure in the arm-chair, turning the leaves in search of some hopeful promise to assure her heart concerning these absorbing interests! How plainly I remember her earnest face and tone as she said, 'I feel the burden of the sin of the world'! That was a frequent utterance with her.

"Mrs. Kennedy had a remarkable memory for hymns, and it was my delight to persuade her to repeat one or two for us. Leaning back in her chair, she would close her eyes, and recite in a soft voice, in a kind of half-chant, marking the emphasis occasionally by a slight lift of the hand. Her favourite hymn was that that begins—

> ' Come to our poor Nature's night
> With Thy blessed inward light,
> Holy Ghost the Infinite,
> Comforter Divine.'

In this connection I may mention that her last visit to me was to bring a leaflet containing a hymn by L. S., printed for private circulation, and entitled, 'My Lord and I.' She said, 'I cannot stay to-day;' but I begged her just to stay, and read me the hymn, which she did with keen enjoyment of its devout meaning, for it was truly her own experience.

"Our real farewell was taken a week or two before. Mrs. Kennedy seemed for many months in the attitude of Christiana, only waiting for the Master's call to enter the river. Her strength decreased and her step grew feeble. She came to me one morning, and stayed talking of the new movement to give women a recognised position in the Churches, and of other more intimate subjects. Rising to leave, she put her arms round me

P

and said, ' And if, dear Mrs. Braden, you hear soon that I have
gone home, you will know that I go only trusting in the
merits of my Saviour Jesus Christ.' There was a quiet, happy
solemnity in her manner and voice that made me realise that
our parting was near, as indeed it proved, for in about three
weeks the message came that she went home.

"Her friendship was a rare and beautiful gift, for which
I thank God. Agnes Braden."

The other member of this little company was Miss Bull,
till her removal from Acton.

Letters to Mrs. Kennedy's Niece, written after our return from India.

In the previous parts of this biography will be found
extracts from letters to the same correspondent. The
two first given express condolence with her niece on
occasion of the death of her eldest son, a most promising
young man. ,

"Portobello, *September* 15, 1880.

"I cannot say we were unprepared for the news of this
morning. Miss Ely had most kindly and thoughtfully prepared us for it, and yet we ventured to hope. God has seen
meet to order it otherwise. I feel as if I could only sit down
and weep with you. Words are of little avail, but He who
stood by the bier at Nain and raised the widow's son to life is
no less near you, and no less compassionate than He was then."

"Portobello, *September* 22, 1880.

"How much I have been thinking about you during these
sad days! The last rites are now over, I doubt not, and life
has resumed its wonted channels. It is then, I think, that the
loneliness and desolation begin to be really felt. One is stunned

at the time, and until the precious remains have been committed
to the dust there is always more or less requiring one's attention.
Now there is nothing to do for the beloved one, and the eye of
faith alone can follow into the invisible world. But what joy
that you can think of your Claude as safe and for ever with the
Lord! How much care and anxiety have we about those who
remain, however well they may act! All this is at an end in
regard to him, though your own poor heart will bleed for many
a day, and the blank can never be filled in this world. We
remember you and yours constantly in prayer. May He who
has been with you in even a greater sorrow be very sensibly
with you now, to comfort and sustain you, and to give you
many glorious views of "the land which is far off, the goodly
land beyond Jordan"!

Another most promising son, rising into young man-
hood, was carried off by death in the beginning of 1888,
which drew forth the following letter:—

"ACTON, *January* 18, 1888.

"You have, I need not say, been much in our minds during
the last fortnight. You have indeed been called to pass through
deep waters, and we know well that even with all the help the
Gospel gives there is an ever-recurring struggle between faith
and sense. For a time the terrible silence from the other side
is well-nigh overwhelming. We follow the loved ones gone,
and long unutterably for some token to eye or ear, but there is
no voice nor any that answereth.

"Then we go to the blessed Book and to the feet of our
blessed Saviour, and try to say, though with faltering lips,
'Thy will be done.' Well do I know the struggle, and He
who wept at the grave of Bethany does not forbid our tears.
May He sustain and comfort you, and very greatly sanctify
this solemn event to your other dear ones! I remember dear
Mr. Aitken saying to me, after our sorrows of 1853, 'God has
taken them off your hands.' You had your cares about the

education and future of your dear boy, and now he is safe with the Good Shepherd. No more care or anxiety for him.

"I hope you have got your uncle's letter, written on hearing of your new and great trial.

"We have been having dark gloomy days in London for a long time. Those are very miserable who have no 'sunshine within.'"

"PORTOBELLO, *November* 21, 1881.

"I do not think it likely we shall remain at Portobello after May 1882. It is a very cold place. The east winds are so trying in spring. Truly we are strangers and pilgrims on the earth, as our fathers were. May we be more and more followers of them who through faith and patience are now inheriting the promises! It seems so strange to have the wide world before us, and be free to choose our future habitat. . . . Do you know the hymn, 'He leadeth me'? We would, I am sure wish to be led and guided by Him who led His people of old by the hand of Moses and Aaron."

"ACTON, *November* 16, 1889.

"It is always a great pleasure to hear from you, and your last made me feel that I would like just to sit down and have my return talk at once. I am not so able to do what I wish in many ways, but in true love and affectionate sympathy there is no falling off. I thought of you about your birthday time, and the half-century of your life seemed to pass in review with its many changes, bright and happy days not a few, with some as sad as our poor human nature can know—sad as regards our earthly horizon, but it may be the brightest of all when seen in the light of eternity. You have had your full share of life's bitterest sorrows, but you have the blessed hope of meeting your dear ones again in the home above. . . . The last big book we have both read is Farrer's new book, 'Lives of the Early Christian Fathers,' two volumes. There is not much perhaps in it that one had not read before in Church history, but it is gathered and condensed in a most pleasing way, and not nearly so rhetorical as his books generally are.

" We had observed the movement in several of the castes of India against drinking, and are most thankful for it. The doings of our people in many countries in regard to alcoholic drinks are unspeakably sad. Germany too is fearfully depraved on this point.

" I wonder if you ever see the *Indian Magazine*, published in London, or the *Christian College Magazine*, published at Madras. Both are well written, mostly by natives—that in London by youths from India, of whom there are a great many. They give one much information as to progress in certain directions.

" There seems a great seething in many Indian minds at present, and we know to what it tends in the *great* future. What the near future may be it is not so easy to predict, nor do we need to know. 'The just shall live by faith' is four times repeated in Scripture. Had we not the sure promises of Him who cannot lie, truly the present state of the world would be a labyrinth of confusion. Mystery it is, but with certain clear lights sufficient for our guidance.

" May all your and our dear ones be guided by these lights to Him who is the light and life of men ! "

" ACTON, *August* 14, 1890.

" Your brother and his wife have told us of your proposed breaking up next month. You were particularly in my mind on Sabbath last. I have gone through so many changes myself that I can sympathise very truly with you. You are beginning to have the years behind you, and to see your dear ones one by one entering on their own different paths, while others, parts of yourself, have gone to their eternal home above. You are not yet among the shadows, but the noon-tide heat is over, and has given place to a quiet subdued mellow light, coming more from the great light on the other side than from anything here. Be of good cheer ; if the shadows gather here, the heavenly inheritance seems to grow larger and brighter as we approach it, and we enjoy our wayside mercies all the more because we have

gracious foretastes of the glory beyond. . . . Doubtless God
has His own in all sections of the Church, but Ritualism, as
generally understood, would be to me only a chain to bind me
to earth."

"ACTON, *March* 3, 1891.

"I have been wishing to write to you for some time and to
thank you for your last most welcome letter.   I am always so
glad to hear from you and all your dear ones and of their
doings.   You see that my hand shakes now-a-days in writing,
a reminder of my having passed my seventy-seventh birthday,
though sometimes I can hardly believe it.

"We have had a terrible winter here, intense cold, pipes
frozen, and all our water carried for nearly seven weeks.   Then
we had ten days of fog, often of dense darkness.   Indeed we
have now only begun to see the sun, and to look about us with
anything like the joy of spring.   I have just got some bunches
of beautiful snowdrops, which remind one that after the night
cometh the morning, and after the long, dark night of death
the everlasting day."

The letter from which this extract is made was probably
the last written by Mrs. Kennedy to her niece.   In it she
tells her of the joyful prospect of seeing her son and his
wife from India, of the arrangements for their reception,
and of plans for the summer and autumn.   She expresses
the hope of seeing her niece in summer or autumn.   She
did not anticipate, could not anticipate, that in two months
and a half she would have left earth for heaven.   She had
long been ready for the change, and when the Master
called she joyfully responded.

Mr. and Mrs. Pledger, and Mrs. Pledger's sister, Miss
Bull, resided for a time at Acton.   Mrs. Kennedy and
the ladies, after a brief acquaintance, were drawn to each
other by strong spiritual affinity.   After their removal
from Acton they corresponded with each other.   Miss

Bull has kindly sent me the letters she received, and I have made from them the following extracts :—

To Miss Bull.

"ACTON, *January* 15, 1889.

"' Your absence, and that of your dear sister, makes quite a blank in our Acton circle. Even the Church seems less full to what it used to be. To myself personally, the blank is still greater. What a glorious ingathering have we in prospect! So many loved ones have travelled with us a brief portion of our journey, then the paths are divided, and all that is left is a pleasant memory. I trust this is not altogether the case with you, for I hope when summer comes you will be able to come and pay us a visit."

To Miss Bull.

"ACTON, *February* 23, 1889.

"I am downstairs again, after a severe attack of illness, which kept me to my room for a considerable time, and am trying to resume my ordinary ways. I think of you and your sister in your nice snug little house, with pretty garden, enjoying your quiet life and good books, still having, now and then, regretful thoughts for absent friends.

"We have had a long dreary winter in London. I had an attack of illness before Christmas, which was not properly attended to, as I never like giving in. Less than a month ago, bronchitis returned in a much more severe form, and I seemed brought to the very gates of death. I had perfect calm and peace within, I am thankful to say. The thermometer had to be kept, night and day, at 60°. I have said too much about myself."

To Miss Bull.

"*June* 29, 1889.

"I am so glad you have a pleasant home, though, from what you say, you have still to 'guide the spindle and direct the loom,' and, therefore, sometimes too much tired. Is it not difficult to let our work and will be entirely in the hands of our Heavenly Father *with restful confidence ?* It is easy, I well know, to speak to others, but I have had not a little experience of the ups and downs of life, and can all the more sympathise with you."

To Miss Bull.

"*November* , 1889.

" You and your dear sister are most lovingly remembered by us, especially, I need not say, by myself. We had settled down in Acton for the evening of life, and had made some warm friendships, when, one after another, the cords were broken, so far as personal intercourse is concerned. Such is the kaleidoscope of life, and it would be sad indeed if we had not the good hope of the higher life beyond. . . .

" The miserable bigotry that would raise a wall of separation between Christians is very pitiable, and would make one smile if it were not so sad.

". . . Alas ! there is in all Churches at the present time a sadly down-grade as to doctrine. May we, dear friends, be little centres of life and blessing wherever we are !

" These are eventful times in which we live. The forces of good and evil are mustering for the battle. May it be ours to watch and pray . . . !

" This is a lovely day for November. The bare trees are very beautiful, though what is called ' Nature ' has pretty much retired to its laboratory for another spring. How little do we know ! how little *can* we know here !

" We had a most delightful month in Scotland in July. Edinburgh, Aberfeldy, Inverness, Elgin, Aberdeen, with little trips from each. I remember, when a girl, feeling sad that in heaven we should have none of the beauties of sea or sky, flowers, birds, shells, &c. It is such a mistake to say so to children. But I should soon lose myself in theories, and must stop. Fairbairn's ' Typology of Scripture ' has some beautiful expositions and vistas of thought."

"*March* 24, 1891.

"You know, my dear friend, that second causes are just the strings which God pulls, and that all the steps and stops in our way are ordered by His unerring wisdom and love.

"The past winter has been so unusually severe, it has tried us all. The fogs you have escaped, I hope, but here they have been such as we never knew before. Spring is long in coming, but it will come. Even now 'the flowers appear on the earth, and the time of the singing of birds is come,' though flowers are few, and the voice of the turtle-dove is scarcely yet heard. So will it be after all these earthly troubles have wrought their work of sanctification in our souls, by the blessing of God resting on them. The 'Bridegroom cometh; let us trim our lamps and be ready.' You will have guidance as well as grace day by day. I well know how easy it is for me to say so, but I do not speak without experience of affliction and trial in many forms, and truly while it lasts it is not joyous but grievous."

In less than two months the Bridegroom came, and she was found ready with her lamp trimmed to meet Him.

REMARKS ON SERMONS.

It has often been said that preachers have a great advantage over their hearers. They may say what they like, and no one dares to contradict them. If silence be enjoined in the church, hearers, when out, have their full compensation. The preacher's sermon is discussed with a freedom which often gets into license. The Scotch are said to be *par excellence* sermon critics. From the criticisms on sermons in former parts of this narrative, and from those I am now to give, it is plain that Mrs. Kennedy did not hesitate to exercise her judging faculty. It must be remembered these views were given in letters

to her husband, which she was sure would not be turned
to bad account :—

"We had a miserable sermon last Sabbath. It was on
Christ's baptism, and this will explain to you why I thought it
miserable. Some of the preacher's statements were extra-
ordinary, such as 'Baptism is merely a sign of the subjection
of one man to another, as his spiritual guide and teacher.'
'An outward rite can only be the sign of an outward profession.' Here I would fain have asked him the meaning of
the Lord's Supper. Then he took the Baptists' views to pieces,
and held up the different parts as at best childish. Oh, this
unfairness! How it disfigures and mars the best men at times!"

"We went to hear Dr. Candlish, but the preacher for the
day was a stranger. The text was the request of the mother of
Zebedee's children, 'Grant that these my two sons,' &c. A
sweet mellow sermon, though its connection with the text was
not apparent. It was all about the way God answers prayer
and the sufferings of Christ. The particular request was not
even touched upon. You know my dissatisfaction with this
style of preaching."

I must now give one of Mrs. Kennedy's severe strictures
on a sermon she heard. It is in her indignant strain. It
was not by any one of the pastors she had in succession :—

"Two-thirds of the sermon was a talk about *proportion.*
'Those who understand proportion are the men who get on
in the world.' We had Professor's talk about Euclid. Little
stories were brought in, but much was really wild and silly.
'The world is on the eve of wonderful changes—such a
revolution as has never been. Who are the men to be most
afraid of just now?—the men with fixed ideas.' One would
have thought we were in a chance world, with nothing stable.
There was a fling at Spurgeon, as 'an accuser of the brethren.'
The last part was a very poor application of the value of pro-

portion in regard to estimating things present and the things
to come ; but what these things are no one could have gathered
who did not know. . . . I must confess my soul has been
stirred within me. I wish I could take things more calmly,
and do the right thing in the right spirit, but sometimes we do
well to be angry."

I find her some time afterwards in a very different
mood as a hearer. Writing on a Monday she says :—

"I was out twice yesterday. I did not enjoy the morning's
service. The preacher (a stranger) had a most peculiar and
unnatural voice. His subject was 'Christ's weeping over
Jerusalem.' In the evening, though I went with small expectation, we had a noble sermon. It might have been preached in
Mr. Aitken's or your father's pulpits fifty years ago, and the
good folk would have pronounced it 'a gran' sermon.' The
subject was 'The truth as it is in Jesus.' I was so fascinated
by the matter that the voice seemed to disappear. The sermon
would shine beside any of the Erskines' sermons." *

In this biography reference is several times made to
Mrs. Kennedy's divergence from the Church views of her
early days, and the broadening of her sentiments on
various subjects. The extract I have just given, expressive
of her delight in hearing sermons pervaded by evangelical
truth, similar to those she had heard in her youth, shows
how firmly she rested in everything essential on her old
footing. She continued to the last to regret the setting
aside to a large extent in families of the Assembly's
Shorter Catechism, which, with a few modifications and
additions, she deemed an admirable compendium of divine
truth. She continued to live and revere her Covenanting

* The reference is to the sermons of the Revs. Ebenezer and Ralph
Erskine, the founders of the Scotch Secession.

forefathers, though she deemed them in some points mistaken. She could not forgive Sir Walter Scott for his want of sympathy with them, and his caricaturing of them by fastening on a few of the most fanatical. She became reconciled to the organ, but she never liked it, and was much disturbed by the elaborate music of some of the anthems. She could not accept what is called the Voluntary Principle. She did not regard any of the existing Church Establishments as scriptural in their foundation and administration, but she thought there could be a State Church of the right order; only, like a full acceptance of Independency, she feared it must be deferred till the Millennium. Roman Catholics ought not to be persecuted, but, with their avowed subjection to the Pope, she thought too much political power had been granted to them. Her position was that of many in a transition period like ours, who are largely affected by surrounding present influences, who strive to keep an open mind, keenly test what is set forth as truth, and at the same time are led by intellect and heart, and also in some degree by prejudice, to cling tenaciously to the past.

Mrs. Kennedy looked back with deep thankfulness to the services held on successive days in connection with the celebration of the Lord's Supper in Presbyterian churches. They had been very useful to her. She knew they could not be held where the Lord's Supper was observed frequently, and that frequent observance she had come to like; but, with me, she often regretted the slight way in which the ordinance was often administered, with very little, or perhaps nothing, in the preceding sermon bearing on it, and only a few words of address, along with the prayers and thanksgiving, in the dispensing of the elements.

She also regretted the well-nigh absence of exposition from the pulpit. The habit in Scotland in former days, and I suppose in many places is still, was to devote the forenoon discourse to what was called lecturing—the exposition of the books of Scripture in order. It must be acknowledged that too often the lecture was the loose paraphrasing of Scripture, giving very little beyond the impression made by a careful reader on himself; but when it was the fruit of thought and close study, it was very instructive, and greatly enriched the minds of the hearers. Mrs. Kennedy to the last lamented that nothing of the kind was attempted in England. In a letter I had from her during a temporary absence from home she observes : "I went to my class in the afternoon, and waited for the after-meeting, which is held once a month. We had an address by a lady from Ealing—very sweet, but, like most ladies' addresses, all exhortation. My lesson—rather the International—was John the Baptist. I at least tried to give the girls some instruction from the prophecies regarding him, his birth and different appearances, ending with his death. The want of true scriptural exposition is surely one of the great pulpit defects of our age." One of her fixed ideas was that ladies could not expound—surely a mistaken idea.

CHAPTER XVI.

LAST MEMORIALS—EXPRESSION OF FEELING IN RHYME—CHARACTERISTICS.

This biography began by the record of Mrs. Kennedy's early religious experience, given in her own words. I now give place to three letters to her children, left along with others to be read by them when she should be taken from them. The biography throughout bears testimony to the love she bore to her children, and her intense longing for their spiritual welfare, to which these letters give fervid expression. They were, I believe, written on Sabbaths, when I was from home :—

"Acton, *January* 18, 1884.

"My beloved Children,—I have this day reached my threescore years and ten—a long term of life, yet very brief in the retrospect. Truly I can say, ' goodness and mercy have followed me,' and also add with humble confidence, ' I will dwell in the house of the Lord for ever.' Your dear father and I cannot expect to be much longer here, but we know in whom we have believed, and have the blessed hope of the far more blessed life beyond the grave. We have not been without our own share of the trials of life, but in all we have been cheered and helped by faith in Christ and the assurance of our Heavenly Father's love, as we could not have been in any other way. Our trust and highest happiness has come from this. We have many a pleasant road and sunny spot to look back to, as well as here and there the ' Hill Difficulty ' or ' Valley of Humiliation,' but by Divine grace our faces have been kept toward the Celestial

City, and as we draw near to it the prospect broadens and brightens marvellously. Alas! that my own life has so poorly illustrated the power of God's grace and truth! We leave you six, for we cannot expect to be much longer here, thankful for the very much that is pleasing and amiable. I do not make distinctions, though you will do so yourselves. We long for signs of thorough spiritual awakening. 'If any man be in Christ he is a new creature.' I know young people are reticent, especially towards their parents, but the new life will show itself in many ways. Often I hope regarding most, I may say of all, my beloved children, that there is some good thing in you towards the Lord God of Israel, but we long to see unmistakable signs of conversion and the new life. Oh, what do those lose who do not know Christ savingly! It is a feeble figure to say that it is like being blind to this beautiful world and all in it. The one is for a few brief years, the other for ever and ever. Our prayers are for you daily and hourly, our beloved children. May we meet, an unbroken family, in heaven! This brief note is not meant for any of you now, but to be put aside till I am gone to my blessed Saviour and rejoin our darlings in the better world, 'whom we have loved long since and lost awhile,' and many besides—parents, brothers, sisters, friends. Then we shall look for you each one. To Thee, O Lord, I commit my beloved ones; living and dying may they be Thine! Re-unite us in the many mansions!"

"ACTON, *March* 14, 1886.

"I am alone this Sabbath afternoon, and the thought comes strongly over me that soon all our children will have of me and of their dear father will be a memory, even as it is with us in regard to our parents. I have entered on my seventy-third year, and am not without warnings that soon 'the silver cord may be loosed and the golden bowl broken.' For many years I have seemed to live in Bunyan's Land of Beulah, far beyond the sight of Doubting Castle, hearing often the songs of birds on the other side of the river, and getting glimpses of the goodly land beyond Jordan.

"Anon, the descent and the river to be crossed have looked very dark, and are at no time pleasing to flesh and blood; yet calmly, trustingly I would go forward, assured that He who has been with me in many trials and brought me through many sorrows will be with me still. 'Yea, though I walk through the valley of the Shadow of Death I will fear no evil, for *Thou* art with me.' So would I live that when the Home-call comes I may be able joyfully to say, 'Even so come, Lord Jesus,' like Christiana ready and looking for the Post.

"My great concern is about our beloved children, and Thou, O Father, only knowest how great that concern is. We have so much to be thankful for in regard to them, and we hope that in their hearts the good seed is hidden germinating, or to germinate in Thy time. Yet we long for the full consecration of heart and life. They were dedicated to Thee from their birth, and we have sought, though with much shortcoming, to bring them up in Thy nurture and admonition so far as we had them with us. It is the outpouring of Thy Spirit upon them we look for, and we plead the promise with confidence, 'I will pour My Spirit upon thy seed and My blessing upon thine offspring.'"

"*November 2,* 1886.

"I am alone to-night communing with the mighty dead. It is not now 'how many are gone,' but 'how few remain.' I think of the many loved ones who are gone, and try to follow and to imagine what are their employments now.

"I kneel and pray, read the Blessed Book, *meditate, think,* and *pray* again, 'but wait and see' is the answer to my too minute questions. There is enough for faith, nothing for curiosity. 'In knowledge, purity, and happiness, the dead in Christ are far beyond us here.' We have many cares and anxieties about our beloved children; not about their worldly circumstances, but about their saving interest in the Lord Jesus Christ. Would rather they were poor in this world a thousand times than live for the present life only"—(Here she names most lovingly several of the children)—"I am depressed that my own example was not more free from failure. I am conscious of earnestness in seeking to teach and lead my dear children to the Saviour, yet humbled on account of much shortcoming. I have the comforting assurance of God's Word that He will lead them all to Himself. ' Lord, do as Thou hast said.' I know in whom I have believed for myself, and for them I trust."

Mrs. Kennedy had great facility in rhyming, but she exercised it rarely. In the course of conversation with me she now and then got into rhyming, but she thought her effusions so ephemeral that she objected to my writing them out. I find among her papers an amusing satire on a mismanaged arrangement for a Missionary Conference, in which she hits off in a very good-natured fashion the different members of the Committee, her own husband included. This was not, however, a vein in which she allowed herself to indulge. I find among her papers two pieces of rhyme which she sent to me when absent, the first when I was on a missionary tour in Kumaon, the other when I was out on deputation work in England for the London Missionary Society. I omit some stanzas in which she pours out her affection for myself, and retain those in which she gives expression to her motherly love. I also give place to the piece she put into my hand on the morning of May 1, 1890.

> Father, I thank Thee that so long
>   Our lives in one have met ;
> Oh ! grant the time may not be long
>   That we must separate.
>
> Even now fair visions often rise
>   Of Beulah's land in sight ;
> And though we each must cross alone,
>   The Lord will be our Light.

Q

And when on Jordan's farther bank
   We each the other see,
We'll meet our early loved and lost,
   From sin and sorrow free.

Yet there I think we'll watch and wait
   Till each loved child comes home,
Our hope, our trust, our daily prayer,
   The Lord will not disown.

RANEE KHET, *February* 1876.

SOLITARY MUSINGS.

Life's busy tasks are well-nigh done,
   The evening shadows gather ;
Yet more dependent every day
   We each are on the other.

Our lives in one have gently flowed,
   In bright and cloudy weather,
And, parted, do not seem the same
   As when we are together.

But when the call of duty comes,
   We must not then consider,
But, prompt and ready, only say,
   "Dear Master, tell us whither."

The Lord to us hath ever been
   A good and gracious Giver,
And well we know, for He hath said,
   "I will forsake thee never."

And when the gathering shadows fall,
   And we are at the river,
Come, blessed Lord, and bear us through,
   To be with Thee together.

ACTON, *November* 1886.

Now fifty years have come and gone
    Since our divided lives were joined,
Since which as one we've travelled on,
    In union sweet, *one heart, one mind.*

It has not all been sunlit road,
    We've had our dark and cloudy days,
But mercy so has mixed with all,
    We well may Ebenezer raise.

Our " olive plants," some gone before
    To the bright world of joy and love,
More spared their work on earth to do,
    And be prepared for heaven above.

For hopes fulfilled, for fears dispelled,
    For each, for all, we bless Thee, Lord,
And still we wait Thy promised grace,
    And rest upon Thy faithful Word.

Now twilight shadows come apace,
    And darkling cross our onward way,
But faith and hope beyond them sees
    The world of everlasting day.

ACTON, *May* 1, 1890.

During the last few months of Mrs. Kennedy's life she
often gave utterance to words that appeared to me of so
poetical a tone, that I begged her to write two or three
hymns.   She said she wondered I did not know her better
than to suppose she was capable of so high a work.

MRS. KENNEDY'S CHARACTERISTICS.

For Mrs. Kennedy's character and career I must refer
the readers of this biography mainly to the narrative of
her life and the testimony of those who knew her well,
but it may be fitting for me to supplement their statement.

She had a keen, active, inquisitive mind, and a kindly disposition, which prepared her to be loved and esteemed by those with whom she might come into contact. Her crowning excellence, which dominated her entire life and made her what she was, came to her not by nature, but by grace. She passed at an early period, as she tells us, through a severe mental and spiritual struggle. From the time she was awakened to the unutterable importance of divine things, her whole soul was bent on the quest for truth. She felt nothing else was for a moment to be compared with it in value, and she could not rest till she obtained satisfaction. The issue was a strong intelligent piety, which moulded her character, and by its depth and thoroughness prompted her to the habitual use of the means by which godliness is sustained; among which she ever gave the chief place to the study of the Scriptures and close and constant communion with her God and Saviour. Of her it may be emphatically said, she exercised herself unto godliness.

To the end of life she felt deeply thankful that in her early days her mind was stored with divine truth by her pastor and parents, especially by her father, though, as has been already mentioned, she thought that, from the best motives, the parental training was unnecessarily severe to the youthful mind. The knowledge with which her memory was stored, without any welcome from the heart, became to her instinct with life and preciousness when the heart embraced it as a loving message from her Heavenly Father to draw her to Himself. The great fundamental truths of man's guilt and sinfulness, of the provision made for man's salvation by the Messiah, the incarnation, life, atoning death, resurrection, ascension, and reign of the Son of God, and regeneration by the

Holy Spirit, were with her not notions, opinions, but truth turned into living, life-giving principles, which she treasured as her very life. As time advanced, with her much reading and thought, her views broadened. The universal aspect of our Lord's propitiation was very precious to her, and had a more prominent place in her faith than in early years. Her pastor, Mr. Aitken, was not a hyper-Calvinist. The universal aspect of Christ's sacrifice was always implied in his teaching and appeals. She was also more inclined, as years advanced, to see more of Christ in certain classes, to regard more hopefully indications of character than she had once done. She delighted to dwell on those passages of Scripture which pointed in glowing and yet general terms to the triumph of the Redeemer in the rescue of souls, and tried from them to enlarge her hopes for the future of mankind. She at the same time clung to the supreme authority of Scripture, as alone entitled to decide the great question of man's present and future state. She was abundantly satisfied that the Bible all through bore God's impress, and she shrank with all the shrinking of her spirit from tampering with its teaching. She read much, as I shall presently observe, and thought much, but she rested with unwavering trust on the truth as it is in Jesus, to the end of her life—rather, I should say, on Christ Himself, as the way, the truth, and the life. The last portion of Scripture she was able to hear continuously was the first chapter of St. Peter's First Epistle. As I read, she said, "How precious! very especially the words 'Redeemed by the blood of Christ, as of a lamb without blemish and without spot.'" I may be allowed to mention here that a few days before her last illness I read to her the first part of the essay since published under the title "The Propitiation of our

Lord in its Bearing on Ethics." She expressed her approval in unusually warm terms:—"It is so opportune, so true! Be sure to publish it, whatever it may cost us." She said she so wished to hear the whole, but she did not live to hear it. Nothing grieved her more than to hear, as she sometimes did, sermons from pulpits acknowledged as Evangelical which had not to her mind a tinge of Evangelical thought and sentiment. She had no such complaint against those whom she regularly heard. With me, she regretted that our Lord's propitiatory sacrifice had not a more prominent place in the preaching of the day, even in the preaching of those who adhered firmly to Evangelical truth.

Mrs. Kennedy's life furnishes an illustration of the compatibility of earnest living piety with the discharge of the most homely duties. She looked well to the ways of her household, both in India and England. She had, in the opinion of those who knew her well, marked administrative talent in domestic management. It was a principle with her that observance of the laws of health in the matter of food and other things was the fulfilment of duty, and largely tended to the soundness of body which is so favourable to soundness of mind, with all the efficiency which bodily and mental soundness secures. This wise attention to homely duties was often observed by those who came into close contact with her.

Some excellent housewives are so taken up with domestic duties that they lose their capacity for work beyond their homes. Far different was the case with Mrs. Kennedy. She had public spirit in a high degree. She was deeply interested in her fellow-creatures at home and abroad. She was very desirous to know what was going on in the world, and was ever ready to do in her own sphere all she could for the good of others. Not a few devout persons, especially of the gentle sex, confine their reading to books bearing directly on the divine life. The more emotional and devotional they are, the more highly they are prized. Mrs. Kennedy, on the other hand, read extensively in different directions. Considering the numerous pressing duties devolving on her during the greater part of her life, her reading was singularly large and varied. For fiction, it was very limited. Some of the best novels she read, and as she read she was, like others, under their spell; but now and then she commenced some of high repute, which she found page after page so full of the most silly talk, that she could not go on with them. History was always attractive to her. Gibbon's " Decline and Fall of the Roman Empire," the works of Macaulay, Froude, Lecky, and of many others were carefully perused. She had a special delight in Church History. Dr. M'Crie was the most prominent minister in the Old Light Anti-Burgher Church, of which she was a member in her youth. She had met him, and heard him preach on several occasions. His works, Lives of Knox, Melville, and Henderson, and " The Rise and Suppression of the Reformation in Spain and Italy," were read and re-read by her. Her love and reverence for the Covenanters she retained to the last, though she thought that in some matters they were greatly mistaken. With their doings and sufferings she was very familiar. I remember well how eagerly she read D'Aubigné's " History of the Reformation " when it appeared. She afterwards read Neander's " Church History," nine volumes, and every other work in that department on which she could lay her hand. Books of travellers—as Livingstone, Speke, Grant, Cameron, and many others—with their innumerable

and sometimes wearisome details, were read with a patience
and interest which surprised me. She was thankful for
what she had seen of the world, but she wished to see more,
if it were possible. The prospect of a vast extension of
knowledge in the world beyond was a favourite theme.
There were no books which drew forth so much of her
intellect, heart, and conscience as those which aimed at
opening up Scripture, and which bore on the Gospel in its
many aspects, both in its doctrinal and practical bearings. In her youth she highly prized the writings of
John Foster, and in later years those of Vinet and Isaac
Taylor. As with all Christians, she was refreshed, stimulated, and encouraged by the biographies of the wise and
the good.

Her soul was athirst for knowledge, and she took large
draughts of it. She often lamented she had not learned
Latin and Greek when she was young, and that she had
acquired the merest smattering of geology and astronomy.
She read Isaac Taylor's "Physical Theory of Another
Life," but was disappointed. She did not obtain from it
much new light.

As an illustration of her reading, I may observe that
on the appearance of Mr. G. A. Smith's first volume on
Isaiah, she read it with great interest, finding much in it
which did her good ; but she doubted his transposition of
chapters, and regretted his tendency to represent the
prophet as a great sage, who, by his own insight, foresaw
the future, and was now and then mistaken. She regretted
still more Mr. Smith's giving only a secondary application
to the Messiah of passages which she thought referred
primarily, in some cases exclusively, to Him. She left
untouched books on what is called the higher criticism.
She knew enough about them to dread their specula-

tions. To turn the early books of the Old Testament into historical novels seemed to her the sapping of the foundations on which the authority of Scripture rested, turning the rock of history into the quicksand of legend.

Years ago she had read the late Dr. Fairbairn's (of Glasgow) " Commentary on Ezekiel," and she was perusing it for the second time when seized by her fatal illness.

Mrs. Kennedy was what is called an omnivorous reader. She read very rapidly, and, if the book was interesting, very eagerly. She often complained that though she had an excellent verbal memory, she remembered little of what she read, which gave me occasion to say her mental appetite was beyond her mental digestion—that she would know more if she read less. I do not remember her ever leaving a duty unfulfilled for the perusal of a book, but for her own mental progress her reading was excessive.

Mrs. Kennedy often told me of some of her early friends, who held the opinion that in the Millennium Presbyterian Church government would be universally adopted. That notion never got hold of her. As time advanced, she entertained on this subject what would be deemed latitudinarian views. To Lord Bishops, to Prelacy lording it over Presbyters and people, she retained all her Covenanting dislike; but she thought Superintendents, permanent Presidents—in Presbyterian phrase, permanent Moderators—of the wisest and the best, were required in some stages of the Church. Independency would do well for the Millennium, but was too good for the present. On the whole, Presbyterianism was best in ordinary circumstances till the Millennium should come.

These views are pithily expressed in a letter I received from her a few years ago, when I was absent from home. She had heard of disturbances in an Independent church, and she wrote:—

"Eh me! if Independency be good, the people are often far enough from being so. I think I hear you ask me, 'Are Presbyterians always good?' No, far enough from that; but— there is a but—Presbyterianism seems to suit better the present half-sanctified state of the Church. When our education is complete we shall all be Independents! You are very forbearing with your incorrigible wife, though quietly I don't think we differ very much."

I told her she was not worthy of instruction on this subject, as she was not a sufficiently serious learner.

She was, however, a conformist with a good conscience. As her husband was a Congregationalist, she joined Congregational churches wherever she went. She was much gratified by her minister, Mr. Aitken, writing to her to congratulate her on her marriage. When she came home in 1850, she called on him when she went to Aberdeen, and was cordially received. He said to her that if he were at Benares, as she was, he thought he would join the Independents. Firmly attached though he was to his own Church, as was shown by his declining to join the Free Church when many of his brethren did, he had a catholic spirit, though by his position and training often prevented from showing it.

Mrs. Kennedy had a great, and to some extent I think a mistaken, aversion to women addressing public meetings and taking part in public teaching. She took Paul's words against women speaking in the Church, and applied them to women in our day, more strictly perhaps than Paul would do if he were with us. No one could go beyond her in her high estimate of woman in her true dignity, her duties, her responsibility, and her influence—an influence often far more powerful than authority; but she believed Nature itself pointed out two distinct spheres, each supplemental to the other, and both requiring to be rightly occupied to secure human welfare. She was slow to believe in prophetesses. Both at home and in India she took an active part in conducting services with women and children, though she shrank from taking the lead when many women were present.

During the fifty-one years of our married life, I never heard her voice in prayer, though many of her own sex did. She had no hesitation in conducting worship with children and servants in my absence. With women's true rights she had the fullest sympathy, but she disliked what is called "women's rights," which, if granted, she thought would do them wrong.

What Mrs. Kennedy was as a friend and as a visitor and helper of the sick, the distressed, the bereaved, and the poor, what she was as an active worker for the advancement of Christ's kingdom, is shown by the details already given, and by the testimony of those who knew her best.

She had a great esteem and love for some poor people whom she visited and helped, but a few by their constant applications tried her much. One of that class she sent off more than once with sharp words, but they were no sooner uttered than they were regretted, and the request refused was granted. She acted in the spirit of a distinguished magistrate in India, of whom it was said—the story of course is apocryphal—that when he sent a man to gaol, on the man coming out he was sure to get a present in compensation for the suffering inflicted. In giving she had great delight, but to receiving, except when there was not only the need but a most fitting reason for receiving, her dislike was almost morbid. I could not but say to her at times she had in her nature a good bit of the Lady Bountiful.

In several of the letters received Mrs. Kennedy is called " a happy Christian." It may most truly be said the joy of the Lord was her strength. Gloom and austerity she regarded utterly unworthy of the Christian. She often mentioned an expression used by a lady whom she casually met in the grounds of the Crystal Palace. Seated near her, she indicated, as she was wont to do, where her heart was. The lady responded, " My husband is a very religious man, but not miserably so," suggesting that much religion was incompatible with happiness.

What shall I say about her in the closest of all relations, as wife and mother? What she was in these relations I must leave well-nigh entirely to be inferred by the readers of this biography. All I can venture to say is, that while I am assured many wives of missionaries, as well as of others, have been as devoted to their husbands, as sympathetic and identified with them, as loving and wise in the management of their children, as Mrs. Kennedy was to me and mine—it would be downright folly and uncharitableness to think otherwise —she may well have a place among those who have distinguished themselves in those sacred relations. However fondly attached husbands and wives may be to each other, however ready to help each other, their work may be so widely different that the help cannot go beyond sympathy and good wishes. In many cases the

wife cannot enter into the intricacies and details of
the husband's life.   In the case of missionaries, husband
and wife are engaged in the same work, enlisted in the
same enterprise, hand in hand and heart in heart prosecuting the same aim.   Their departments are different,
but so closely related that the one is the supplement of
the other, and success depends on constant hearty co-
operation.   Mrs. Kennedy was identified with me in all
my engagements, and I ever felt the deepest interest
in hers.   When she was not with me I felt my right
hand was tied up.   We told each other constantly of
what we were doing, and took counsel of each other as
to what should be done.   I cannot conceive a wife more
interested in her husband's work, more closely identified
with him, more ready to help in every way in her power,
and more able to help than she was.

While this was her bearing from the commencement
of our married life, as time advanced she was, if possible,
more and more sympathetic and helpful.   Her character
mellowed with years under her large experience of the
.discipline of life, and she bore more and more manifestly
the image of her Saviour, with whom she held increasingly close communion.   Her natural temper was quick,
but it was kept under severe control.   She often quoted
a remark of Hannah More, that "old people should grow
old gracefully," and she largely succeeded, not by any
special effort, but by habitually keeping steadily before
her mind the true end of life, in acquiring gracefulness
of character.

As to her children, they all with one heart and voice
call her blessed, and well they may.   Our eldest son
suggested the epitaph on her tomb, "Devoted wife,
loving mother, fellow-worker in the Gospel of Christ,"

in a very few words expressing what she was in domestic life and Christian work. Above this epitaph, as expressing our assured hope, are the words, "Until the day dawn and the shadows flee away."

Though in Mrs. Kennedy's character and life there was a combination of qualities which are not always found even in very estimable persons, but which, when combined, are very attractive, far be it from me to say that she was perfect. There was no difficulty in finding traces of the imperfection which cleaves to the best. She took ever lowly views of herself. While conscious, as true Christians are, of a heart-bent Godward, and of never consciously harbouring any wrongful thought or feeling, she often spoke of her falling below the high standard set before her. She was almost rude in rejecting the claim to perfection which some of her friends seemed inclined to advance. She questioned these closely—she herself was my informant—as to what they meant by perfection. Did their minds never wander in prayer? Did they at once drive away every low motive which came in with the higher, so that not even the stain of it remained? Did they never utter a hasty unadvised word, or do an unkind deed? Could they approve without reserve all they thought, felt, said, and did? The reply she got was, "These are natural infirmities clinging to our present state." She affirmed they were clear proofs that spiritual perfection had not been reached. No one could maintain more heartily than she did that this was the goal towards which we should ever press, and which, by Divine grace, we could even in the present life more and more nearly approach.

I have perhaps dwelt too long on Mrs. Kennedy's character. From my relation to her, it is natural for me to let affection say too much; but I do not think those who really knew her will condemn me. Instead of condemning me, they will confirm my statements. How they esteemed and loved her is shown by the extracts from their letters I proceed to give.

CHAPTER XVII.

IN MEMORIAM—TRIBUTE TO CHARACTER AND USEFUL-NESS FROM INDIAN AND ENGLISH FRIENDS.

PERSONS to whom Mrs. Kennedy was unknown may be inclined to think that her friends have indited their eulogiums in inflated terms. Their words are unusually strong. All who know these friends, and some of them are widely known, may be sure they were written in all sincerity, and have simply said what they felt and thought. They are not given to hollow exaggerated language. I must acknowledge that I have been not only gratified, deeply gratified, but surprised by the warmth of their utterance. I was well aware she was esteemed and loved, and that those who knew her best were those who held her in the highest regard; but I was not aware till she was gone of the extent of the esteem and the warmth of the affection. From many letters received I give no extracts, as they simply express love and sympathy. It will be observed that most of the letters from which extracts are taken were written on her friends receiving tidings of her death. The letters of Mr. Adeney, Mr. Bolton, and Dr. Weymouth were written on my informing them of my purpose to write her biography.

I give the first place to letters received from India and letters received from friends who knew Mrs. Kennedy in India.

*Letter from the Native Members of the London Missionary
Society's Church in Benares.*

"BENARES, *July* 15*th*, 1891.

" To the Rev. JAMES KENNEDY.

" DEAR SIR,—We, the members of the London Missionary
Church at Benares, have heard with deep regret of the death
of your beloved partner. We beg to express our deep sorrow at
the removal from this world of our great friend and benefactress.
While she was with you in our midst for several years, she
spared no pains to come to our houses, to inquire into our
circumstances, both temporal and spiritual, to talk with us and
our dear ones most affectionately, to bring us nearer to Christ
by word of instruction and advice, to encourage us in our
toilsome pilgrimage, to console us in our trials and in our
afflictions—in a word, to do all the good work of a faithful and
devoted missionary's wife in love. We assure you, dear sir,
many of our women were brought by her personal influence
of character and devotedness sincerely to love and adore the
dear Redeemer, and to do some work for the extension of
His blessed kingdom. We therefore feel your loss is the loss
of our little Church, and fully sympathise with you in your deep
sorrow in your old age, and earnestly pray that the good Lord
will comfort and console you by His Spirit, and enable you to
work on now singly for His glory and the good of sinful souls,
with the same degree of love, faith, and hope as all the days of
your life in India. We are assured dear good Mrs. Kennedy
is most happy and blessed in the midst of holy angels and
saints round the throne of grace in heaven, where several of
our old beloved members, whom you knew well and trusted for
their faith and love, have also gone.

" You will be glad to hear that under the faithful and loving
ministrations of our beloved missionaries and their worthy wives
our little Church has, by God's blessing, been steadily making

R

progress in the right direction, to the praise of the Lord their Master and to the salvation of their souls.

"With our loving sympathy and prayers for you, dear sir, we remain, on behalf of our Church,

"KASHEENATH DUTT,"
and several others.

From Mr. RAM CHANDRA BOSE.

"DEAR SIR,—It does not become me to say anything to console you. The Master whom you have served all your life, and in whose service Mrs. Kennedy spent and was spent, is doing that. All that it becomes me to do is to approach you with assurances of the deepest sympathy and condolence. She was a mother in Israel, and a mother to many poor native Christians, who, like me, were unworthy of her regard. She manifested the spirit of Christ, and did His work of seeking and saving the lost.

"If I am to-day not an alien from the household of Israel, living in the world without God and hope, a great deal of the happy change will be traced by the Master to her firm yet tender way of bringing sinners to Him. I believe she is now holding converse with some of those she strove to lead to Christ, in the better land, and before long she will have the satisfaction, the pure pleasure, of seeing others entering into her present joy, which is the joy of her Lord. I have just written a line to Mr. Pringle to say I have never seen a lady more deserving of reverence than Mrs. Kennedy, and certainly no lady, European or Native, has done me so much good as she did. Israel has lost a mother, and many native Christians of the London Mission of Benares in bygone days have lost a mother. I should not say more.

"With assurance of deepest sympathy, I am yours very truly,

"RAM CHANDRA BOSE."

"Lectures on the Evidences of Christianity, Based on the Miracles of Christ." By RAM CHANDRA BOSE, M.A. Published in India, and afterwards republished in London by the Religious Tract Society.

. *Dedication of the Indian Edition.* .

"To Mrs. M. S. KENNEDY.

" MY DEAR MADAM,—These lectures, written amid multifarious work, have been printed by order of the Publishing Committee of the Methodist Mission, Northern India. Though disfigured by the blemishes incident to hasty composition, they are expected to subserve the end contemplated in their publication, viz., that of contributing a mite towards obviating objections current among educated Indians. The little good they may accomplish in this way will be connected by the Good Master with the great good done me by yourself and Mr. Kennedy. The truth one plants and another waters is almost daily illustrated in the history of missions in India.

"The good seed sown in me by the Free Church missionaries in Calcutta was for years watered by yourself and your colleagues in Benares, and has during the last seven years been receiving increase from God, through the instrumentality of the Methodist missionaries under whom I am now serving. I cannot be sufficiently thankful for the exuberance of kindness with which I have always been treated by my missionary teachers and missionary employers.

"It is, however, a fact, and ought to be stated, that no person, countryman or foreigner, has watched over my spiritual and temporal interests with such solicitude and tenderness, and for such a length of time, as yourself and Mr. Kennedy, and that no lady has favoured me with so many and such rich tokens of what cannot but be called motherly affection, as you have done.

"I believe, as I have often said, that if my own mother had

been alive, and as intelligently pious as you are, she could not have written letters kinder than those with which you have honoured me in the course of regular correspondence extending over years—a correspondence never interrupted; for when on account of my sins I would shun you, you would, in the spirit of the Good Shepherd, literally seek and save me.

"To you, my dear madam, and to Mr. Kennedy I beg to dedicate these lectures; and though names so justly revered in and out of India ought not to be associated with such unworthy productions, you will, I am sure, look upon them as tokens of a gratitude that really knows no bound.

"That the Lord may bless both you and yours in rich abundance, has been for years the prayer of your affectionate and obliged servant,

"RAM CHANDRA BOSE.

"LUCKNOW, 28*th Feb.* 1880."

Mr. Ram Chandra Bose was for some years the headmaster of our principal school in Benares. He had been strongly recommended for the office by the late Dr. Ewart, and proved a very efficient teacher. When he came to us, he was young in years and character. During a part of the time I was Superintendent of the school, and had ample opportunity, both in the school and out of it, of knowing him well. Mrs. Kennedy and myself became much attached to him, and our attachment to him was fully reciprocated by him. He left Benares for a Government appointment. We got tidings of his conduct which deeply grieved us, and we both wrote to him as faithfully and kindly as we could. He responded to us in a way which was very gratifying. Instead of resenting our counsel and warning, he thanked us for our faithfulness, and acknowledged he had gone astray. By God's blessing our letters were the means of leading him to retrace his steps. We have had several opportunities of meeting him and of having

him as our guest during the many years which have elapsed
since he was with us at Benares. All onward, while widely
separate and withdrawn from personal intercourse, we held
correspondence with him, I writing to him occasionally,
and Mrs. Kennedy very frequently. Many and very
interesting have been the letters we have received from
him. Mrs. Kennedy's last letter to him was written a
short time before her death. She often said that outside
our own family there was no one in whom she was more
deeply interested. For many years he has been chiefly
engaged in writing books and delivering lectures on the
highest subjects, with the evident earnest aim to bring
his fellow-countrymen to the Saviour. In Calcutta, and
still more all over the North-Western Provinces, he is
known as one of the ablest advocates of Christian truth.
He has passed through many vicissitudes and trials, which
I am sure have proved wholesome discipline. I had much
wished to give some extracts from Mrs. Kennedy's letters
to him, but I regret they have not come into my hand.
Towards us he has always acted a filial part.

In a lecture on Raja Ram Mohun Rey as a hymnologist,
in which he contrasts his hymns with those imbued with
Christian sentiment, he gives a touching account of the
death-bed of two of Dr. Duff's earliest converts. Towards
the conclusion of the lecture he gives emphatic expression
to the faith of himself and his fellow-Christians of the
highly educated class. Speaking of one whose death-bed
he describes, he says, " The clouds thickened, and death
appeared so palpably that it could not be mistaken.
This was indeed a critical moment. Did he repent of his
apostasy from the Hindu faith ? Our Hindu friends
generally represent us converts as doing nothing but
perpetually mourning over the rash step we have taken

in embracing a foreign religion. We may assure them
that we never do so. We do mourn over the follies we
have perpetrated after conversion—over the bad examples
we have set—over the little we have done to set forth
the excellency of our religion—but we never even in
our dreams recall the fact of our being separated from
Hinduism but with lively emotions of gratitude. In the
stillness of the night, when deep sleep cometh upon us,
we frequently revisit the homes from which we have
been thrust out, see around us the bright faces which
once hung over us with all the yearning of tender affection, and live once more the sunny days of our childhood.
But we say the truth in Christ Jesus, we lie not, our
consciences also bearing witness, that we have not even
in our dreams bowed the knee before a god or goddess
of the Hindu pantheon; we have not even in our dreams
wavered in our conviction that there is none other name
under heaven whereby men can be saved except the name
we adore." He then gives a hymn which cheered his friend
in his last hours, beginning with the words—

> " The hour of my departure's come,
> I hear the voice that calls me home."

A short time after Mrs. Kennedy's death, my very dear
friend for many years, the Rev. D. G. Watt, M.A., at my
request, wrote an article for the *Missionary Chronicle*, as he
knew her better than most of her friends could have done.
A briefer, and perhaps more suitable, article appeared in
the *Chronicle*, and now I give Mr. Watt's article :—

" HERNE HILL, *June* 1891.

" It is fifty years ago this month of June that I stepped
into the Mission-House of the London Missionary Society at

Benares. Its occupants then were Mr. and Mrs. Kennedy. He had been a fellow-student, and had, with his wife, cordially invited me, being unmarried, to make my residence with them, 'the same which I was forward to do.' I had just completed a journey by Palki-dak from Calcutta, and was in a somewhat shattered condition, owing to an attack of fever which had been made upon me on the eve of setting out on my long journey. I needed rest and nursing, and though I had never seen Mrs. Kennedy, she took care that I got both. It was so also as long as I remained. The unsuitability to me of the Indian climate brought other ailments, in which she was an unwearied succourer.

"By the time of my arrival she had acquired sufficient fluency in the vernacular to enable her to exercise thorough control over the mingled elements of an Anglo-Indian household. Many could testify, if they are still in the flesh, that she showed them 'hospitality without grudging,' when India had no railroads, and travellers' Rests were few and far between. Besides the household cares, there came to her those in regard to the provisioning, &c., of the orphan children supported by the Mission, and also of teaching the native Christian women and others the principles of the doctrine of Christ. She continued all her life long as she had begun, making full proof of her ministry. When she retired from India, it was not a cessation of work. Mrs. Kennedy found, as she had always done when absent from India, that brothers for whom Christ died were within her reach, and might be helped, and by love she served them to the last.

"She acknowledged that her early training had narrowed her views of Christ's work in the world, but those who afterwards got glimpses of her inner life saw that that training had inclined her to bow to the sovereignty of duty at any personal cost. Under this sway she verged aside from some of the paths into which she had been taken when young, and walked onward in a new confidence that God in Christ was the Saviour of all men.

"Through what tremors and mistakes she had to pass only they can guess who have had to tread a similar path, but at length she seemed to reach that strand from which she could see her whole horizon filled with the supreme authority of Jesus Christ, and could trace, with increasing distinctness, His footprints on the sands of time. So she waited on Him alone to lead her in thought and conduct, and thus was prepared unto every good work.

"Her early training appeared also to have given her an interest in the doctrines of the Bible and their bearings. Conversation with her on these subjects did not elicit little more than monosyllabic responses. She could speak pertinently and suggestively, and, as her life developed new experiences, the old truths, which she had found to be of God, she spoke of as still trusted to for spiritual nourishment, but as appearing in larger and more varied forms of supply.

"Mrs. Kennedy endured the chastisement whereof all are partakers—afflictions on herself, husband. and family; among these, the fiery trial of the Sepoy mutiny, when for weeks she and other fugitives were in hourly terror of an unruly soldierlies' assault—a trial which wrote upon her heart, as with a pen of iron, a song of the mercies of the Lord. They made her more deeply convinced of the presence of the Redeemer from all evil, and of His leading her by the way she should go to the land of uprightness.

"Does she rest from her labours? At any rate, the long toil on the battlefield is over. Enlisted for it, and sustained in it, by the grace of Him who makes war arrayed in a garment sprinkled with blood, she listened for His voice, she looked for His sign, she was striving to be more helpful to His interests among men, as every loyal soldier of Jesus Christ is. Now she has been ordered out of the ranks to go into the presence of the King, and to hear from His lips the unutterably grateful words, ' Well done, good and faithful servant.'

"D. G. W."

During a few of our early years in Benares, the Rev. George Small, M.A., of the Baptist Mission, and his very excellent wife, who was killed by an explosion of gunpowder in the neighbourhood of their house in 1850, were among our most intimate and valued friends. The intimacy with him and his second wife has, so far as circumstances have permitted, been maintained through all subsequent years. Mr. Small, in a letter dated Leytonstone, June 6th, 1892, says :—

"I am glad to hear that you are getting on with the Memoir of your beloved wife. The compiling of it must have been at once a sorrowful and a solacing occupation. I am sure the work when published will be extensively read, and prove a source of great spiritual blessing. It is now not far short of half-a-century since I made the personal acquaintance of you both at Benares, and what opportunities I have had since then both in India and at home of knowing her character and worth ! With the possible exception of my own dear wife, her great friend, so suddenly called to glory in 1850, I don't think I ever knew a Christian lady so spiritually minded, and who lived so consecrated and consistent a life. Her conversation and correspondence were always felt by both of my wives, as well as by myself, to be a means of reviving grace."

From Mrs. Fuchs, widow of the Rev. J. Fuchs of the Church Missionary Society, long working in Benares. Mrs. Fuchs is now resident in Germany. The letter is dated Constatt, June 7th, 1892 :—

"It was at the commencement of 1848 I first met Mrs. Kennedy on your returning from the Hills. She received me as a younger sister, and so she behaved to me *always.* Many a good advice and valuable counsel I got from my kind, wise, loving friend. She loved the brotherhood of all the various divisions of the Lord's servants. Her unostentatious, gracious, kindly hospitality, her holy life, her devotion to the mission work, and her domestic virtues were an example to us younger missionary wives. When later I came to England, a sad and sorrowful widow, her friendship was a consolation and comfort to me.

From the Rev. James Ross, for years pastor of the Union Church, Calcutta, and now pastor of the Eglinton Street Congregational Church, Glasgow :—

"GLASGOW, *June* 1, 1891.

"Mrs. Kennedy's removal carries my memories back to a long-past date, when as a boy I was wont to hear you preach in the church in Elgin, in Mr. M'Neill's time, and when you had your children around you. When at a much later date I met you both in Calcutta, it seemed like a renewal of early days to see your well-known faces, and again I had the same feeling when I met you both in Portobello. I shall ever feel thankful that I had the opportunity of knowing you both, and especially for the conversations I had with Mrs. Kennedy in Calcutta and Portobello, and came to know the depth and earnestness of her piety, and the strong good sense, as well as mental vigour, that mingled with her devout loyalty and love to her Lord."

From the Rev. James Williamson, M.A., for years Presbyterian chaplain in Northern India, and now minister of the Dean Parish, Edinburgh. Mr. Williamson often visited Benares to preach to the Presbyterian soldiers— preached to them in our place of worship, and on those occasions was generally our guest.

"Mrs. Williamson and I send our sincere sympathy with you and your family in your bereavement. . . . I do not know that I ever met with any Christian worker of whom I could have firmer confidence that she would hear the approving reward, 'Well done, good and faithful servant.' She has left her impress for good on the native Christian community at Benares especially. I say no more, but I feel that I have lost a friend who made this world richer for me."

This letter is dated May 25th, and was written on Mr. Williamson receiving the intimation of Mrs. Kennedy's death. With her an intimacy had been formed, which has been maintained ever since. In October I sent to Mr. Williamson an account of the circumstances of Mrs. Kennedy's death, and I immediately received from him the following letter :—

"EDINBURGH, *October* 14, 1891.

"I was much pleased to get your letter this morning, telling me about your dear wife and my much-valued friend. She was a true mother in Israel, and many have had reason to rise up and call her 'blessed.' I read with great interest her modest truthful article on 'Female Missionary Work' in Benares fifty years ago. It is when we go back fifty years or so that we see the wonderful progress in missionary work, and how much reason we have to be grateful to the pioneers of missions like yourself and Mrs. Kennedy."

From the Rev. Edward Storrow, for years pastor of Union Church, Calcutta, and now resident in Brighton :—

"Mrs. Kennedy's name was familiar to me some time before I had the pleasure of her friendship. Benares being 500 miles from Calcutta by the old road or river route, it was seldom, except when missionaries passed through the latter to the former, that we saw them. In 1857 she, with numbers from the North-West Provinces, broken in health, and not seldom broken in heart, found a temporary resting-place in Calcutta from the terrible storm of revolt and rapine which for a time imperilled our empire. Some remarks she then made struck me forcibly, as not only true in themselves, but indicative of the strong Biblical quality of her own piety. She said, with what force and impressiveness, in the various crises of the mutiny, many passages in the Psalms, such as xliv., xlvi., lii., lv., lvi., lvii., which in ordinary times seemed to have lost their significance, came into her mind as the most adequate expression of want and desire.

"But it was when Mr. and Mrs. Kennedy came to reside at Acton that my intercourse. with them became close, frequent, and most agreeable. I believe I was always a welcome guest; undoubtedly I was always a happy one. Her kindness was great, but her sympathies were too much under the control of truth and holiness to allow of pleasure in various kinds of society, but to those of congenial tastes she was a warm and delightful companion. Like most who have resided some years in India, their house was open to other old Indians whose missionary and evangelical proclivities were pronounced, and who were content with the plain, familiar hospitality they delighted to offer.

"Her bearing was always affable and courteous, her conversation always intelligent, distinguished by large charity, and ever moving toward grave, dignified, kindly, and important themes. Our recollections of persons are too often of a very mixed nature, but of her—her character, her life, her conversation, mine are uniformly pleasant, elevating, and approaching to the sacred.

"Mrs. Kennedy was mindful of others, especially of the unfortunate and poor; grave, but with a vein of cheerfulness and Scotch humour; well read in solid literature; active in spheres of usefulness, and sympathetic with the great movements of our times. But her three most marked characteristics were *great devoutness, fidelity to evangelical principles,* and *missionary ardour.*

"*Her religion* was not as a dress; it was a part of herself. It was in her every-day life, in her thoughts, feelings, speech, actions. No one could be with her without the consciousness that in all things she 'set the Lord before her.' But this was without ostentation or obtrusiveness. It was because piety was natural and habitual to her. As if the prayer of her daily life was the verse of Bishop Kenn's too little now appreciated hymn :—

> ' Direct, control, suggest, this day
> All I design, or do, or say ;
> That all my powers, with all their might,
> In Thy sole glory may unite ! '

" I have seldom met a woman more familiar with the *Bible* and the *leading doctrines of evangelical religion*. She had been well grounded in her maidenhood in the formularies of the age, and the result was seen in a piety which was strong, deep, intelligent, and beautiful ; for though there is much in the theology of the present day she judged to be weak and erroneous, she had learned to be tolerant of opinions other than her own.

"Mrs. Kennedy was a *model wife for a missionary*, a help-meet in the truest and happiest sense of the phrase. Her husband's work, with all its aims, hopes, joys, and sorrows, was hers, not only through loyalty to him, but for the grand, divine principles which lie at the root of the missionary enterprise. In the native schools, the converts, the women especially, and the preaching of the Gospel to the heathen, she was profoundly interested. Nor was this a merely temporary, or local, or professional interest. It went out toward the work of others ; it was not confined to India ; it remained fresh and vigorous to the end. I never was with her, I believe, without mission work in one or other of its forms being the prevailing feature of conversation.

" In her one ' of the excellent of the earth,' one of ' the salt of the world,' has passed away.

" E. Storrow.

" Brighton, *June* 1892."

From the Rev. John Hewlett, M.A., one of the most devoted and efficient of missionaries and affectionate of friends, who has been recently and very suddenly taken from the work on earth to the service of heaven. At the date of this letter he was absent from Benares.

"Mrs. Kennedy's excellences of mind and heart and character must have made her to you during the period of more than fifty-one years of your married life in a higher degree than most wives can be to their husbands, more than all the the world besides."

In a letter to my eldest son, who had sent to Mr. Hewlett an account of his mother's death, Mr. Hewlett says:—

"During the twenty-five years in which I had the joy of her friendship, I seemed never to have been in conversation with her nor to have received a letter from her without being made to feel that I was under her influence, breathing a fresher and more invigorating spiritual atmosphere, so that I can well think how precious, how inspiring must be the memory of that last week of your dear mother's earthly life, in which she evidently received grace to glorify the Saviour in a fitting termination to her long life of highest consecration to His service."

From Mrs. Hewlett, of the same date :—

"We feel that we have lost a true friend in dear Mrs. Kennedy's death. She was always so loving and sympathetic. We have often thought and spoken of you both, and of our pleasant visits to you at Acton during our recent sojourn in England, and I have often longed for dear Mrs. Kennedy's help and counsel in our mission work among the women in Benares. Many of the native Christians there remember her and love her, and will grieve to hear that she has gone."

From Mrs. General Chamberlain :—

"SPRING GROVE, *May* 28, 1891.

"No one can enter into the depth of your grief nor know the extent of your loss. I know what a friend I have lost in her, whose sympathetic help and wise advice were always given whenever I needed them. Our loving friendship, which became so intimate in Ranee Khet, makes me feel it is no ordinary friend I mourn."

From the Rev. W. F. Adeney, M.A. (now Professor in New College), North End, Hampstead:—

"*May* 12, 1892.

"I am looking forward with much interest to the publication of your Memoir of Mrs. Kennedy. Although I did not know her during the time of your great missionary labours in the East, what I saw of her when it was my privilege to enjoy her friendship while she was a member of my church makes me feel that a permanent record of such a life as hers must be of value.

"I have often thought that the supposed advantages of pastoral visitation were reversed in my visits to Mrs. Kennedy. Although I called on her as her minister, I felt that it was I who received spiritual profit from the rich funds of her spiritual experience. I never knew any one to whom the things of God seemed so perfectly natural. She spoke of them as though she was quite at home with them, because she lived in the habitual contemplation of them. I always came away from a conversation with her with a deepened sense of the reality of the spiritual world.

"At the same time a conversation with her was of intellectual interest. Mrs. Kennedy has often amused me with her description of the doctrinal and disciplinary rigour of the Church of her fathers. Deep as was her respect for the religious character of that old Scotch Communion, I could see that her largest sympathies had never been satisfied with its cramped ideas and purposes. It was most interesting to see how in her old age she rejoiced in every fresh thought that seemed to open up larger views of the love of God.

"Mrs. Kennedy was a true missionary to the last. When in feeble health, she would persevere in visiting our mission-hall mothers' meeting, and delight the laundry-women with her descriptions of the very different life of the women of India, and of the attempts that are now being made to bring some cheering rays of light into the secluded harems of the East. She also did good service as a house-to-house visitor in a poor district, when I know the effort to mount the stairs was very trying to her.

"One quiet, simple, and obtrusive effort of hers was always a source of encouragement to me and a secret of strength to our church, though few knew of it. Mrs. Kennedy met with two other devout women to pray for the blessing of God on our Church. It was literally the two or three. They met in Christ's name, and I am sure He was with them, and I believe their prayers were heard."

From the Rev. William Bolton, M.A., successor to Mr. Adeney as pastor of the Congregational Church, Acton :—

"ACTON, *May* 2, 1892.

"I am very glad you are preparing a memorial volume of Mrs. Kennedy. I am sure that there are many who felt for her great affection and respect to whom it will be welcome.

"During the comparatively short time I knew Mrs. Kennedy there were two aspects of her character which particularly impressed me :—

Her warm sympathy.—She was always ready to help all to whom she could bring blessing, without distinction of any kind. There are very many in Acton who greatly miss the special comfort and cheer she was able to give. After she passed away, the expression of the sense of loss from such varied people was indicative of the wide-spread yet deep hold she had upon many hearts.

"*Her wide charity.*—She was strong not only in her own faith, but in her care for the form by which she found it could be best expressed, but she was willing to hear what others had to say, and was ever ready to believe the best about them. Her great goodness of heart was remarkably manifest in this way. Under forms different from those to which she had been accustomed she would look for the real likeness to the Master and expect to find the touching-point of life.

"The memory of her unfailing energy, which often threatened to outrun her strength, of her habitual brightness, of her calm joy, with which she realised the oneness of heaven and earth, and waiting for the clearer vision, happily worked the while, will not easily fade, and will be an abiding encouragement to all who knew her."

From Dr. Weymouth, formerly head-master of the Mill Hill School, now resident at Acton :—

"*April* 30, 1892.

"It is a pleasure to me, and by no means a surprise, to hear that you are writing a Memoir of dear Mrs. Kennedy. I can never forget those many delightful hours that I have spent in her company and yours when availing myself at times of your kind general and oft-repeated invitation to join you at the tea-table.

"Her conversation was always interesting and instructive, invariably tending towards the sublimest subjects. In it was manifested not only high intellectual power, with breadth of knowledge of books and of mankind, but a rich Christian experience, with all that tenderness of feeling, gentleness of temper, warmth of heart and refinement of taste, which, by the grace of God, such experience fosters and matures.

"She was an eminent Christian, one of God's holy ones, and of the most exalted type. During all my life hitherto I have known few to compare with her, scarcely any to equal her, none by whom she was excelled."

From Mayo Gunn, Esq., Superintendent of Sunday School, Congregational Church, Acton :—

"ACTON, *May* 26, 1891.

"Mrs. Kennedy was so much loved, and so active in every good work, that her wise counsel and ready help will be greatly missed in many directions of our Church work."

s

From a dear friend, the Rev. John Wemyss, M.A., Edinburgh :—

"EDINBURGH, *May* 25, 1891.

" Mrs. Kennedy was possessed of so happy a disposition, and so quiet and composed a mind, proceeding from an unfeigned faith in the love and goodness of God, combined with a sound judgment, that we always felt it was pleasant and did us good to meet with her."

From Mrs. Small, Acton :—

" *May* 26, 1891.

" I shall miss, oh ! so much, my dear kind sympathising friend, with whom I have had so many times of sweet converse since our rather short acquaintance of three years ; but her words of help and encouragement will often come to my mind, and I shall think of one more bright and happy spirit to meet again in the heavenly mansions above."

From Miss Bull :—

" *June* 1891.

" Kindly allow me to express our sincere and deep sympathy with you in particular, and all who mourn the dear departed. With her we know it is well. It has never been my lot to meet with any one her equal for large-hearted nobility and beauty of character in every way ; and while I live I shall never cease to think of her with admiration and gratitude, for she made Christianity to me a very living reality, and I have often longed to be in some faint degree like her. You will say ' Like Christ ; ' yes ! yes ! like Christ. She was more like Him in life and spirit, I do think, than any lady I have had the honour to call a friend. She was always so kind and loving to me and mine in our various trials and sorrows."

From the Rev. J. Radford Thomson, M.A. :—

" *May* 26, 1891.

" Your dear wife was indeed a good, happy, and most intelligent Christian. You cannot but feel your loss acutely. Yet thank God you have sweet recollections of the past and bright hope for the future."

From Miss Ely, Bournemouth :—

" February 1892.

" It is a pleasure to me to think of the bright little visits I paid to Acton, where I learned more of dear Mrs. Kennedy's lovely spirit, feeling that when she was gone the world became so much the poorer."

From H. J. Glanville, Esq. :—

" May 26, 1891.

" My wife and I feel, like many others, we have lost a true and faithful friend. To know Mrs. Kennedy was to respect and love her. We look back to many kindnesses received from her. We feel that one of the excellent of the earth has gone, and her departure leaves a blank which will not easily be filled up."

As this work is being sent to the press, I have received a letter from my much esteemed friend, the Rev. Dr. Sewall, Professor of Sacred Rhetoric in the Theological Seminary, Bangor, Maine, U.S.A., containing the letters sent by Mrs. Kennedy to Mrs. Sewall. We met Dr. and Mrs. Sewall on the occasion of the great Missionary Conference in 1888, and felt so drawn to each other by deep Christian sympathy during our very brief personal intercourse, that we have maintained ever since most friendly correspondence. I informed Dr. Sewall of my being engaged in writing a Memoir of Mrs. Kennedy, and in his reply he says :—

" We feel very deeply your great loss, and our own also. We are very glad you have it in mind to publish a Memoir of your dear wife. So useful a life, and so sweet and saintly a character, certainly deserve to be commemorated, for the instruction and example of those who come after. We can well imagine what a hallowed task, both delightful and sad, it has been to you."

I give an extract from a letter of Mrs. Kennedy to Mrs. Sewall, dated September 9, 1890, which gives expression to views she firmly held :—

" Our Churches in this country sadly need the quickening and saving power of the Holy Spirit. We have the down-grade here as you have in America. Happily we have the many times seven thousand who drink from the fountain-head and are the salt of the ear'h.

" You will see from the papers the sadly tumultuous times we are passing through as regards labour and capital. Indeed, you have had your own difficulties across the Atlantic in perhaps greater degree. We must hope that in the end good will result, though much temporary suffering and ill-feeling are a present consequence. Our Heavenly Father will, by His own divine alchemy, work all those discordant elements into His own glorious plain, and build up a Church for Himself, 'without spot or wrinkle or any such thing,' when the work is complete.

" But, dear Mrs. Sewall, does not the mystery grow ?—the fate of those outside ! In youth we seem to see little difficulty in some parts of what is revealed ; but as we look more narrowly and get larger experience, the clouds gather and faith is more sorely tried. I feel this is 'too high for me.' He does, and will do, all things well, and ' what we know not now, we shall know hereafter.' This is solid rock in a stormy sea. May we have grace to rest on it more calmly and fully ! "

Printed by BALLANTYNE, HANSON & CO.
Edinburgh and London.

www.ingramcontent.com/pod-product-compliance
Lightning Source LLC
Chambersburg PA
CBHW020900020726
47497CB00005B/1488